ROUNDTREE
DAYS

ROUNDTREE DAYS

A
JEFFERSON DANCE
WESTERN MYSTERY

GERALD ELIAS

LEVEL
BEST BOOKS

To the Utah desert, which has everything it needs to sustain vibrant life, if only humans would let it.

Praise for Elias Mysteries

"Fans of ratiocination will be pleased with Utah concertmaster Elias' witty and acerbic debut."—*Kirkus Reviews*

"This richly plotted mystery will thrill music lovers, while those not so musically inclined will find it equally enjoyable." —*Publishers Weekly*

"A musical feast for mystery and music lovers."—*Library Journal* (Starred review)

"...the twists and turns of his plotting will keep readers guessing. The real hook here, however, is the insider's view of the musical world..."—*Booklist*

"Brilliant and captivating on every level."—Starred review, *Booklist*

"Elias has a nose for creative detail and a refreshing impatience with pomposity. Indulge yourself in his artfulness."—*Kirkus Reviews*

"There's just one word for this book: bravo!"—Starred review, *Publisher's Weekly*

Chapter One

7:00 a.m.

JEFFERSON DANCE

I was soon to confront murder in a devilish form, but at the moment it was upon Meg's much more angelic form that I found myself idly gazing. I lowered my cup of coffee and gave her a closer inspection.

She lay naked on her side in unselfconscious repose, a vision of voluptuous feminine pulchritude, daring to be stared at. And stare I did, remarking her every detail. Her pudgy hand with delicate fingers—which had never seen a day of work—supported by her bent right arm and dimpled elbow, propping up her smooth, glossy cheek. Her Mona Lisa smile at once coy and suggestive, framed by tawny, curly locks wreathed in a garland of hemlock. Her teasingly pouting lips and the nipples on her breasts rosier than those which nature bestows, contrasting against the alabaster whiteness of her complexion. Her left hand, caressing her hip, clutching a diaphanous kerchief tantalizingly draped over her nether parts, preserving what little modesty there remained that could be preserved. Her name was Meg—Roaring Meg, to be totally accurate. I knew that because that was the name engraved on the nameplate beneath her. And though she was constructed of wood and plaster and paint and hung in bas-relief above the gilt-edged bar mirror and below a Tiffany-style chandelier, I smiled back at her, my singularly arresting breakfast companion. They say worshiping graven images is a sin.

1

Fortunately, I'm not religious.

My eyes found their way to the mirror below Meg, where I saw a man looking into it who I determined after some considerable inspection must have been me. Though the mirror was as spotless as everything else at the Vermillion Arms, which in my youth was called the Loomis City Grand Hotel, the glass must've been of the vintage variety because it skewed the mouth and chin a bit to the right, like at a carnival. Or could that have been the souvenir of a broken jaw courtesy of an intoxicated ranch hand on a Saturday night long ago? The right eye seemed alert although, with some justification, on the tired side. The left eye was covered with a patch—my error, not the rattlesnake's for its natural instinct to protect its territory. It was a lesson learned—thankfully not a fatal one—not to bed down too close to rocky overhangs.

One might have discovered a touch of gray, had the over-worn Stetson been lifted off the head. If I recall correctly, there were fewer facial wrinkles the last time I looked, and the weathered complexion under them might have been the result of worry or simply of a lifetime of reluctance to living indoors. Probably the latter, as it had long been my philosophy to leave the lion's share of worrying to others. My image in the mirror lifted a mug of coffee and took a long draft, and after giving the issue serious consideration concluded that the overall visage probably would not be of the type to greatly endear him to Roaring Meg.

Three coffees ago I had entered the Vermillion Arms dining room, leaving the cool, dry morning air, fragrant with desert sage, and exchanging it for the aroma of sizzling bacon and blueberry buttermilk pancakes. A fair trade. Dawn was just making its presence felt, but the place was already abuzz with activity. A sea of tourists, mostly elderly, had inundated Loomis City, Utah for the annual *Roundtree Days Festival* weekend and filled every seat in the restaurant—and the whole town for that matter—which is what had necessitated setting my keister on a stool at the polished mahogany and brass bar.

Meaning no disrespect to Meg, it was the impressive head of a bighorn ram, boasting a pair of magnificent spiraling horns and mounted to the left

2

of Meg's ruby-red painted toenails that was giving my heart palpitations. In twenty-four hours, my friend Poot Ahern and I would embark upon a long-awaited bow and arrow hunting expedition, the object of which was to come home with a trophy of our own. After years of submitting our names in the lottery and coming up empty, we finally were granted two of fewer than forty permits issued by the state to hunt the Utah desert bighorn, arguably the most coveted big game in the West. Loomis City would be our starting point, conveniently situated as it was in the middle of Utah's vast desert wilderness.

While I waited for Poot to arrive, my gaze alternated between the ram and Meg, both of them vying for, and stimulating, my wandering imagination. Poot had free time on his hands. He had recently resigned from his position as the ranger at Antelope Island State Park in the Great Salt Lake because some state legislator had the brilliant idea that converting the water in the lake from salt to fresh and stocking it with fish would make it more of a tourist attraction. How that could be accomplished with water five times saltier than the ocean, how much it would cost, and what that might do to the overall ecology of the land even if it were possible (which it wasn't) were issues that seemed not to have troubled the esteemed senator. But that brand of alchemy was more than enough foolishness for Poot, who decided that after our hunting trip he'd forgo a return to public service and devote his energies to his ranch, where the only bureaucracy was his Angus herd, and the only debate occurred where they congregated at the trough.

What had brought me back to Loomis City after all these years was an invitation from Merle Tuttle, the sheriff of Castle County. Tuttle had been a friend of my folks before we moved out of Loomis City, and because his deputy was on leave for a hundred-forty-member family reunion up in Provo he needed help with traffic and crowd control at this year's festival, which began two days ago, on Friday. The summer-ending festival had grown every year since its inception, and this year's continued the upward trajectory. Though the town still only had a few dozen parking spots and a single traffic light at the intersection of Center and Main, Tuttle didn't think it would be too much of a challenge for me to keep the herd of several thousand humans from stampeding. "You've always had a knack for making molehills out of mountains," he said by way of a compliment, kindly noting that on previous occasions I had volunteered my assistance to law enforcement around the state. To make things official, Tuttle appointed me acting deputy sheriff and even gave me a badge.

Catching the eye of the young lady who was the breakfast bartender, I pointed to my mug for yet another refill, which I'd allowed to get cold while I was wasting my time musing over the wall hangings. With a smile and a wink, she promised me a heater as soon as a fresh pot was ready, and I turned my attention to my copy of the local weekly newspaper, the *Public Pinyon*. Page one was divided between news of the festival—this year's was record-breaking in every quantifiable category—and a story about the beginning of fall practice for the high school football team. The Scorpions' coach was reported to have expressed optimism they would improve upon last year's record of two wins and seven losses. Let's hope his optimism will be rewarded, since odds were that they couldn't do much worse. Page two was a summary of the recent selectmen's town meeting, which got me hoping that the fresh pot of coffee would be ready soon. I shifted my attention to an eye-catching ad for a grand opening of a new steakhouse. It was called Buffalo Grill, accompanied by the slogan, *"Won't Ya Come Out Tonite?"* I decided to decline the cordial invitation, not that I was ever averse to a good medium-rare rib eye, but because I was mildly allergic to bad puns and misspellings, intentional or not.

Turning the page, I found a whole foldout section of festival activities, which I took a pass on, and I had just begun perusing the *Loomis Lore* column on the back page when my phone rang. The call wasn't about traffic control.

I glanced at the mirror and behind the image of my face, which was taking on a progressively more somber aspect, I spied Poot scissoring his way toward me, parting the gray sea with a series of "pardons" and "excuse me, ma'ams."

"Truck's packed for our hunting trip tomorrow morning," he said without preamble.

"Well, you can unpack. We got to go out to Merle Tuttle's place. Seems someone burned down his stable."

"Okay."

Without waiting for my fresh coffee, I left an Andrew Jackson on the bar counter for the waitress in consideration of her good intentions. Though I couldn't swear to it, it looked like the bighorn ram was smirking, as if he had designed to place obstacles in my path in my hunt for his brethren. So, I tipped my hat to Meg instead, not that I expected a response. After all, she hadn't moved since they nailed her up there in 1878.

CONRAD MICHENER

The longer Ashlee's cellphone rang, the more my "Wee Willy"—as she so charmingly referred to it—shrank.

"Are you trying to break the world quickie record?" she pouted. Maneuvering to give me a little manual CPR with her left hand, she answered the phone with her right, which did little to enhance the aura of romance. Nor did the bed, which apparently was as vintage as everything else in the Vermillion Arms and squeaked like a stepped-on mouse.

Ashlee swiveled off the bed and abandoned me to her phone, her divine posterior alluringly positioned six inches from my face. Not that I minded the view—it was voted (informally) one of the ten most glorious asses in Hollywood—but I soon got the distinct impression she had forgotten I was there. I was tempted to reach out and squeeze those delectable cheeks, both to remind her of my presence and, as the saying goes, because it was there. Whoever had called her was doing most of the talking, with Ashlee just shaking her lustrous locks from time to time. That probably was not an effective conversational tactic for a phone conversation, but seeing her long, blond tresses tossing from side to side almost got me going again. I took a clandestine photo of her on my own phone as a little keepsake.

Finally, before hanging up, she got in the last word.

"Ugh."

"Who was that?" I asked.

"Inez."

"What's she want? It's the middle of the night."

"It's almost eight o'clock."

"Like I said. What'd she want? She told us we don't have to be anywhere before ten."

"Merle Tuttle's stable's burned down."

"So what? Sometimes things burn down."

I hoped this ingenious line of reasoning would be sufficiently convincing to get back to business, and I wrapped an arm around Ashlee's waist and probed her belly button with my index finger, something I could usually count on to get the desired result. For some reason, she shouldered me away.

"You don't get it," she said.

"What's to get?"

"It didn't just burn down. Someone burned it down."

"How does Inez know that? She's a publicist, not Christiane Amanpour."

"It's her job to know stuff."

I was about to argue that certain "stuff" was not relevant enough to impinge upon my lifestyle, when there was a knock on the door.

"Who is it?" Ashlee asked.

"Room service. Your breakfast."

Ashlee opened the door, buck naked, and grabbed the tray from the bellhop quickly, not to protect her modesty but because he was so flummoxed it looked as if he was about to drop it.

"Thank you!" I called from the bed. "That will be all." Except for his tongue, which had unfurled down to his knees, the bellhop hadn't moved, but not from the reason Ashlee thought. Sometimes the obvious eluded her.

"Sorry," she said, "I can't give you a tip. I don't have anything on me." She closed the door with him still standing there.

God bless Ashlee, she has the appetite of a Green Bay linebacker in the offseason and had ordered the Mother Lode breakfast special. She returned to the bed with the heavily laden tray, and while she tore pieces of rye toast, dabbed them into her fried eggs, and stuffed her face, I gorged myself on home fries and sausages. And that was just for starters. By the time we finished, we were feeling much better. It was almost as good as sex, but not quite. And I know this because the sex we had for dessert was better. Wee Willy rides again!

Since there was no smoking in the hotel, I could only imagine the cigarette I would have lit after we'd consummated. I was feeling good. At least until Ashlee whispered what I was hoping were going to be sweet nothings in my ear. But what she said instead was, "You didn't burn down Merle's stable. Did you?"

"Why do you even think that?"

"You know why."

"No, I didn't burn down Merle's stable. Scout's honor. Did you?"

So much for conjugal bliss.

Chapter Two

8:00 a.m.

JEFFERSON DANCE

We headed out to Merle Tuttle's ranch in my truck, which was built the same year as Voyager One and probably had as many miles on it. Poot's was better, but he still had his horse trailer hooked up to it.

In Loomis City, you could usually walk a block in thirty seconds. This weekend, with all the festival traffic and jaywalkers, driving one block took ten minutes. Like all Utah towns and cities settled by the Mormons, by nature and training an orderly people, the streets of Loomis City were arranged on a grid in an effort to create order within an untamed landscape. The center point of the grid was the intersection of the two major streets, Center and Main, which ran exactly North-South and East-West, respectively. From that center point, streets radiated outwards in the four cardinal directions, always the same distance apart, and were numbered by the hundreds. For example, the intersection one block north and one block east of the center is called 100 N and 100 E. It might not be poetic, but even a blind man could navigate any Utah city as long as he knew where he was starting.

We finally made it to the local Suzi Q's Pik 'n Pak on the outskirts of town and stopped to buy Tuttle some precut sandwiches, coffee, and chaw tobacco. I didn't know his favorite brand but figured he'd appreciate the gesture, nonetheless. If he didn't like it, he could always spit it out. The cashier at the register had a nametag that identified her as Lindsie. The smiley face insignia on the tag was well-chosen, as the young lady was a cheerful, blue-eyed high school girl, no doubt happy to have a summer job, or more accurately the paycheck that went along with it.

A mile beyond Suzi Q's the traffic thinned out, civilization disappeared in the rearview mirror, and the desert took over. At the point where State Road 12 narrowed to one lane in each direction and the speed limit changed from thirty to forty miles per hour, a big hand-painted banner over a roadside souvenir stand read ROUNDTREE DAYS SALE! WELCOME! in bold red, white, and blue. A couple of Navajo families had removed a well-worn canvas tarp that covered their merchandise and were in the process of removing a second. Rough boards and the ground served as display shelves, on which were arranged the typical tourist wares: rugs, bowls, baskets, turquoise jewelry, statues, flutes, and dream catchers. Next to the souvenirs a few enterprising Navajo children interrupted setting up their lemonade stand to wave as we drove by. Their poster read ADE IN AMERICA! ONLY 50¢!

The speed limit ratcheted up to fifty-five, and shortly thereafter we veered off to the right onto a dirt road that was only a road because someone had driven back and forth enough times on the desert floor to make it one. We were in high-country desert, meaning that while there were no Sahara-style sand dunes, what grows there—a gray-green sea of pinyon pine and juniper, Mormon tea, yucca, black brush, and prickly pear cactus—has the tenacity to survive on precious drops of rain that are few and far between. But the notion there is not enough rain in the desert is a misconception. It may be true for man's survival, but for what thrives in the desert it is exactly the right amount.

It wasn't hard to spot Merle Tuttle's house at the end of the road, as it was the only one. It was harder to spot the stable, because so little was left of it. Curiously, the house, which was barely more than twenty yards from the stable, seemed to have survived unscathed.

Tuttle's visage was as black and smoldering as the charred ruins he stood in front of, an unwelcome, angry black stain of smoking wreckage intruding upon the otherwise benign landscape. And if I had any doubts about my perception of his mood, the rifle Tuttle was pointing directly at us tended to remove them.

When we got out of the truck and he saw who I was, he lowered his weapon and his face softened. Though Tuttle and I had never been close, either in terms of our relationship or geographically, he had a soft spot for me because he and my father had cut their teeth as ranch hands together. I thought him to be a decent man, which one wouldn't necessarily assume from his gruff bearing. But when one's property is violated, it can excite the worst ugliness in even the gentlest of souls.

"This is my friend, Poot Ahern," I said to Tuttle by way of introduction.

Tuttle tipped his hat.

"'Meetcha," he said.

"'Meetcha." Poot tipped his.

"Sorry about this, Merle," I said.

"Needed a new roof anyway."

"Accident?"

"Nah. It wasn't no accident. Can't ya smell the kerosene? I don't keep no kerosene in the stable."

"Any ideas who might've done it?"

Tuttle hesitated. He looked off into the horizon, which had only started to lighten. A few high morning clouds teased moisture, but we all knew they were just imposters who would soon be moving on.

"Nah," he said finally. "If I made a list of everyone I've ever locked up, anyone who might've had a bone to pick with me, there'd be more names than Utah Republicans. Well, better go into the office and start finding out, I suppose."

"Why don't you let me and my partner figure that out for you?" I offered.

Merle caught the innuendo. I'd seen lawmen who'd been victims of crimes, and as much as they tried to remain objective, it was darn near impossible and things usually turned out badly, or worse.

"You're thinking I'd make this too personal. Is that it? You don't think I can do my job?"

I was thinking how close he came to shooting me two minutes earlier, but

I didn't say that.

"Nah. It's just that traffic control really isn't my cup of tea," I said instead. "We can leave that to Gimpy. He's more than capable. 'Sides, you need to handle the hard part."

"What's the hard part?"

"Insurance company."

Tuttle almost smiled.

"You got a point, Jefferson. Got to find somewhere to house the horses too. Once I find 'em all, that is. The fire spooked 'em good."

Tuttle looked at me for a moment that seemed to stretch as long as salt-water taffy on a July afternoon. Whatever he was considering, it made his eyes narrow. Then he shook his head as if he were waking himself up.

"Okay," he said, "You're one of us even if you haven't been here for a coon's age. Consider yourself promoted. I'm making you acting sheriff."

That was more than I needed or wanted. I asked him as diplomatically as possible whether he had the authority to make an appointment like that, right there on the spot.

"The selectmen have pretty much given me a free hand when it comes to hiring and firing. Just look at Gimpy. He'd worked on the ranch with your pappy, too, 'til he hit the bottle. I hired him twenty years ago because he needed a job and all he's ever done is take up space. No one's complained yet. So don't worry. If there's any heat, I'll be the one to take it, not you."

"Much obliged," I said.

"You need some help rounding up your horses, Sheriff?" Poot asked. "I brought my horse down here with me."

Tuttle gave Poot the same gaze he'd fixed on me. He sure took his sweet time considering, though if my stable had just been burned down, my thinking would probably be a mite on the logy side, too.

"You can call me Merle," he said, which was a nice thing to say except that it didn't answer Poot's question. So we waited some more.

"Nah," he finally said. "There's only eight horses. I can handle 'em myself."

"That being the case," I said, "how about Poot taking over my position as deputy so I don't have to do double duty?" I presented Poot's bona fides to

11

back up my request.

While he considered that new wrinkle, I handed Tuttle the bag of sandwiches, coffee, and tobacco to sweeten the deal.

"I suppose," he said.

We all shook hands and I promised to keep him informed when we found something out.

On our way back into town, I asked Poot, "Where are you stabling Sally? Way too hot to leave her in the trailer all day."

"A nice young lady in town. Sixth grader. She's a member of the 4-H club and a horse lover. They have to do a volunteer community service project and she chose Sally."

"You trust her?"

"Girl's name is Sally, too."

"Match made in heaven."

"Seems so. The two of them fell in love at first sight. She's given Sally a hose-down and grooming every day."

That kind of woke up a thought in the back of my head.

"You notice the ground was muddied around my truck when we were at Tuttle's?"

"I did. That clay stuck in my boot real good."

Yet it hadn't rained for weeks. There might have been an easy explanation for the mud: Tuttle had tried to hose out the fire. But the mud wasn't that close to the ruined stable, I hadn't noticed any closer in, and Tuttle had been holding a rifle in his hands, not a hose. All of a sudden, I had more questions.

"Let's go back," I said.

"Okay."

I did a U-turn onto the desert floor and drove back through the dust cloud that had been our creation. Tuttle, a kerchief wrapped around his nose and mouth, was already working up a sweat, sledgehammering scorched timbers that were still jutting up like accusing fingers, which would have been a safety hazard had they remained in their precarious position. He hadn't touched the sandwiches, but he did have a rather large wad of chaw in his cheek.

"Merle, what time did the stable burn?"

"Between five and seven this morning."

He knew I'd want more explanation but stopped. I had no reason to think he had anything to hide. I chalked it up to him being the type that preferred to just move on in life after a bad spell without dwelling on the badness of it. If I pestered him to elaborate, chances were he'd tell me next to nothing and go back to his hammering, so Poot and I let our eyes wander toward a red-tailed hawk hovering on the far horizon, on our muddied boots, on anything but Merle. Our silence coaxed him forward.

"And I know that," Merle continued, his voice filling the vacuum, "because I left the house at five, same's I do every morning, to let out the horses, and when the sky's just light enough to mend fence 'fore it gets too hot. When I got back to the house for some breakfast 'fore going to work, the place was up in smoke."

"Fire department come to put it out?" Poot asked.

"I guess you're new to the area. Fire department's in Granstaff."

There was an edge to Tuttle's voice, which Poot wisely chose to ignore.

"You put it out yourself, then?"

"Nah. Was too far gone. Just let it burn."

"How do you reckon it didn't burn your house or set off a brushfire?" I asked. "As I recall, there was a bit of a breeze this morning, and it hasn't rained here in months."

"Because wouldn't you know the sumbitch was so dang considerate? He watered the scrub around the stable so the fire wouldn't spread. With my own dang irrigation system! The sumbitch."

It was a relief to hear Tuttle let out what he'd been bottling up.

"What kind of a system do you use?"

"Sprinkler. Center pivot. Tried and true. Keep it close to the ground."

"Well, thanks," I said. "That gives us something to chew on."

"You do that."

Poot and I got back in the truck, hoping this time we'd make it all the way into town. The drive gave us time to consider the situation.

"So, the arsonist wanted to make sure Tuttle wasn't around when he torched it," Poot reasoned.

13

"Or his horses."

"Meaning it was intended to cause property damage but not to kill or create general havoc, because he doused the perimeter. Revenge maybe? Or to scare him for some reason?"

"Tuttle doesn't seem like the type of man to scare easy. Could've been he wanted to make sure Tuttle didn't see him, so he waited 'til Tuttle was gone. Maybe it's someone Tuttle would've recognized. And also, he knew Tuttle's habits because he was already there before dawn, waiting for him to leave his house."

"He also knew that if he let the fire burn uncontrolled, with things dry as they are, it could've started a serious brushfire."

I was glad for that precaution. It was a specter I did not relish considering. A few years back I'd been on a helicopter crew that parachuted into the midst of a brushfire outside Delta, tasked with establishing a firewall to keep the flames from enveloping the town. The fire had been started by a couple of teenagers setting off Fourth of July fireworks in a campground where signs had been posted warning of high fire danger due to exceptionally dry conditions and prohibiting campfires. The boys apparently felt that their patriotism was exempt from the restrictions and within two days thirty thousand acres of wildlife habitat had been scorched. It took three days and the life of one of my crew to control the fire, and weeks more before it was fully extinguished. What remained—what had been burned—would take years to return to something resembling normal. And that hadn't even been the peak of fire season, which it now was.

If we were right in all our assumptions about this current arsonist, it meant he was probably a local. That eliminated a few thousand tourists and those associated with the TV show, leaving only a few hundred folks to consider. And narrow that down to someone who might have a vehicle with clay caked in the tire treads and who had bought several gallons of kerosene in the recent past. But those were big ifs, and such speculating was both premature and overly optimistic. Nevertheless, it made sense, and not wanting to spook either the festival or the culprit, it was important to get ahead of the curve and keep the arson from public knowledge.

Poot interrupted my thoughts.

"Suppose it could've been Tuttle did it himself?" he asked.

"I hadn't thought of that, but I might've worked my way there sooner or later," I said. "Why would he?"

"Insurance money?"

"For what? To build a new stable? That'd cost more than they'd give him, probably."

"Maybe for something else."

"Possible. It would be a stretch. But possible."

We stopped back at Suzi Q's for our own sandwiches and a bag of pork rinds on the way to Tuttle's sheriff's office in town.

"How's it going, Lindsie?" I asked, without looking at her ID tag. She seemed genuinely pleased I'd remembered her name. I handed her my credit card.

"Have you heard?" she replied, clearly excited about something and happy to have someone to tell it to. When I had a job at a convenience store as a teenager, passing the time was as exciting as watching the spin of the Slushy machine, so big news, like Herb Warner's sow giving birth to a drift of piglets, was a welcome interruption of the monotony of the job.

"Depends," I said. "We expecting rain?"

"No such luck," she said. "Sheriff Tuttle's place burnt down."

So much for getting ahead of the curve.

"Where'd you hear something like that?" Poot asked.

"Oh, I don't know. Everyone who's come in has been talking about it. Some people think Alexis did it."

When we got back in the truck, I said, "Remind me who this Alexis is."

"Alexis Honeycut Roundtree is one of the main characters on the 'Roundtree' TV show. Vernon Roundtree's wife. Seems they're separated but deep down inside they still have an abiding love for each other. They're both just too proud to admit it. Didn't you read your festival guide?"

When we were back on the road, my cellphone rang. I fished it out of my jacket pocket and, since my truck is the opposite of what one would call soundproof, I pulled over to the shoulder and put the phone on Speaker so both Poot and I could hear.

"Jefferson Dance?"

"Speaking," I said.

"Linda Benallie. Editor of *Public Pinyon*."

"Read it this morning. Very informative."

"You read it?"

"Isn't that what newspapers are for?"

"Sure. But, you know, it's mainly just us locals who actually read it. Out-of-towners mainly use it for the motel listings and restaurant ads and for wiping cow pies off their shoes. Look, I'm calling about Merle Tuttle's stable being burnt down. He's not answering his phone, so Gimpy Okleberry said to call you."

I looked at Poot. He shook his head, confirming my thoughts.

"No comment at this time," I said, and hung up. After driving another thirty seconds I pulled over again and redialed her number. "Sorry I hung up on you. No offense intended."

"None taken."

"I was thinking, maybe you could help us shed some light on the subject."

"Sure. Come on over to the office. It's just three doors down from the hotel, in the back of the copy center. You can't miss it."

CONRAD MICHENER

I stepped out of the shower and wrapped a towel around my manly torso, preparing to sneak back to my room, which was next to Ashlee's. A father-daughter carnal relationship, even if the father-daughter part was TV make-believe, would not go over well with the public. We needed to make sure we didn't fail the smell test.

Ashlee had the TV turned on to the Mormon Tabernacle Choir singing hymns of faith and devotion. Not the best way to relieve a hangover. She had begun the mysterious ritual of applying her makeup, which would take up the bulk of the rest of the morning. She peered into the mirror on her dressing table like she was Galileo searching for Uranus in his telescope.

"Isn't there anything better on?" I asked.

"It's Sunday morning and it's Utah," she said to her reflection in the mirror. "What do you want?"

"How about 'Never on Sunday'?"

She ignored my witty retort. I examined my own face in her mirror and was not displeased with the manly image.

"They say I look younger in person," I said.

"Don't flatter yourself."

"You think they're wrong?" I asked. "Do I look forty-something to you?"

"That's cuz makeup spends two hours getting you to look like my father."

"Details."

"What should we do about Merle?" she asked. I guess she was tiring of me talking about me.

"Why should we do anything?" I protested.

I picked up the remote on Ashlee's dressing table and changed the station to a spirited infomercial about how to increase yields with a new type of alfalfa seed grain. *"Ten percent, twenty percent, thirty percent more per acre!"*

"I guess you're right," Ashlee said. "It's just that..." I knew that the dot, dot, dot at the end of that tapering statement meant trouble.

"What do you mean, 'It's just that'?"

I spotted some sheets of paper that someone must have slid under the door while I'd been scrubbing *eau de Ashlee* off me in the shower. I picked them up, gave them a once-over, and cleverly changed the subject.

"Look, conscientious Inez has slipped us our schedule for the day. Once we leave the friendly confines of this esteemed hostelry, we're pretty much booked until midnight. Even if we wanted to do 'something' about Merle, there's no time."

I switched the TV station again to a discussion of fishing lures you can buy, only by calling immediately to operators waiting by the phones, to guarantee reeling in a huge crappie. *"And if you call now, we'll give you absolutely free—"*

"Whatever," Ashlee said. "I just thought."

"And it was a nice thought. Don't get me wrong, baby. But Merle is a grown man and can take care of his own business."

"A *grown* man. I'll say."

"Knock it off."

"How do I look?" Ashlee asked. Most of our conversations veered toward that topic eventually.

"Adorable," I said. I put my hands on her boobs from behind and gave them a suggestive squeeze. "I'm the proud father of a beautiful, intelligent, caring young lady."

She pulled my hands away, but good-naturedly.

"Do you get off on that?" she asked. "Sometimes I think you're kinky enough to pretend it's true."

"No more than you fantasizing you're doing it with your doting daddy."

"And if I'm naughty, is my strong, silent, daddy going to spank me?"

"Don't forget hairy-chested."

"Hairy-chested."

"Only if you say please."

She sighed, which could've meant any number of things.

"Too late," she said, bouncing up. "Gotta get ready for a book signing."

"That's not till noon."

"Which is why I have to get started now."

Chapter Three

9:00 a.m.

JEFFERSON DANCE

Like most businesses in Loomis City, the newspaper office was near the center of town, but with the weekend crowds, the closest parking spot was a quarter-mile away, which gave Poot and me a chance to loosen our legs. The buildings along Main Street—some brick, some wood, even a few red sandstone—had been restored to their original late nineteenth-century and early twentieth-century glory, conflicting with my vague childhood mental image of them as being bleak, starkly intimidating, and run-down. If one eliminated the swarms of people, automobiles, and every other modernization from that visual perspective, I could see how a Western series could be successfully filmed here. Once the town was rid of the crowds and the souvenirs decked out in window displays, and the cars moved off Main Street, it wasn't hard to imagine that Loomis City could be an ideal film set.

Poot and I bobbed and weaved among the throngs of tourists. Dolled-up storefronts and Victorian-style lamp posts, freshly painted in glossy black, sported pots overflowing with pink and purple petunias. Folks sitting in outdoor cafés were intermittently sprayed with a fine mist to keep them cool, as the day had already warmed considerably and the humidity hovered close to zero. With the annual rainfall in these parts averaging around ten inches, one could argue there were more urgent needs for the water–like crop irrigation or watering livestock–than for decorative flowers and creature comforts. I suppose it's a sign of the times that tourism trumps traditional economies, where the new livestock were the tourists.

Poot and I were approached for our autographs more than once by adoring but misguided "Roundtree" fans who mistook us for cast members. Poot had his black Stetson and handlebar moustache, and my eye patch seemed to attract particular attention. "Hey, which one of you is the bad guy?" a portly gentleman in Bermuda shorts shouted at us. "Wanna draw on me, pardner?" With his pointed index finger and raised thumb, the man fashioned his right hand into a handgun, whipping it from an imaginary holster, and aimed it at Poot. "Gotcha! Right through the heart." Poot smiled, tipped his hat, and kept walking.

If small-town newspapers have the reputation for operating on shoestring budgets, the *Public Pinyon* wore loafers. We found the office at the back of the modest copy center. It consisted of four gray metal file cabinets, a water cooler that didn't seem to be able to stop bubbling, a Mister Coffee with a full pot, and a pole fan that would have to be turned on before long. A country-western singer crooned on the radio about his girl's love not being real, or it really was real but he had failed to realize it. The singer used the word "real" a lot. A stuffed Gila monster and a desktop computer perched atop an imitation wood-grained desk, completing the décor, except for Linda Benallie, who sat behind it on a folding chair.

Magnified by a pair of horn-rimmed, bottle-lensed eyeglasses, her blue-gray eyes contrasted incongruously with her bronzed Native American complexion. In her right hand she held a handsome, expensive-looking fly rod, which she handled like an expert angler. But instead of trying to hook a fish, she was working a black cat into a frenzy as it darted about, trying to corral the fly. Benallie gave the rod a sudden flick, which jerked the fly up and behind the cat, who responded with a back flip.

"Don't worry, no hook," she said in response to my inquiring gaze. "Just practicing my technique. Meet Little Zeke, my business partner and live-in rodent repeller. If I don't constantly entertain him, he'll break my heart and leave me for another."

Benallie wore a plain white sleeveless dress, an unostentatious turquoise necklace around her neck. Her hair was done up simply in a no-nonsense, raven-black ponytail. She rose gracefully from behind the desk and spread her arms wide.

"Welcome to *The New York Times* west."

I consider myself tall, but Linda Benallie had the better of me by half a head, and from the look of her bare arms could probably hold her own in an arm wrestle. Whereas Roaring Meg might be described as curvaceous, Benallie was more like what my Aunt Flora used to diplomatically refer to as "big-boned," especially when she spoke in regard to one of her own well-fed progeny.

Benallie requisitioned two folding chairs from the vacant copy center, which was closed for business on Sunday.

"What can I do for you gentlemen?" she asked, gesturing for us to sit.

"We need some background," I said. "We're trying to figure why someone might've wanted to burn down Tuttle's stable. Whether it might've been intended as a threat or warning. I saw you've got this *Loomis Lore* column about town history in your paper. Maybe there's something in there that'd be pertinent."

"I guess I've become the unofficial town historian. And it's quite a history for such a small place. Whether it'll be of any help, though... Want some coffee?"

We didn't refuse, and the coffee could have been worse. I repaid the hospitality with a compliment as we all sat back down.

"You're pretty nimble with a fly rod," I said.

"My ex and I used to spend all our free time working streams around here, what there are."

"He taught you how to fish?"

"*I* taught *him*. But that's ancient history. Family history. What you're after is town history. Politics. You ever been to Loomis City before?"

"Born here, but my folks left when I was just a kid. Changed a lot. From what little I remember, anyway."

"That it has," Benallie said. "Until recently, you could have called Loomis

City a backwater town, except that wouldn't be accurate because there's no water.

"What *is* true is that Loomis City is the largest town in Castle County here in southeastern Utah. But that's not saying much, since the county's the size of Delaware and includes all of fifteen-thousand-odd hardy souls. And as we like to say, some are very odd. There was a time, a century or so ago, when they thought there was enough silver hidden in the surrounding hills to make every Tom, Dick, and Harry into a Vanderbilt, Carnegie, and Astor. So, they kicked us Native Americans out while the prospectors flooded in. Pretty soon brothels lined Main Street and business got so good that the women of the night were adding day shifts. When more genteel, 'civilized' folk arrived, a grand hotel emerged, among the more tawdry erections, so to speak.

"For a time, folks flocked in, but then the silver rush went bust as fast as a five-dollar trick, and folks flocked right back out. Loomis City dried up like a puddle in the desert sun. A few hundred ranchers and farmers, real diehards, continued to scrape out a hard life. As you know, the land is unsympathetic and the climate's unforgiving, but they continued to call the town their home. The Main Street brothels had long gone the way of all good things, of course. It could be argued that the boarded-up shops that replaced them were not much of an improvement to the town's pockmarked complexion. Here and there, you could spot a few enterprises that held on by their fingertips, but just barely. My mother had a saying: like a rock climber with a mosquito on his nose."

"That's kinda what I remember," I said. "There were the Sears catalog store, the John Deere dealership, the All America insurance agency. I guess they were the ones who stuck with the town through thick 'n thin."

"A few healthy teeth in a mouthful of gum disease. The Loomis City Grand Hotel still stood, barely, held up mainly by the plywood boards that covered its windows." Benallie took off her glasses and gave me an appraising look. "Is this any help?"

"Could be," I said. "That's pretty much the picture of how things were. When did all that change?"

"Eight years ago, when the Loomis City board of selectmen was approached out of the blue by TV producers planning to do a contemporary Western cable-TV crime series."

"Why Loomis City?" Poot asked.

"The selectmen asked the same question. They were suspicious why anyone would show the slightest interest in our hangdog town.

"The producers said they'd done a year-long, painstaking search among dozens of small towns in the West, and the consensus was that Loomis City was the best choice. They went on and on about its 'glorious desert environment,' wide open spaces, big sky, and get this: 'vintage' architecture, and the absence of heavy traffic with a congested downtown that would otherwise make filming a Western a logistical nightmare."

"In other words, Loomis City was blessed to be a ghost town," I said.

"That's the gist. What the producers didn't say was how little money they figured they'd have to throw at the selectmen to persuade them to convert dilapidated Main Street, which in a strange, perverse way had been preserved by benign neglect, into exactly the set the producers craved. The selectmen had a midnight meeting and responded before the producers had a chance to change their minds."

"And the townsfolk bought in?"

"Some of the old guard who liked things just the way they were objected, but the vote to put Loomis City back on the map passed by an ample majority."

"Which side was Merle Tuttle on?" I asked.

"At first he was a nay, but then he said he had a 'come to Jesus' moment when he had a vision of what would happen to Loomis City—namely, go extinct—if they didn't jump in, and so he changed his tune, which won him some friends and lost him some others. The producers actually patterned their TV sheriff, Vernon Roundtree, a little bit after Merle. They did some interviews with him for background. Around here we've got a saying: 'The actor who plays Roundtree, Conrad Michener, is ruggedly handsome, and that Merle is rugged, but one out of two ain't bad.' And whereas Roundtree solved eight murders a year, Merle said he considers himself lucky never to have come across a single one."

"From the look of things, it seems the producers spent more money sprucing up Loomis City than they bargained for."

"They decided they needed to make it presentable to TV viewers who needed an image of small-town America they could be proud of. But their investment paid off. 'Roundtree' became an overnight success, and after six seasons Loomis City is now one of the most popular tourist destinations in the state, though some locals chafe that the town's TV name, Vermillion, is what all the visitors to the annual *Roundtree Days Festival* call us. They even have banners up: 'Welcome to Vermillion, The Friendliest Town in the USA.' But with the exception of the diehards, most Loomis Cityites don't mind what people call it as long as the coffers continue to be filled."

"When I was a kid, there weren't any paved roads or sidewalks. And that wasn't too long ago, either."

"Once the ball got rolling, new tax money poured in and the cement poured out. All the stores that had been shuttered got repurposed and reopened. Restaurants, coffee shops, bars, boutiques, souvenir shops, art galleries, jewelry stores, recreational gear, and all the services needed to maintain them. You've seen them."

"And they all advertise in the *Public Pinyon?*"

"I can't complain."

Considering that the town was filled to the brim and hopping with activity, I had to conclude "Roundtree" must be an entertaining show. Personally, I've never seen it, and probably wouldn't even if I owned a TV.

"Were you raised here?" I asked. "You know a lot about the town."

"No, sir. It's just that I'm nosy. I've only been here four-and-a-half years. I grew up in Four Corners and went to college at UC Davis. My father's an Anglo archeologist, and my mother's from the reservation. One day she volunteered to help on one of his digs. They met over Anasazi potsherds and the rest is prehistory."

"You took your mother's name?"

"It has a better ring to it than Throckweiler."

I couldn't argue with that.

"Why is it almost all the tourists seem to be seniors?" Poot asked.

"Go figure. The show never really caught on with the Millennials. I think it's partly because Vernon Roundtree's kind of a father figure even though he's a sexy hunk. And the old folks love the festival because it reminds them of their childhoods, whether real or imagined. It's geared to their down-home tastes, like the Marionberry pie contest, which everyone knows is Vern's favorite pie. Or the evening pit barbecue at the corral outside town where it's all the ribs you can eat. The whole thing is like a retiree's Disneyland. All along Main Street, they jostle one another to buy as much of the paraphernalia as the producers can churn out, from 'Roundtree' T-shirts in every color of the rainbow to imitation Western outfits. And who can pass up the chance to buy Vernon Roundtree's favorite cologne and breakfast sausage? But what they like most of all are the celebrity sightings. The actors make unscheduled cameo appearances throughout the weekend decked out in their TV personas. They're like Pied Pipers, except instead of rats there's a trail of old folks behind them."

"I understand tonight's the big sendoff," Poot said. "All the stars assembled together, mounted on horses, for the Vermillion Grand Parade, climaxed by the most extravagant fireworks display in southern Utah. At midnight on Larson's Bluff, above the fairgrounds."

"How'd you know all that?" I asked.

"Because, thanks to you, Tuttle's folks gave me the job to keep the crowds off the street once the parade starts."

"Well, this is all very interesting," I said. "But it doesn't shed much light on who burnt Tuttle's stable. You know of anyone who had an ax to grind with him?" I asked Linda.

"As sheriff, Merle's had to deal with a lot of little problems here and there. Most folks respect him." The way Benallie's voice tailed off at the end was suggestive.

"But there's someone you're thinking of who might not be among 'most folks'?"

"Well, sort of. There's Fiddler, but he couldn't have done it."

"Who's Fiddler?"

"Oh, he's just our local pothead. He's been around for decades. Causes a little mischief now and then, especially during festival weekends."

"Why during the weekends?"

"He says all the crowds and commotion disrupt his 'stasis'. That's what he calls it, his 'stasis'."

"If he doesn't like the crowds, why doesn't he just leave town? There's a thousand square miles of nothing that starts right outside town limits. Seems to me he should be able to find his stasis out there."

Benallie shrugged.

"Good question. Maybe he just likes being a nuisance."

"And this Fiddler, he's crossed Tuttle?" Poot asked.

"Merle arrested him for throwing a rock through the window at Chuck's Wagon when it opened up a couple years ago. Fiddler called Merle the Antichrist and threatened to excommunicate him. And last week Merle locked him up for a night to dry out because he was wandering drunk on Main Street and harassing some of the early arrivals."

"What's Fiddler's real name?" I asked.

"Just Fiddler. He just showed up one day. No ID. No means of support. But somehow, he manages. That's been the hallmark of the whole town for the past hundred-fifty years so no one ever asked."

"I'm going to ask the obvious question."

"The answer is no, he doesn't fiddle. He plays guitar."

"Where's he live?"

"Out by Reilly Wash, west of town. In a shack past a stand of old cottonwoods. Can't miss it for the smell. But I'm telling you, I think you're barking up the wrong tree."

"Maybe, but it wouldn't hurt to sniff him out."

Poot and I got up to leave. Benallie came around to our side of her desk.

"Much obliged for all the background," I said. "Almost makes me feel I never left."

I went to shake her hand and received a bear hug in return.

I smiled and, as soon as I could free up an arm, tipped my hat.

"My pleasure," Benallie said. "Merle Tuttle's a good man. You find whoever burned down his stable. And I hope you'll remember to call me when you find something out."

She slipped her business card into my hand.

Though it was four short blocks to Merle's office, it was long enough to get some more information from Poot, but not before he managed to inject an editorial comment.

"Looks like you've got yourself a new fan," he said with a smirk wider than his moustache.

"What are you grinning at?"

"Nuthin'."

"You ever watch this TV show?" I asked him, changing the subject.

"I don't. But the wife does. She swears by it. Sometimes she tells me she wishes I were more like Vernon Roundtree."

"What does she say about the show?"

"Seems this Vernon Roundtree himself is no pup, though he's younger than most of his fans. He has a TV daughter, Jordan, played by an actress named Ashlee Vega. Jordan is a young family doctor who went to medical school back east, but she returned to Vermillion to tend to Native American children on the reservation."

"Free of charge, I'd guess?"

"Of course. Occasionally, she reluctantly accepts a handmade turquoise bauble as compensation."

Now I understood why every storefront selling trinkets on Main Street had been featuring The Jordan Collection.

"Roundtree has an estranged wife, Alexis Honeycut Roundtree, played by Maddison Hadcock, who the missus says is a famous actress. Alexis is not merely Vernon's appendage. She's a successful businesswoman in her own right. She's the proprietor of the Vermillion Arms but has a blind spot about her husband Vern's good qualities—honesty, integrity, and loyalty—because he tends to be tenaciously single-minded at his job—"

"And, like the traditional cowboy, has an inherent reticence expressing himself when it comes to matters of the heart?"

"I thought you said you've never seen the show."

"That's right. Just a guess. Didn't mean to take the wind out of your sails."

"Whatever. Alexis is the daughter of Lyman Honeycut, a ruthless mineral baron, who connives to run the town behind the scenes and is an adversary of the unremittingly honest Roundtree. Honeycut has always felt that his daughter is too good for Vern Roundtree's blue-collar worldview. Providing an extra spicy twist is that in a rebuff to both her father and her husband, Alexis is having an affair with DeWitt Cheney, a devoted environmentalist who has a difficult time fending off her many personal charms, try as he might."

"Sounds like you know a lot about this show without ever having watched it," I said. "I don't believe I've ever heard you talk that much about anything except horses, maybe."

"Once in a while, I'd look over the wife's shoulder."

"Once in a while."

I thought about Merle Tuttle dolled up to become Vernon Roundtree and Loomis City dolled up to become Vermillion, and Roaring Meg, with her cupid smile, dolled up there on the wall of the bar. And as much as you knew she was just wood and paint, if you tried hard enough you could believe just about anything was real.

CONRAD MICHENER

I dreaded that sound. Always did. The knock on my door, like the KGB. Doom. I covered my head with a pillow.

"Wardrobe, Mr. Michener."

"Leave it outside."

"I can't. Mr. Michener, you know that."

As my agent, Stewie Morgenstern, would say, "Why is this day different from any other day?"

I pulled the sheet off the bed and wrapped it around my waist. I dragged it with me, holding it in one hand, opening the door with the other. I turned around even before Emelda, the wardrobe girl, entered the room.

"Put it anywhere." I got back into bed. It was going to be a long enough day. Endless, in fact. If I didn't have to be anywhere until ten o'clock, I sure as hell wasn't going to waste an hour getting ready.

"Yes, Mr. Michener."

Whether she or anyone else knew that I had spent the wee hours engaged in fun and games with Ashlee Vega was anyone's guess. Personally, I didn't particularly care, except that the gossip columnists were worse than a swarm of locusts. It wouldn't look good to the public if they found out the hero of "Roundtree" was boinking his TV daughter.

Now that I thought of it, it would look even worse if they knew about her and Merle, what with his stable being burnt down. As Roundtree might say, it was "none of our affair." But still, once the locusts got hold of it, who knew how it would end up?

I was having a hard time replumbing the depths of my beauty nap, so I gave up trying. I didn't feel like another shower, so I stuck my head under the faucet for a while and slapped my cheeks a few times to wake up, after which I checked on my hundreds of thousands of followers on various social media platforms. I'd do anything, even that, in order to postpone as long as humanly possible having to don my cowboy regalia.

Along with the usual requests for intimate dinners, offers for one-night stands, measured opinions about other characters on the show—"DeWitt Cheney must die!"—and advice on how to solve cases, there was a new thread on my Facebook fan page started by someone who had apparently lost his sense of reality even more than the others. He wanted to start a movement for Vernon Roundtree to run for president. Seriously. Hundreds of others on the thread had already commented and shared and liked and whatever else they did to make themselves feel important. I groaned out loud. The price one pays for being a celebrity, Inez reminded me, over and over. Without social media, she insisted, life on earth as we know it would cease to exist. Well, maybe I didn't want to know it, especially after scrolling through more messages.

I decided I had to make a detour before my first scheduled activity, whatever it was—cow tipping?—and if I was late for it as a result, so be it. I needed to put this Tuttle stuff to bed if for no other reason than to make

Ashlee see that it was none of our business. If I walked out the door now in a pair of Bermuda shorts and sunglasses, as I would have liked, chances are nine out of ten people wouldn't recognize me. But my contract said, no, I must be Vernon Roundtree as soon as I step outside my hotel room door. So, I donned my buckskin jacket, rawhide pants, and who the hell knows what kind of leather cowboy hat. I was a marked man. I was Vernon Roundtree, hero sheriff of Vermillion, Utah. *Yee haw*!

Chapter Four

10:00 a.m.

JEFFERSON DANCE

Gimpy Okleberry, Tuttle's dispatcher, had explained to me that normally on Sunday the only officer on duty at the office, adjacent to which was the jail, was Gimpy himself. But with the jail's two cells currently empty, Merle had assigned Gimpy and everyone else in the department, plus as many local volunteers as he could muster, to be out and about tending to the tourists. While maintaining law and order among the senior citizenry wasn't exactly the Wild West, it did have its challenges. The volunteers had spent the past week practicing the Heimlich maneuver on each other until their sternums were bruised and had attended a seminar on how to triage heat stroke and heart attack while awaiting the EMTs.

So Poot and I were not expecting to see someone sitting in a folding chair outside Tuttle's second-floor office door, intent upon his cellphone. He gave the appearance of a cowboy but the red bandanna around his neck was a little too laundered, the boots a little too polished, and the day-old beard a little too manicured. Nevertheless, I must confess it was a reasonably close approximation.

"Well, I'll be," Poot said, holding out his hand. "If it isn't Conrad Michener, himself."

"That's me!" Michener said, shaking it. "Is Sheriff Tuttle around?"

"I'm the acting sheriff," I said. "Jefferson Dance."

I unlocked the office door and ushered Michener in. Poot followed behind and closed the door. It was a nice, homey office with rough pine paneling, upon which hung photos of Merle on various hunting and fishing trips with friends and what appeared to be family. A taxidermist had done an admirable job with a tiger trout perched on the wall behind Tuttle's oversized oak desk. I judged the fish was at least a ten-pounder, maybe twelve, and must have taken a skilled hand to haul it in. I made myself comfortable in the swivel leather chair behind the desk. Michener pulled up a chair on the other side. Poot stood by the door.

"What can I do for you?" I asked.

"I've got this problem, sir. Word's gotten out that Sheriff Tuttle's stable has been torched."

I waited for a follow-up, but Michener seemed tongue-tied, as if he had practiced a message but now, in front of a live audience, the words seemed inadequate. Maybe Michener was a natural for his laconic Roundtree persona.

"Spit it out, friend," Poot said. "We won't lasso you." Poot didn't even crack a smile.

That seemed to have pushed Michener forward, like a slap on the back to dislodge a misdirected bite of sirloin.

"Well, it's like this," Michener said. "Lots of people waited a whole year and saved up a lot of money to come here for the weekend and celebrate *Roundtree Days*. They drove here from all over the country. Far away as China."

I did not take kindly to what it sounded like he was getting at. "And you don't want to see their fun spoiled by a little local inconvenience like an innocent man's stable being burned down."

That seemed to have startled Michener, whose eyes widened.

"Hey, look, maybe that's what the producers are worried about, but it's not what I meant. Let me explain better. I'm sorry. It's like this: These people believe with all their hearts that I *am* Sheriff Vernon Roundtree. You know what I mean? They think I'm the law here in this town. They don't

32

even call the town by its right name. They call it Vermillion. They're in this pretend world where they think 'Roundtree' is the reality. They think the stable burning down is, like, one of the episodes."

It took me a minute to catch his drift.

"Your fans want you to solve the crime," I said.

Michener pinched his eyes closed.

"Yes," he said. "They want me to find out who burned down Sheriff Tuttle's stable."

It's a rare moment that one feels the urge to laugh and rail at the same time. I decided to do neither, at least for the time being.

"You sure?" I asked.

Michener handed me his cellphone, opened to his Facebook page. I scrolled down his fan mail and got more than enough answers to my question. I handed it back.

"Those," Michener said, "and the proverbial man on the street. I can't go two steps without someone giving me the thumbs-up."

I still wondered why Michener was bringing this to my attention. It didn't seem like it was anything I could help him with, even if I was so inclined, which I wasn't.

"I have a confession to make," he continued.

"A confession? You want a lawyer before you say anything else?" Poot asked. I think this time he might have been serious. It was hard to tell where Michener was leading. If this had all been a preamble to him telling us he'd burned down the stable, a lawyer might not be a bad idea.

"No," Michener said, with a hint of a goofy smile. Or was it an involuntary grimace. "No, not like that. You see, in 'Roundtree' I've got this screen daughter, Jordan."

Another pregnant pause. For some reason, Michener felt it was an important moment for him to stare at his extended fingers, as if he needed to make sure all ten of them were still there. I'd heard that good actors can make a career on how they manipulate silence. That's a good trick, getting paid for doing nothing. A bear in winter would earn a fortune. But either he needed a better scriptwriter, or he was leading up to something that wouldn't be a waste of our time, so I let him take his.

"Well, it's like this," Michener finally continued. "When we're off set, Ashlee and my relationship isn't quite as platonic, if you know what I mean."

I guess my eyes narrowed, because Michener put up his hands in defense. "Don't be horrified. Ashlee's only eight years younger than me. Okay, ten. We've each been married before."

"Mr. Michener," I said, "what you do in your personal life is your business. We're not here to—"

"No, no, that's not it, either," Michener said.

"Is what you're saying," Poot stepped in, "that it wouldn't behoove you to have your fans know you're having an affair with your TV daughter?"

"No, that's not it either," Michener said. "Or partly. Maybe."

He was getting as exasperated trying to explain himself as I was trying to understand where he was going.

"Let's try this," I said. "What would Vernon Roundtree say? Maybe look me in the eye for starters."

Michener took a deep breath and assumed his TV persona.

"I suppose he would say that the simple truth is that Ashlee told me she was approached in an amorous manner. By Sheriff Tuttle. And I suppose that's something you should know." Michener seemed exhausted by his effort and collapsed back into his chair.

Merle Tuttle? Poot and I looked at each other, then at Michener, who one could argue looked more like a sheriff than we did. But if his accusation was true, that opened up a whole new can of wormy motives that might have led to Merle's stable being burned down. The idea that the arsonist was a local suddenly became more wishful thinking than principled deduction. If Michener's admissions turned out to be a useful lead and helped solve the crime it mattered little to me whether his adoring public gave him the credit.

Before we could pursue that line of thought any further, Gimpy Okleberry hobbled in on his clubfoot. He'd been like that since birth, he'd told us, and by now no one who knew him even noticed it. Gimpy took one look at Poot and me, and another at Conrad Michener. He took his hat off and said to Michener, "Sorry, Sheriff. Didn't mean to interrupt anything, but you sure look younger in person."

"Just who are you calling Sheriff?" Poot said. If anyone could disguise his irritation, it was Poot. This time, though, it was as well concealed as a poked rattlesnake. But I didn't mind so much. I was hardly more of a sheriff than Michener was. It was almost amusing.

"Sorry, sir," Gimpy said to me. "We seem to have a missing person."

"Seem to?"

"There's a woman outside who says her husband's missing."

"How long?" I asked.

"Since about nine."

"That's not very long."

"That's why I said 'seem to'. But she's really upset. Could you talk to her?"

"Okay. Tell her to hold on a minute."

"Where are you staying?" I asked Michener.

"The Vermillion. Like all the cast. Room twenty-four."

Out of curiosity, I asked, "And Ms. Vega?"

"Twenty-two."

I called out, "Okay, Gimpy."

Gimpy opened the door, and an elderly woman entered cautiously, wearing sensible walking shoes. Her hair matched her trim gray pantsuit in both color and tidiness. Not knowing who was in charge, she looked at each one of us and tried to smile, especially at Michener, but it was obviously an effort.

"Have a seat, ma'am," I said. Poot gave Michener a look that meant, don't be a boor and give the lady your seat. Michener obliged, first giving us his cellphone number before leaving. The woman clearly recognized Michener as Vernon Roundtree, and as her eyes followed him out the door, the adulation her gaze conveyed seemed to momentarily eclipse her immediate distress.

Gimpy brought the woman a glass of water and once she was settled, I said, "We'll try to help, ma'am. Let's start with who you and your husband are."

"My name is Harriet Wohlmer and my husband's is Harold. Our friends call us 'the two Harrys.'"

35

"Do you live in Loomis City?"

"Loomis City?" She looked momentarily perplexed. "Oh, you mean Vermillion. Heavens, no. We're from Necedah. Necedah, Wisconsin, and we drove our Winnebago here for the festival, you see, like we do every year."

"Mr. Okleberry says you think your husband is missing."

"That's not exactly right. I *know* Harold is missing."

"Though it has only been a short time that you haven't seen him."

"Yes, but he was supposed to meet me at the Cowboy Waltz Jamboree and never showed up. I looked everywhere for him. I went back to the Winnebago and all his things were there. His wallet and his cellphone and his prescriptions."

"Medications?" Poot asked. "Is he ill?"

"He's been diagnosed with dementia, you see," Mrs. Wohlmer said, who was doing an admirable job maintaining her composure. "He has his good days and his bad days. Sometimes he gets lost. And he gets anxiety attacks when he misses his medications. I'm so worried because it's already almost ninety degrees out and he could be wandering out in the desert without any identification."

She had a point. It was a hundred miles to Boulder in one direction and another hundred to Blanding in the other. In between were desert, mountains, and more desert, with little water or shade to speak of.

"Where was the last place you saw Harold, Mrs. Wohlmer?"

"We had just finished our cinnamon buns at that new bakery in town. The one with the funny name?"

"Alpaca Lunch?" Gimpy offered.

"No. Not that one. The other one."

"Knead The Dough?"

"Yes, that's it. Knead The Dough. Harold said he would just be going back to the Winnebago, but I don't know if he ever got there."

"Where is the Winnebago parked?"

"At the high school. On 300 South and 100 East. They made the parking lot available for visitors' RVs."

Mrs. Wohlmer pulled an embroidered lace handkerchief from her purse and wiped her eyes.

"This was going to be our last trip together before…"

"Mrs. Wohlmer," I said. "You mentioned you had driven here from Wisconsin."

"Yes."

"Who did most of the driving?"

"Harold, of course. He did all of it. Why not?"

There was an obvious answer to that question. I chose to let it go unsaid, but Mrs. Wohlmer answered it for me with a fuller explanation.

"Harold's a retired trucker. He's a reliable driver, even with his…condition. He's never had an accident, never gotten lost while he's driving."

"Where's the next place you were going to meet him?" I asked.

"At the Vermillion Arms. For lunch. In a half hour."

I looked at my watch.

"I know," she said. "It's early for lunch, but then we take our nap. It keeps us going. We want to be wide awake for the fireworks. Harold loves the fireworks."

"Do you have some friends here in Loomis City?"

"Oh, yes. The Lawrences and the Muscvardsens. They come every year, too. They're from Black River Falls, which isn't too far up I-94 from Necedah."

I pulled my wallet out of my pocket and removed some cash.

"Gimpy," I said, "why don't you escort Mrs. Wohlmer to the hotel and buy lunch for her and her friends? Mrs. Wohlmer should have some companionship until we find her husband."

Before they left, Mrs. Wohlmer texted a photo of her husband to my cellphone. Harold Wohlmer was a robust, healthy-looking Midwesterner. He might have had seconds on pork chops once too often, but otherwise appeared as fit as anyone his age, even more, as if heavy exercise had at one time been a part of his daily life. You just don't think people like that would suffer from dementia, but I suppose that's a naïve thought.

"A good-looking man," I said, not lying.

"He's the handsomest man I've ever known," Harriet Wohlmer said. "And I love him."

I promised to send the photo out to everyone associated with both the local police and with the festival, with instructions to keep an eye out for her husband.

"I'll bet he shows up real soon," Poot said, not batting an eyelash, but I knew he wasn't so certain.

"Thank you," Mrs. Wohlmer said, forcing a smile. "You boys are almost as good as Sheriff Roundtree."

After Mrs. Wohlmer left, I called Merle Tuttle with a progress report. I didn't mention that I knew anything about him and Ashlee Vega just yet. He had enough on his hands at the moment and I acknowledged it.

"Don't worry about me," he said. "Take care of the old lady's husband. I'll be all right. I'm going to be tied up with insurance stuff for a couple days but once that's done I'll nail the sumbitch who did this even if I have to do it myself."

After I hung up, Poot suggested we should find Ashlee Vega and have a chat with her, and then go find this Fiddler fellow. They both seemed like long shots, but one has to start somewhere.

CONRAD MICHENER

Little did I ever expect I'd talk myself into visiting the Loomis City Sheriff's office. Seeing Merle Tuttle was the last thing I wanted to do, but it seemed the best way to rid myself of this arson business unscathed. As I walked down Main Street, I became increasingly convinced I'd made the right decision, because the eyes of the morons on the street lit up when they saw me and they'd say idiotic things like "Mornin', Sheriff," and "We've got your back."

When I arrived at the office wouldn't you know it was shut tight. What else would you expect in a hick town on a Sunday morning? I banged on the door in case someone was sleeping in there, which there wasn't. The office being on the second floor, you'd think they could have managed to put a sign out downstairs saying they were closed so I wouldn't have had to unnecessarily walk up a flight of stairs. But no. At least there was a folding chair outside the door, but it was not ergonomically designed and killed my back. I figured I'd give it fifteen minutes and if no one showed, no one could say I hadn't given it the old college try. I got out my cellphone to while away the time and saw that the dreaded Facebook thread had grown long enough to circle the globe eight times. As my agent would say, "Oy."

Just before I was about to get up and leave, two lanky locals showed up. One was tall and clean-shaven with an eye patch, the other a head shorter with a handlebar moustache. They both looked like cowboys, even though their clothes were clean, maybe because it was Sunday, and they were on their way to church and then to go a-courtin'. One could only imagine their intelligence level, though some of these yokels occasionally do seem to respond to stimuli. I mildly wondered what they were doing at Tuttle's office, and hoped they would just keep going so I wouldn't have to talk to them.

Shorty, God love him, recognized me and called me by my real name. He held out his hand, which was clean, so I shook it. When I asked where I could find Tuttle, the tall one, Jefferson something, informed me he was the acting sheriff.

He unlocked the office door and I followed him in. The office was the one that the production crew duplicated to shoot "Roundtree." I guess it's what the fans would call rustic nostalgic. I call it a dump, but don't tell anyone I said so. Shorty came in last, closed the door behind me with a definite click, and stood next to it. All of a sudden it occurred to me, how the hell did I know if One Eye was actually telling me the truth? These guys might have been the desperadoes who burned down Tuttle's stable and had come here to destroy evidence or something. Now I was alone with them. They could beat the crap out of me, and no one would ever know.

One Eye sat behind the desk, so I sat on the other side. He asked me what I wanted. I figured I'd go along with things and be real polite, hoping to get out alive.

"I've got a problem, sir," I said. "Word's gotten out that Sheriff Tuttle's stable has been torched."

I waited for the guy to say something, but he just sat there. So, I just sat there. Where was the scriptwriter when I needed him?

"Spit it out, friend," Shorty said. "We won't lasso you."

Ha-ha. Funny guy. Like I said, where's the scriptwriter?

I tried to explain that there was a lot at stake, and that arson kind of was complicating things. One Eye did not seem pleased with my effort at nuance. Or was it innuendo? The guy clearly had a chip on his shoulder. I glanced over mine to make sure that Shorty wasn't going to stab me in the back. But I had to make a decision. If they're not going to kill me, maybe the guy really was the acting sheriff. I'd go with that and see where it led.

I tried to explain with words so small that even they would understand that the hoi polloi thought I was a real sheriff and were expecting me to solve the crime.

I watched One Eye mentally process this information. No doubt it was a challenge for someone of his ilk.

"Your fans want you to solve the crime," he finally said.

Bingo. The primate stirs. To provide corroboration, I opened my cellphone to my Facebook page and handed it to him. Maybe he'd be good at understanding words that had pictures with them. He spent a while scrolling around and handed it back to me. Then he sat there for a while, looking at me, not intimidating, but just kind of sizing me up. I guess I started to trust him a little and opened my big mouth when I probably shouldn't have.

"I have a confession to make," I said.

"A confession? You want a lawyer before you say anything else?" Shorty asked.

Boy, was this guy a doofus. I couldn't keep the smirk off my face.

I started telling them about me and Ashlee, but man, I really should've shut up. One Eye just sat there, waiting. He kept looking at me, not staring, just waiting. What was I going to do, stand up and leave? That's what I should have done, in hindsight. But I didn't.

When I admitted the lady and I were engaging in off-set nooky, the way the guy was looking at me changed. I started wondering maybe he's one of those Holy Rollers who thinks sex is a sin and now he's really going to kill me and condemn me to eternal damnation. It's a good thing I didn't tell him I hadn't used a condom. Though maybe I should've told Ashlee.

They still didn't get it. I went round and round in circles with these two rubes until One Eye ordered me to look right at him. Have you ever tried to look a one-eyed man in the eye? I mean, should I or should I not try to not look at the eye with the patch? What would Martha Stewart say? Whatever. I spelled it out for them that Ashlee had confided in me that Tuttle had tried to get it on with her.

The two guys looked at each other. For the first time, they seemed a little surprised. Let them be. Fortunately, at that moment some old guy limped in like Grandpappy Amos. He looked at the three of us and said to me, "Sorry, Sheriff Roundtree. Didn't mean to interrupt anything, but you sure look younger in person." Jesus, not another one. Shorty didn't take kindly to that remark being addressed to me, and I have to admit I didn't blame him.

Limper announced that there was a missing person, which wasn't any of my business, so I didn't pay any attention. I just wanted to leave.

After One Eye asked me where I was staying, Limper went to the door and brought in an old lady. I gave them my phone number and then got the hell out of there.

Chapter Five

JEFFERSON DANCE

Trying to walk along Main Street against the current of *Roundtree* hordes was like shouldering through a herd of cattle on its way to a watering hole. Halfway to the hotel, we were accosted by a pair of substantial women in their sixties. One would have expected persons at that stage in life to have been more savvy than to try to squeeze themselves into tight-fitting, iridescent orange Bermuda shorts and T-shirts inscribed with *"I ❤ VERN"*. Surrounding the logo were a number of hand-scrawled autographs. Whether they had been inscribed while the women were wearing the shirts was a vision I chose not to ponder.

"Howdy, pardners!" the lady with large, pointy sunglasses said.

I tipped my Stetson and kept walking.

"Can you sign me?" the other said. "Please?"

She held out a Sharpie and proffered her ample chest for us to add our John Hancocks to those celebrities who had preceded us.

"We're big fans of yours," the first one said.

"We loved how you cowpokes saved Jordan's horse when the stable was on fire," said the other.

Before I could think of a polite way of disabusing the ladies of their mistaken identity and inform them that it was a real stable fire we had to urgently attend to, a lanky, twentyish man in black jeans and a black T-shirt with the image of a golden coiled rattlesnake on it pushed his way toward us.

"Get the hell outta here!" he yelled at the women, waving his arms. "Go on! Scram! You're disgusting!" Though it was undeniable I had wearied of playing pretend cowboy, there was no excuse for the young man's rudeness.

The two women, whose only crime had been a shortage of good taste, were clearly alarmed. They retreated into the crowd, which determined that Poot and I were no longer safe objects of its attention and fell back upon its other passion, window shopping.

"What's your name, son?" I asked the young man.

"What's it to you?"

"That's not the right question," Poot said to him. Poot is generally good-natured as a pup, but when he's crossed, he can snap hard as a hungry coyote in a lean winter. Maybe I should have warned the kid.

"It ain't?" the kid answered. "And you think you're gonna tell me what's the right question?"

"Here's the right question, son," Poot said. "What would be the best way to apologize to my friend for your disrespect? You've got ten seconds to think about that. At eleven seconds you'll be flat on your back for a very long time."

Poot was a good five inches shorter than the young man, but somehow you can tell that he's had experience backing up his words. The kid took a long look at Poot and considered the odds.

"I just don't like what's happened to this town," he said.

"That's not an apology," Poot said and took one step forward.

"Okay, so I'm sorry."

"Accepted," I said, before Poot had time to debate the issue. We already had one crime and a missing man on our docket. We didn't need to have this kid laid out, especially in public. "Now, tell me your name."

"Jalen."

"Jalen what?"

"Jalen Taggert. Jalen Ray Taggert. Sir!" He gave me a mock salute, which I ignored.

"And what is it you don't like about the town anymore, Jalen?" I was curious. He was almost too young to remember when Loomis City had one foot in the grave, which it had when I was a boy here. Yet he apparently thought of that era as the good old days.

"Well, look around! It's like a theme park. I mean, over there's a Vietnamese restaurant! What's a Vietnamese restaurant doing in Loomis City? These foreigners invade our town, and we can't even walk down the dang street!"

"Look, Jalen," I reasoned. It was neither the time nor place for a history lesson, so I made it short. "There's less than one day left of this Roundtree business, then everything will be nice and quiet again."

"But—"

"Hold on. I get that the new normal may not be to your liking, but sometimes you've got to take the bad with the good. Why don't you head on up to the hills with some friends for the next twenty-four hours? You can let off steam, shoot at some road signs, and talk about how great things used to be when this town was dyin'."

Jalen looked at me and then at Poot and decided that agreeing with my proposal was healthier than disagreeing. He gave us no more trouble.

We made it to the Vermillion Arms without further incident, intent on finding the whereabouts of Ashlee Vega, and then checking in on Gimpy and Mrs. Wohlmer to see if her husband had shown up. The glistening hotel lobby, richly restored to the opulent fin de siècle tastes of the most extravagant miner baron, bustled with *Roundtree Days* activity. Everything seemed normal. That is, until we spotted Gimpy next to the front desk talking quietly but urgently to Conrad Michener, who was so pale he looked like he might pass out. Glancing behind the desk, the clerk and a pair of tourists were engaged in a similarly somber conversation.

"What's going on?" Poot asked Gimpy.

"Maddison Hadcock is dead," he whispered. "I think she's been murdered."

Poot gave me a look that said, "Jefferson, you were a dumbass for accepting this traffic duty job right before our hunting trip." The look I gave him back said I agreed.

"Where?" I said to Gimpy.

"Here in the hotel. Two guests—an older couple—reported it to the desk clerk. I cordoned off the room and told Rusty Carlisle to stand guard there 'til you got here and told the guests and the clerk to stay right here and zip their lips."

"Who's Rusty Carlisle?"

"My nephew. He doesn't talk much, but you can trust him."

"You call the coroner?"

"You betcha. Doc Albers. He's already up there."

"Good job, Gimpy," I said.

"Thanks, sheriff. Room 12." Gimpy saluted. That was the second salute I'd gotten in the last half hour, but this one almost made me smile. Almost.

"Stay here," I told Gimpy. "Make sure the clerk, the two guests, and especially Michener, stay put. I'll be taking statements from all of them soon as I've checked out the room." I was about to walk away, but then added, "And don't forget to notify Merle."

We found Rusty sitting in front of Room 12, his chair leaned back against the wall, putting the finishing touches on tying an elk hair caddis fly.

"Sorry to interrupt," I said.

"'S'nuthin'," Carlisle said. "Doc's inside. Door's unlocked."

"Don't let anyone else in."

"Yep."

It was an ugly scene. Maddison Hadcock, aka Alexis Honeycut Roundtree, lay on her back, scantily clad, on a Victorian-style canopied poster bed. Doc Albers was at her side. He pointed with a latex-gloved index finger to a half dozen gaping wounds in Hadcock's chest.

"Been stabbed multiple times," Albers said.

"I can see that."

Her eyes were closed, and her left hand was next to her cheek as if she were still trying to look seductive. Her skin was pale and glossy and her entire disposition, unaccountably, seemed almost reposeful. The alabaster image of the wooden Roaring Meg one floor below seeped unbidden into my mind. Yet repose hardly could have been the case, because the room looked like a herd of bulls had been in the China shop. Upended Chippendale-style chairs, a broken Tiffany-style lamp. Breakfast scattered over the floor. Coffee drippings stained one wall, a delicate porcelain cup shattered at its base. I touched the coffee stain. It was still damp. The bed on which Hadcock lay was relatively undisturbed, as if it had been a sanctuary among the chaos. Ironically, though, that's apparently where she was murdered as, except for the bed, there didn't seem to be blood anywhere.

"Weapon?" I asked Albers.

"Knife."

"About four inches? Serrated?" Poot asked.

"Yes! How did you know?" Albers asked.

"I think it's right there, over in the far corner," Poot replied. He knelt down beside it and pointed without touching it. It was lying halfway under an armoire on the Oriental rug, not in plain sight, but not totally hidden, either. I inventoried the strewn breakfast more carefully. Dishes, grapefruit, toast. A silver spoon, fork, both initialed VAH. No knife.

"Poot, does that knife have the initials VAH on it?"

Poot nodded in the affirmative.

It looked like we'd found where the weapon came from.

"We'll bag that for prints," I said. "When did it happen?"

"This morning," Albers said. He lifted up Hadcock's left wrist. "I'd say at approximately 9:47."

"I'd heard you were good," I said, "but I didn't realize you were that good."

"I'm not," Albers replied. "I'm basically the town's GP. That's just what her wristwatch says. It's stopped and the glass is shattered. I'm guessing that's about when she was killed."

We went back to the lobby. Poot talked to the clerk while I talked to Michener. I asked the two guests to stick around and thanked them for their patience.

The hotel had a guests' business room behind the lobby that was pretty soundproof. Michener followed me in, and I closed the door.

"Go ahead," I said.

"I don't know what the hell's going on," Michener said. "After I left you, I

46

came back to the hotel. Madsie and I were scheduled to do a photoshoot in the saloon at one o'clock. I called her cellphone and there was no answer, so I went to the front desk to leave a message there, too. That's when the clerk told me. My God!"

"Where were you before you came to the sheriff's office?"

"You don't think I had anything to do with it!"

"Answer the question. But I've got to tell you, first you implicate your girlfriend and TV daughter in an arson and now your TV wife is dead. At the moment, things aren't looking promising for season seven of 'Roundtree.' "

Michener's hand went to his pants pocket, a little too quickly for my taste, or maybe I was just jittery. Mine went just as quickly to the .45 in my holster. He froze when he saw my reaction.

"It's my cellphone," he said. "I took a photo this morning that proves where I was. I'll hand it to you nice and slow."

"You do that," I said, and relaxed my grip.

He showed me a photo of a woman whose blonde hair cascaded down to her naked buttocks, which the phone indicated was taken at 7:38 that morning.

"Ashlee Vega?" I asked.

"None other. Not bad, huh?" Michener said, misinterpreting the amount of time I was taking to study the photo. The surrounding furniture in the photo would leave little reason to doubt it was her hotel room once we checked it.

"And after 7:38?"

"I went back to my room. My dresser, Emelda, came between nine and ten," Michener added. "She'll confirm I was there the whole time."

I told him he could go but ordered him not to mention to anyone that Hadcock was dead. He wobbled off, a mite unsteady on his feet.

I went back to the lobby and found Gimpy sitting with the two guests at a small, ornate wrought iron table tucked under the overhang of the sprawling Victorian stairway. On the table was a cribbage board and a deck of cards. I instructed Gimpy to go and corroborate Michener's statement with Ashlee Vega and Michener's dresser, and, finally, to have Michener show him the photo of Vega and confirm that it was taken in her room. I didn't think Gimpy would mind that part of the assignment.

Bob and Dot Melanson were a diminutive couple whom nature had construed to look like a pair of matched beetles, with Bob's trimmed goatee being the only obvious distinction between them. In their early to middle seventies, they told me they had driven to Loomis City all the way from Salem, Massachusetts. They bragged about having attended every *Roundtree Days Festival* since its inception and had "fallen in love" with the Vermillion Arms.

"It's like going on a honeymoon every year," Dot said. "We're hoping to win the team cribbage contest this year. Last year we came in second."

"We can win a year's worth of *Roundtree* swag," Bob said. "I hope they don't cancel it just because Alexis was murdered."

"You mean Maddison Hadcock," I corrected.

"To us she's Alexis," Dot added. "She owns the hotel."

"Tell me what you saw."

I found myself wanting to hear what they had to say not only because it was standard procedure and perhaps relevant, but also because this was my first up-close-and-personal encounter with authentic Boston accents. A question entered my mind: At what point does an accent become a dialect and then an entirely new language? It was a question I'd have to ponder at a future time, and I turned my attention back to the Melansons' narrative, which I could with some confidence define as still being the English language.

"Bob and I had just finished a practice game, right here, and I had pegged out with His Nobs and I double-skunked Bob, who, as usual when he loses, thought I was cheating. But I would never cheat. I won fair and square. He's just a sore loser and—"

"And then?"

"And then I said, 'Okay, if that's the way you're going to be, I'll just go upstairs and get a clean deck from the room, so you know I'm playing fair and square.' I went upstairs—"

"We're in Room 14," Bob interjected. "Thirteen is unlucky."

"And I saw that the door to Room 12 was open a little. When Bob and I travel, we want our privacy and we think everyone is entitled to theirs, so I went to close the door but, umm…"

"You couldn't help poking your nose inside, could you?" Bob said. "And now, you've thrown me off my game."

"What did you see?" I asked Dot.

"That the place was a mess. Some people are like that, you know? It's their nature. But then I saw Alexis lying on the bed, all bloody, and I said to myself, 'Oh, my God!' This was definitely not in the activity guide. So, I ran downstairs and told Bob, and then we went straight to the clerk at the desk. And he found Mr. Okleberry. Do you know he has a clubfoot?"

"And we've been sitting here ever since," Bob said, "while everyone else is getting ready for the finals."

"When you were upstairs this morning," I asked both of them, "did you see anyone acting suspiciously? Anyone who you thought shouldn't have been there?"

Bob and Dot looked at each other.

"There was a young guy dressed like a cowboy running around," Bob said, "not just on our floor. All over the hotel. But he wasn't any cowboy."

"How do you know he wasn't a cowboy?" I asked.

"Because he was wearing red Nikes! Cowboys wear boots. You ever seen a cowboy wearing red Nikes?"

I had to admit it was a perceptive observation. I got Bob and Dot's phone numbers and wished them well on their cribbage tournament.

Before I left them to their game, Dot said to me, "Sir, did you see the last episode of season six?"

"I'm afraid I missed that one."

"Well, you should know that Alexis was having an affair with an environmentalist!"

"I might have heard something about that," I said.

"Well, that could be important because her father, Lyman Honeycut, is trying to buy out mineral rights at Bears Ears National Monument right out from under the federal government's nose!"

"I'll keep that in mind," I said, and tipped my hat.

49

Poot's report from his talk with the desk clerk corroborated what Gimpy and the Melansons had said, but the clerk offered little more other than to stammer out apologies for the hotel, adding vague guarantees that nothing like this had ever happened. Poot got the sense that the clerk's main concern was that he'd be fired as a result of the hotel losing money from the bad publicity resulting from a murder on his watch. My experience in such matters, however, suggested the opposite—that people were attracted to sites of violent crime like moths to light.

The Melansons' hometown, for example, where the draw of the Salem witch trials was still going strong after more than three centuries. Hadcock's murder could add just one more legend to the *Roundtree* mystique.

Poot and I went into the Vermillion Arms dining room, where only a few hours earlier I'd been enjoying a quiet cup of coffee and communing with an imaginary vixen. We purchased two orders of Vern Roundtree's Famous Smothered Barbecue Chicken to go and brought it up to Rusty and Doc Albers. I asked them if Hadcock's body was ready to be removed. Doc answered in the affirmative. Poot suggested it would be better to move the corpse without the general public knowing. Doc scratched his head.

"Not sure how."

Poot had an idea.

"Wait five minutes and then take her down the service elevator and out the back alley."

Poot and I returned to the lobby. He found a spot near the registration desk where everyone would be facing him with their backs to the elevator banks. As per his instructions, I took a place in the rear.

"Ladies and gentlemen," Poot announced in a loud voice. There was still a lot of crowd noise. He cleared his throat in dramatic fashion.

"Ladies and gentlemen, I have a special announcement to make. Who would like to meet Jordan Roundtree up close and personal at the fireworks tonight?" That quieted things pretty fast. "And who would like to get a chance to shake the hand of Sheriff Vernon Roundtree, himself?" The interest level of the buzz crescendoed from mild to keen.

"Where do we sign up?" I shouted from the back of the lobby, the obligatory shill.

"Hand me a piece of paper and a pen," Poot said to the clerk. "Fast."

"Everyone, get in line," he said to the crowd. "No pushing, please."

Over my shoulder, I saw Doc and Rusty unobtrusively exit the back door, a covered gurney between them. They could have been kitchen staff delivering a meal. But it didn't matter. I think the president of the United States could've walked in and those folks in the lobby wouldn't have noticed it. I hoped they wouldn't be too disappointed when it would be announced that the meet and greet had been postponed indefinitely.

CONRAD MICHENER

"Get me the hell out of here, Stewie!"

"Calm down, Connie," he replied. Stewie Morgenstern, my hotshot New York agent, had become a pro at pulling me back from the edge, mainly because he had so much practice at it. But this was different. I wasn't allowed to tell him that Madsie was dead—had been murdered—and that Sheriff One Eye—what was his name?—Walz something?—no, Dance—considered me a suspect. Me, a suspect? The next victim, more likely. So I told Stewie about the arson, which nobody told me not to talk about, and I made it sound as bad as possible because I wanted out. And Stewie was telling me to calm down.

"Okay, I'm calm," I said. But I wasn't, even after the two Xanax I'd taken when I'd arrived back at my room. I just said it to pacify him. Why was I pacifying *him*? "Now, get me the hell out of here. This show isn't going to make it to next year the way things are going. And I'm sick of playing a cowboy. I want to act for a change, before I get typecast."

"You *are* acting," Stewie replied. "And you're doing a damn good job of it if you look at the ratings."

"I mean act as in *act*. As in a real dramatic role. No more, 'Howdy pardner. Reckon it looks like rain today.' "

"Okay. I'm working on it," Stewie said.

"What are you working on?"

51

"I'm talking to a Canadian production company about a series that takes place in nineteenth-century Japan, just after it was opened up to the West. Lead role. Big bucks. And they'll shoot it in British Columbia so you could stay here in the city and go out there only when you need to."

That sounded intriguing.

"What would be my role? Admiral Perry?"

"An American cattle baron, showing the Japanese how to raise Kobe beef."

"Another cowboy."

"Cattle baron, Connie. Cattle baron! It's a big step up from cowboy."

I almost hung up on him. I would have, except all of a sudden it felt like my phone was my life raft, my tether to reality, and I needed to hang on.

"So what should I do now, with people dropping like flies around me?"

"Who's dropping like flies, Connie?"

Whoops.

"Just a figure of speech. As you can tell, I'm a little jittery."

"Understood. Stick it out, Connie. Be Vernon Roundtree just a little while longer. Your fans love you. Your fans adore you. Get through this, kiddo. Be the tower of strength and it'll help get you the next deal. Multi-year. Seven figures, easy. I promise. Hold on a sec? I've got a call on another line."

I hung up. Kobe beef. Aren't they the cows that get massaged and are fed beer? That's the role I wanted. To be a Kobe cow. I peeled off my Roundtree outfit, took another Xanax, and lay down in my underwear, intent upon spending the rest of the day in bed and fantasizing that I'm a drunk cow getting a shiatsu massage from a ravishing geisha. After all, Dance didn't want me to talk to anyone about Madsie's murder. I was just following orders.

I turned on the TV to "Judge Judy." She had begun to lay into a big, bald tattooed idiot for signing his girlfriend's name to bad checks and was about to render her verdict when there was a knock at the door.

"Go away," I said.

"It's me, Inez. We need to talk."

"Go away." The last thing I needed right now was a publicist, sexy though she was, to hound me into doing something I knew I wouldn't want to do.

"Connie, we have an opportunity!"

She said the word "opportunity" as if she'd just found the formula for turning cow turds to gold.

"Go away."

She knew that if I opened the door, I was a goner. Partly because she was a looker—half Persian, half Brazilian, whole seductress—who could wrap me around her little finger. Maybe that's what made her such a good publicist. That, and she never gave up.

"You know I won't, Connie. Open up."

What the hell. I opened the door, turned around, and collapsed back into bed on my back. I covered my head with a pillow to demonstrate my discontent.

"Are we pouting?" Inez asked. She said it in baby talk, which did little to improve my mood.

"Don't you understand what's going on?" I asked. Then I remembered yet again I wasn't allowed to talk about Madsie. Did I blow it already?

"Of course I do," Inez said. "Sheriff Tuttle's stable has been burned down and your fans are asking you to solve it. It's all over Facebook, Instagram, and Twitter."

So she hadn't heard the front page stuff.

"What's this big opportunity you've got lined up?" I asked, though I knew that asking was the kiss of death.

She sat down on the side of the bed and gave my shoulder a friendly shake. The shake of death.

"You're Vernon Roundtree, Connie! You solve the mystery, like you always do. Like your fans want you to."

"What do you mean, 'You solve the mystery'?"

"Do an investigation. Interview witnesses. As Roundtree, you do it all the time. You're the best at it."

"Inez, I have a script when I do it. The questions I ask have already been written out, down to the last raised eyebrow. I spend a week memorizing them. The people answering the questions spend a week memorizing the answers. And when we act and don't get it right the first time, we do it over

53

and over again until it sounds believable. We know the ending a year before we begin. There's no investigation. It's just pretend."

"You're just being modest," Inez said, and she put her hand right where she knew she would get the desired response. I groaned. This wasn't fair. It was below the belt. Literally.

"You always do such a great job," she said.

And so did she. I felt a little guilty, with my TV wife on a slab, though it can't be denied that Alexis and I were estranged because she had cheated on me with DeWitt Cheney. And Ashlee? She'd forgive me. She always did. And look at her and Merle Tuttle! That was a hard one to picture. He was old enough to be her father. So, I was just evening up the balance sheet. In the end, I agreed to Inez's plan. How could I not?

Chapter Six

12:00 Noon

JEFFERSON DANCE

Concluding our efforts at huckstering, Poot and I headed over to Tuttle's office for a little strategic planning. We drew the window shades to keep out the sun, which had already turned the room into a sweat lodge. I went to the lavatory and poured water over my head. Even without the enormity of Maddison Hadcock's murder to turn up the temperature, the heat was made more intense by an unforgiving, cloudless sky. I couldn't forget that not least among our concerns was the general well-being of the tourists, especially the older ones, for whom dehydration and heat stroke were real dangers, and we surely did not need any additional emergencies on our hands. Poot said he would call the festival staff to tell them to send out reminders everywhere for folks to drink buckets of water, wear hats, and apply plenty of sunscreen. The basics that everyone in these parts knows about, but easterners tend to not believe, or if they do, to think that the desert sun will mummify everyone but them. I'd seen unwitting, disoriented victims of dehydration. It was an ugly sight, but one easily avoided.

That thought brought me back to Harold Wohlmer with a greater sense of urgency to find him as quickly as possible. Poot availed himself of the office phone to find out if there had been progress in that regard. The responses were not hopeful. On the other hand, Doc Albers must have been successful in removing Hadcock's body unobtrusively, as no one seemed to be aware that the *Roundtree* constellation had just been diminished by one star.

Our discussion circled back to the two crimes, the arson and the murder. After due consideration, we agreed that even though at first it seemed highly unlikely two such overt crimes occurring within hours of each other could be unrelated, it was even more unlikely that they were related. In the case of the arson, the perpetrator had made considerable effort to minimize injury, first by waiting until Tuttle and his horses were away from his stable, and second by turning on the sprinkler irrigation system to prevent a general conflagration. It was an effort that took careful planning, understanding of the mechanics of the irrigation system, and appreciation of the relationship between water and desert. Maddison Hadcock's murder, brutal and angry, was the opposite. It had all the earmarks of an unpremeditated crime of passion. Since the perpetrator obtained the murder weapon only after entering the room, it's possible he hadn't even planned to kill, that his violence was provoked or spontaneous, in a moment of rage.

These unsubstantiated hypotheses might be intriguing, but without supporting evidence they were little more than flights of fancy and would likely get us nowhere. We really needed some hard facts if we hoped to make any progress. Being low on manpower, Poot and I decided to split up and meet periodically to compare notes. Poot headed off to the county morgue, which was not in Loomis City but in Granstaff, the original county seat of Castle County, where he'd get more detail on the Hadcock murder from the medical examiner. I consulted the activities calendar in the *Roundtree Days* booklet and headed over to the Desert Rows Bookstore and Espresso Bar, not to make Poot feel envious, but for a very special book signing.

The outside of the store was decorated with red, white, and blue bunting and with window posters of a brilliantly smiling Ashlee Vega. The event was already twenty minutes underway so there was a long line of folks spiraling out the front door, fanning themselves and swigging soft drinks. I tapped a bald fellow on the shoulder and advised him to go inside or at least buy a hat, assuring him that the lady behind him would be happy to save his place.

"I used to go to the beach all the time when I was a kid," he said, "and a little sun didn't bother me then."

"Were you bald when you were a kid?" I asked. He didn't see the humor, though some of the folks around him thought it was pretty funny. I guess I shamed him into common sense, because he went into the store.

I followed him inside, and though I'm not a big fan of air conditioning, I couldn't complain that Desert Rows had opted for that luxury. Ashlee Vega sat next to the cashier at a linen-draped table, autographing books and any other "Roundtree" paraphernalia to which a Sharpie would adhere. I pulled a DVD of Season One off a rack, and then spied a couple classic books in paperback by Wallace Stegner and Edward Abbey, the Yin and Yang of wilderness literature, that had been on my bucket list. I paid for it all, went back outside, and made the signing line one fan longer.

Vega was very good at her job. She chatted amiably with one fan after another, as if each was her old friend. The husband of the elderly couple just ahead of me said, "Jordan, we love you so much, can I give you a big hug?" His wife said, "Melvin, don't be ridiculous!" Vega was quick on the draw. "Oh, it's okay, ma'am, but I'm afraid my daddy wouldn't approve of me hugging a strange man. And I've got to do what he says, 'cause he's the sheriff!"

When it was my turn, she looked up at me with a Farrah Fawcett smile, which would have made my knees buckle if I hadn't been pretty sure it wasn't genuine. I also couldn't help but recall Michener's voyeuristic photo of her on his cellphone.

"Nice to see a younger face in the crowd," she whispered, with a conspiratorial wink.

My knees buckled.

"I'd certainly appreciate it if you'd sign my disk," I said, immediately wondering if I'd made the comment sound lewdly flirtatious intentionally or unintentionally, whether she might have interpreted it that way, or whether... Whatever.

"Mmm, I'd love to," she said. "Would you prefer Ashlee or Jordan?"

"Either." Again, with the innuendo. "Let's do Ashlee."

"And would you like me to personalize it?"

The way she said "personalize…"

"Yes, please."

"What's your name?"

She batted her eyelashes slowly. Whoever said you don't sweat in the desert had never met Ashlee Vega.

"Actually, it's for a friend. Could you write his name?"

"Whatever you want. What's your friend's name?"

"Merle Tuttle."

The smile on Vega's lips didn't flicker for a second. But in her eyes, I spied a flash of surprise and maybe even alarm, and I wondered if I had the same effect on her knees under the table as she had on mine standing up. But her hesitation passed as fast as a sun shower in Death Valley, so I couldn't draw any conclusions.

"Merle with an *e* at the end?" she asked. I had to give her credit. She was a professional.

"That's right." I continued more softly. "The brochure says you've got a half hour between this book signing and your next event at the hayride. Please stop by Sheriff Tuttle's office for a quiet chat."

"Okay," she said.

Ashlee gave me a parting winning smile as the next fan approached.

I hurriedly completed what you might call my "stage preparations" a minute before Vega arrived. Whether it was her normal street attire or her Jordan Roundtree getup she was dressed in, the short cutoff jeans and loose-fitting halter top did Ashlee Vega no disservice. My Uncle Wayne—Aunt Flora's husband—would have thought, "She's easy on the eyes." He wouldn't have said it out loud, though, because Aunt Flora would have swatted him on the back of the head.

On the other hand, Vega seemed to have abandoned her smile somewhere between Desert Rows and the sheriff's office, and I had a good guess why. I gestured for her to make herself comfortable in the chair facing the desk, behind which I sat in Tuttle's office chair.

"I know what you're thinking," she said. The absence of agitation in her voice suggested she hadn't yet heard about Maddison Hadcock's murder, and I decided to keep it that way.

"No, I don't think you do," I replied. "What I'm thinking is, it's hot in here, and on such a dry day and after all the talking you were doing at the bookstore, you might need this."

I opened a drawer in the desk, removed a bottled water, and handed it to her. If she was surprised by my gallantry, she didn't show it. Apparently, she was accustomed to being pampered, but it didn't prevent her from drinking half the bottle off the bat.

"I don't know anything about it," she said.

Maybe I was wrong that she hadn't heard about the murder.

"About what?" I asked.

"That Merle's stable was burned down. For God's sakes, everyone's heard. You don't have to play games."

"Tell me about you and Merle."

"What do you know?" she asked.

"Not very much. Fill me in. You don't have to play games, either."

"Let's get this straight," Ashlee said. "Merle Tuttle is a very nice man. We've been good friends, but it was never anything more than that."

I guess she thought I must be some kind of hard-nosed interrogator because she stopped and waited as if I was going to try to trip her up with a hundred confusing questions. I leaned back in the chair, folded my hands on my stomach, and gave her my sympathetic "you're off to a great start" smile. One winning smile deserves another. She got the hint.

"I mean, he's done a fantastic job getting the town ready for *Roundtree Days*," she continued. "Ever since the first festival, he's been incredibly supportive of what we're trying to do here. Not everyone in town is a fan of all this activity every year. It's a pretty dull place except for the big weekend, when it goes insane. In winter it's dead as a doornail. Now, because it's on the map there's a lot more going on and it's really helped the local economy—"

"Ms. Vega," I interrupted. "Let's stay on track, shall we? I was asking about your relationship with Merle Tuttle."

"All right. You wouldn't think such a small town would need so much paperwork. If Merle hadn't pushed hard for all the ordinances and permits and waivers and God knows what else, this whole amazing thing would never have gotten off the ground."

"Why do you suppose Merle's been so gung-ho?"

"Because he genuinely thinks it's good for the town. The first time I met him was at a meeting with the board of selectmen. That's when Alfie made his pitch to film 'Roundtree' in Loomis City. That was even before we had any idea the show would be so popular we'd have a festival."

"Alfie?" I asked.

"Our producer."

"Does Alfie have a last name?"

"Moran."

I wrote it down.

"One *r* or two?"

"You don't know who Alfie Moran is?" she asked. She acted as if I'd never heard of Abraham Lincoln, but I have to confess I would not be able to name a single TV producer if my life depended on it.

"Is Alfie in Loomis City this weekend?"

"Of course he is."

"Good. You were saying you and Moran met with the board."

"Not just the two of us. The whole cast."

"And you wanted to make a good impression."

"Yes."

"Well, apparently you made a big one on Merle."

"What do you mean by that?"

"You tell me."

"We became friends. Every once in a while, we'd have a drink or two at the Vermillion Arms. You know, his wife died, and they never had any kids, so it wasn't like it was, like, illegal."

"Did you and Merle ever get together at times other than at the festival?"

"I came out to visit once or twice."

"Like when the town is dead as a doornail?"

"I suppose. Merle took me hunting. He showed me how to fire a rifle."

"Makes sense," I said.

"What makes sense?"

"That you and Alfie would go to great lengths to make sure Merle continued to support the festival. Especially considering some folks in town weren't buying it."

"It's not like that."

"Well, that's good, because if someone as attractive as you were having a flirtation with Merle while in a relationship with Conrad Michener, I could see how that might inflame some passions. Enough, maybe, to inflame his stable."

"You've got it all wrong," Ashlee protested. "God, I knew you'd get it wrong."

"Set me straight, then."

"Merle wanted as much out of us as we wanted out of him."

"Meaning?"

"He had this crazy idea of wanting to be a screenwriter for 'Roundtree.' He bragged he knew more about life in a town like this than our writers did. So every year he'd bring us a new script, and every year Alfie would politely decline. He had a lot of story ideas—you know, based on his experience—but to write dialogue for TV, a screenplay, it's a profession. It's a skill. You don't just have an idea."

"How did Merle take it?"

"He'd get upset and pout and threaten to cancel the next festival. But then he'd always calm down and everything would get back to normal."

"After a few drinks and a night of commiseration, you mean."

"I told you I knew what you were thinking."

Ashlee shook her head in disgust, and I didn't much blame her. Maybe I was reading too much into their relationship because I wanted things to line up neat and clean. But the scenario fit. Tuttle had hesitated when I asked him who might have burned his stable, as if he had his suspicions but didn't want to say. Maybe he'd said something to Moran or his crew—one of those threats, perhaps—that caused them to get vindictive. Especially Michener, who might've taken umbrage at a small-town cowpoke, and an old one at

61

that, rising above his station to stake a claim on his woman. That smelled as strong as roadkill skunk when he talked to Poot and me earlier. It was just a theory, but it was plausible. How plausible remained to be seen.

"Where were you between five and seven this morning?"

"Are you kidding? In bed. I had breakfast in my room."

"Can anyone corroborate that?" I already knew the answer, but I wanted to hear it from her.

Vega sighed. "Conrad."

"One more question. Where were you between nine and ten?"

"Why?"

"Just answer, please."

"I took a bath."

"For an hour?"

"I like bathing."

I took Vega's cellphone number and told her I'd be in touch. As she was leaving, a thought popped into my head.

"By the way," I asked, "since you're staying at the hotel, might you know a young guy who runs around in Nikes dressed like a cowboy?"

"Oh, sure."

"What's his name?"

"That would be Alfie."

After she left I opened the door to the cloakroom in the back of the office.

"Well?" I asked Tuttle, who had been holed up there at my request. His face was red, and it wasn't from the sun.

"Have to admit," he replied, "she got it just about right."

"You think Conrad Michener could've had it in for you?"

"You mean Vernon Roundtree?" It was good to hear Tuttle laugh, though I'm not sure it was the best moment for it. "Well, you can't rule anything out, I suppose, but he knew I really wasn't a serious rival for his gal's affections. I mean, just take one look at the two of us. And jeez, would a Hollywood actor have known to water my field before burning my stable down? Would probably have been more manual labor than he's done in his whole life. Doesn't add up to me."

"What about this guy, Alfie Moran? He was also seen running around the hotel when Maddison Hadcock was killed. Maybe there's a connection."

"Well," Merle said, "devil's advocate could say that considering he rejected my scripts, I had greater reason to make trouble for Alfie than vicie-versie. And as far as Hadcock, I have no idea what the two of them might have had in for each other. Alfie can be a bur on your backside when he gets in a mood, but I'm told that's not atypical of TV producers."

My phone rang. It was Poot.

"On my way back to town. Thought you might want an update."

"Hold on," I said, and took the phone outside. "Go ahead."

"Stabbing was indeed the cause of death, and the knife we found was indeed the murder weapon. They pulled some prints from it and are running them through the data banks. Minor bruising on her cheek and jaw, too, and a cut on her lip. Could've been a fall, I suppose."

"Or she was hit in the face. Before or after she was stabbed?"

"Doc says before. Means she could've been unconscious when she was killed."

"Anything else?"

"Doc found evidence of semen in her."

"Where?"

"You name it."

"Was she raped?"

"Doc says no. Also been smoking marijuana."

"So, she had consensual sex and got high, then ate breakfast, after which she got knocked out in a fist fight, and then was stabbed to death?"

"Doesn't make much sense."

"It's sure enough a cockeyed chronology. But if they find a match for the semen or the prints, it's likely we have our perp."

"Maybe."

"What about Wohlmer?" I asked. "Any reported sightings?"

"No. Not yet."

I told Poot to meet me at the Vermillion Arms. I hung up and asked Merle a question.

"How did things go, rounding up your horses?"

"They were amenable enough. Not like there's going to be a stampede of eight horses."

"Take you long to corral them?"

"I was out there a couple hours. Then I changed my mind. Decided to let them roam. There's still enough forage for them to get by for now, and as long as they stay away from grazing on the loco weed, they'll be okay. Should try to figure out where I'm going to stable them pretty darn quick, though."

"So they're still out there on the range?"

"Yep."

"Well, good luck," I said.

Merle tipped his hat and went off to do battle with his All America agent. I didn't really suspect Merle of being involved with Maddison Hadcock's murder any more than anyone else. Less, even. If he had been, why would he have surrendered his badge, even temporarily? But he had not been forthcoming about being chummy with the "Roundtree" crowd, had declined Poot's offer to help him round up his horses, and now he had left me to consider the fact that he was yet another person without an alibi between nine and ten that I could corroborate.

Poot and I had a mutual interest in meeting Alfie Moran since he had a connection, if tenuous, to both the arson and the murder. Moran's professional relationship to Merle Tuttle, at least as Vega had described it, had had its ups and downs. Tuttle had promoted "Roundtree" and wanted payback, but hadn't received it, unless an occasional evening with Ashlee Vega counted as such. Witnesses had also spotted Moran cavorting on the second floor of the Vermillion Arms around the time of Maddison Hadcock's murder.

According to the festival schedule, Moran was about to give a presentation in the hotel grand ballroom on *How the Western Was Won*, highlighted by a photo montage of a century's worth of Hollywood Western matinee idols. It sounded interesting. I wondered what John Wayne would've looked like trying to rope a steer in real life.

I'd also been wondering with increased anxiety whether news of Hadcock's death had spread. She was in great demand during *Roundtree Days*, and our meager troops had little experience dealing with murder cases.

Poot and I arrived at the hotel at the same time. I filled him in about Alfie Moran and sent him off to the ballroom. I went upstairs to Room 12. Rusty Carlisle was still sitting there tying flies.

"Hey," he said when he saw me, and set back to his task.

"Any troubles?" I asked.

"Nope."

"Any people come 'round asking for Maddison Hadcock?"

He chuckled. "You mean Alexis Honeycut Roundtree?" he asked and continued with his fly tying.

"Okay. Any people come 'round asking for Alexis Honeycut Roundtree?"

"Yup."

"And what did you tell them?"

Rusty shook his head and sighed. Like many fly-fishing fanatics, he took umbrage at having his nirvana disturbed. I can't say I didn't share that feeling when I had a reel in my hand, but now wasn't the time for dawdling. On the other hand, the fastest way to catch a fish is with patience.

Rusty finally bit. "I told everyone she was off in a secret location planning a special event for the end of the festival and was not to be disturbed. I figured word about that would get around and folks would leave me be. Which they have. Till now."

Rusty's ploy had been a good one, but I was not entirely satisfied.

"But what about the 'Roundtree' production folks? They must be worried."

"Oh, them. I just told them they'd have to call her on her cellphone. Didn't you see the note on the door?" Rusty pointed behind him with his left thumb.

I hadn't noticed it until then. It was typed: "I'm out and about—wink, wink—so if you need me you'll just have to call. MH." It was followed by her cellphone number.

"How d'you know her number?" I asked.

"Front desk. Where else do you think?"

"So what does 'wink, wink' mean?"

"Heck if I know. I just figured with these Hollywood types, they'd know what 'wink, wink' meant."

I headed back down the grand marble staircase, leaving Rusty in peace and thinking that I'd give serious consideration to nominating him for governor if the opportunity ever arose. Between his innate wisdom and the amount of time he spent on his fly-fishing, I suspected he had the makings of an excellent public servant.

A big screen flanked by maroon velvet curtains hung above a stage at one end of the ballroom. Five rows of six round, linen-covered tables, each of which would soon seat eight to ten Western movie fans, were lined up. Soft Muzak played from an overhead speaker. Mantovani? It didn't fit, but maybe it was never intended for folks to actually listen to it.

Poot had corralled Alfie Moran by the podium next to the screen on the stage, and I could see that the producer was as compliant as a colt being saddled for the first time. Poot had his hands in his jeans pockets, his head tilted to one side. I'd seen Poot assume that pose many times over the years. He was letting Moran blow off steam while wondering how people can act so dang foolish. Next, Poot would raise the toe of his right boot, keeping the heel to the ground, and examine it. Which he did.

"His scripts were shit, that's why!" I heard Moran reply loudly to whatever had been Poot's quietly proffered question, no doubt referencing Tuttle. The content of Moran's answer didn't surprise me. What surprised me was the accent. He was a Brit. Producing a Western. Well, why not? After all, didn't that actor fellow, Clint Eastwood, find fame and fortune in spaghetti Westerns in Italy?

"You know what brilliant name Tuttle invented for the town?" Moran continued. "You won't believe this. He named it Carsonoma County! I said, 'Look mate, you can't name a place Carsonoma County. A horrible disease is not the image one wants to portray of the town we want all Americans to call home.' And you know what he said? He said, 'Not carcinoma like in *cancer*. Carson like in *Kit Carson*. Kit Carson plus *Sonoma. Carsonoma*.' I said, 'Mate, it doesn't matter. People are not reading a bloody book. They're watching TV. The *V* in TV stands for vision. They don't see spellings. Carcin, Carson, they sound the same. Look at the demographics. Do you want to remind the entire Baby Boomer population of their imminent slow, painful deaths?' Do you hear what I'm saying?"

Before Poot could answer, Moran continued.

"And his hero's name. Buck Thorn. Buck Thorn? What kind of name is that? From a bloody 1947 space movie? With X-ray guns?"

I sensed Moran was losing steam and interjected a question.

"When's the last time you were in touch with Maddison Hadcock?" I asked.

He looked at me, at first with surprise, since he hadn't realized I was there, and then with disdain. I looked at him a little more closely. He was a short, wiry fellow with a disproportionate stomach paunch. Too much foie gras, I suspect. A boyish face, though lined by years, stress, and excess. His trimmed, graying sideburns would have looked debonair except that they advertised the dye that darkened the rest of his bush of hair. The Melansons had said he was young, and I guess he was, relative to them. As they'd noted, Moran was decked out in Western wear, though the designer jeans tended to out him as a pretender. A bolo tie was secured by a gaudy slice of turquoise engraved with the figure of a bronco-buster swinging a lariat. A pair of red Nikes completed the ensemble.

"What have we here?" Moran said, sizing me up as I had done to him. "Another colorful aboriginal? What clan do you come from?"

Poot said, "He's the sheriff. Answer the question."

Alfie chewed on the inside of his lip, looking at both of us, as if trying to come to grips with an upside-down world in which a pair of country bumkins could be in a position of greater power than a millionaire TV producer.

"The bitch," he finally said. "I've been calling her for hours and she's not answering."

"That doesn't answer his question," Poot said. Though in a way, it answered a bigger one. He thought she was still alive.

"Can I see your phone for a minute?" I asked.

"Why the hell"—then he saw the look in my eye—"not." He handed me his phone.

I tried it and handed it back.

"Punch in the passcode. And no more fun and games, if you don't mind."

I checked his recent calls. He had been telling the truth. There had been spasms of calls to Maddison Hadcock over the past few hours.

"Thank you," I said, and returned his phone. "Why hasn't she been returning your calls?"

"How the bloody hell do I know?"

He passed that test, giving no indication he knew the answer.

"You leave a message for her to call you back?"

"No, I left a message saying, 'Please do not call me back for any reason whatsoever.' What do you think? Of course, I told her to call me back. Many times. In no uncertain terms. Jesus!"

"Tell me the nature of the conversation you had with her the last time you were in contact with her."

"What's going on here?" Alfie asked. "Is she in trouble? Am I in trouble?"

"Did you see her this morning?"

"Yes, I saw her this morning."

He paused to bite his nails and spit them out. I waited.

"So I went to m'lady's bedchamber bright and early," he continued, "where, in fact, we engaged in recreational sex. With a weed chaser. Sue me. For all of twenty minutes. It's how she likes to start the day."

"And then?" I asked.

"Meaning?"

"You gave her a peck on the cheek and said ta-ta?"

"More or less. We both have a busy day today, as you can plainly see."

Folks were starting to wander into the ballroom for the presentation. I needed to end this soon.

"That's not what I heard," I lied. I was thinking about how the furniture had gotten rearranged in Hadcock's room. "I heard you got into a bit of an argument."

"Then you heard wrong," Alfie said, a little too forcefully.

"Sure about that?"

Alfie had run out of nails and started working on his knuckles.

"All right, so we had a minor disagreement."

"About what?"

"About her contract for next year. She wants her role in the show to expand geometrically and her salary to expand exponentially. I corrected her math, and reminded her that as her role was secondary to the star, there was no way she was going to be paid more than an orbiting planet should be paid. And after her father kills her lover-boy tree-hugger in episode six next year, between you and me I don't know where we're going with her character."

"How did she respond?"

"The usual way. She started throwing things."

"And what did you do?"

"I've got to deal with these prima donnas on a daily basis, mind you. So I did the only wise thing. I ducked and left, discretion being the better part of valor."

"What time was that?" I asked.

"A little after nine. I had what you might refer to as a downhome pancake-and-sausage breakfast with the Rotary at nine-thirty. Part of my civic duty. My heartburn will attest to my attendance."

"Where was the breakfast?"

"As God is my witness, we're standing on the very spot as we speak."

"Are you staying here at the hotel?"

"You can't be serious! Who'd want to stay in this creaking dump? I've been provided a manse out in Beauville. Pool, hot tub. All the amenities."

"Beauville? Haven't heard of that town."

"It's not a town. It's a mirage. A gated community in the middle of the desert for the chronically affluent. Still under construction. The new West. They used to corral horses. Now they corral people."

"Thank you for your time," I said. "And good luck on your presentation."

CONRAD MICHENER

Inez, bless her heart, had gone off to notify the networks that there was a *big story* developing: Long-time Castle County sheriff, Merle Tuttle, had been a target of an arsonist on the last day of the world-renowned *Roundtree*

Days Festival, and Vernon Roundtree—aka me—was lending his legendary investigative skills to assist local law enforcement. Thank God, Inez didn't know about Madsie's murder. All I needed was for her to get me involved with *that*. Why did I suddenly feel another migraine coming on?

I had phoned room service, and just finished what the hotel euphemistically referred to as a Cobb salad, when Inez called me from wherever she was. Actually, I hadn't finished the salad. After two bites of the gray rubber the menu said was turkey, I covered it with a towel so I wouldn't have to look at it. What I'd give for a slice of New York pizza. Better yet. What I'd give to be in New York for a slice of New York pizza.

Inez said she thought it was a good idea for me to go out to Tuttle's ranch and nose around, like Roundtree would.

I sure as hell wasn't going to start my "investigation" with Merle Tuttle. He was the last person I wanted to see, and I told her so.

"You wouldn't have to. I'll check to make sure he won't be there. Anyway, I don't think I can get a camera crew out there for a few hours, so it would be a waste of time if you went now. Why don't you interview some people first? That way the news will spread by word of mouth."

"Like who?"

"I don't know. Find out if Merle has any friends or relatives. Someone that might not like him. Gotta go. Kiss-kiss."

Kiss-kiss my ass-ass.

I decided that before I did any real interviews—depending on how you'd define real—I should practice on people I knew, in the hope I'd get the hang of it. I called Ashlee and Alfie to try out my shtick on them. Neither of them answered, and I didn't bother to leave voice messages.

I really didn't want to go back outside. It was too damn hot and there were too many damn "Roundtree" fans, and the thought of putting on my cowboy costume made me want to regurgitate the Cobb salad, as if I needed help with that. Then I got a brainstorm. Family members are always the prime crime suspects, right? I yanked open my night-table drawer. Yes! Right next to the Gideon Bible was what our ancestors referred to as the phonebook. Since there were very few humans in Castle County and probably even fewer who knew what a telephone was, the phonebook should be a concise primary genealogical resource. I opened it up to *T* for Tuttle on page twenty-four.

The good news was that there were a number of Tuttles. The bad news was that they accounted for approximately half the county, from Abby to Zachary. I said I wanted practice, not repetitive disorder syndrome, right? What the hell. I was a hardboiled investigator! I started dialing.

After a half hour I needed to lie down. Things hadn't gone so well. Most of the calls went unanswered, and I didn't want potential arsonists to respond to my personal phone number, so I didn't leave a message. Of those who did answer, I asked, "Are you by any chance related to Merle Tuttle?" Most of them said no. Some of them said, "Which Merle Tuttle?" (That's before I noticed the phone book listed five Merle Tuttles in Castle County.) One person, Bertha Tuttle, answered, "Maybe." I said, "What the hell do you mean, maybe? Either you're related to someone or you're not." Bertha hung up on me. Which was fine, because I was due to head over to the fairgrounds to be the judge of the *Roundtree* horseshoe competition. Though I was no closer to solving the mystery of the burned stable than when I had started, at least the word-of-mouth seemed to have gotten off to a rousing start.

Kiss-kiss.

Chapter Seven

1:00 p.m.

JEFFERSON DANCE

Poot and I split up once again. With Harriet Wohlmer's permission, Poot went to give their Winnebago a once-over to try to find any clue to where Harold might have gone. It was a serious possibility, however, that Harold hadn't even made it back to the RV after leaving Harriet at Knead The Dough.

I returned to the Vermillion Arms hoping for a follow-up with the Melansons, but not unexpectedly they were no longer in the lobby. I next went up to Room 12, specifically to search for Maddison Hadcock's cellphone. I wanted to discover what, if any, voice messages Alfie Moran or anyone else had left. It wasn't there. At least I couldn't find it, so I called Doc Albers and asked if it had been on her person. It had not. A dead end, at least for now.

There was a *Do Not Disturb* sign on Room 14. I knocked anyway.

"Who's there?" came Bob Melanson's voice from within.

"Sheriff's office again," I said.

"Don't you see the sign?"

"Oh, just let him in," Dot Melanson said. "You can take your nap later."

Bob acquiesced and opened the door, but didn't concede fully, as he kept the chain on. That was fine with me, as all he was wearing was a white T-shirt and a pair of striped boxer shorts. I didn't need to see more.

"Well, did you nab him?" Bob asked.

72

"Who?"

"The guy with Nikes, of course. I'm sure he's the one who killed Alexis."

"I appreciate the lead," I said. "I wonder if you or the Missus might have noticed anyone else who looked suspicious."

"Why? You've already fingered the perp."

"I'm sure you're right. But we might need someone to testify. An eyewitness. Or a co-conspirator."

"Good thinking," Bob said. "Now that I think of it, there was a man with a walker."

I considered the general age level of the tourists.

"How do you consider that's suspicious?" I asked.

"Think about it. How did he get up the stairs, I wonder?" Bob said.

"Maybe he took the elevator, Sherlock," Dot said from over his shoulder.

Another dead end. Seems I was good at finding them. Nevertheless, I put the word out to look for a man using a walker. Though there might be dozens, if they found the right person, he could conceivably provide a lead. I uncharitably had an image of a walker race as the newest *Roundtree Days* activity but forced myself to put that out of my mind as soon as it entered. And so it went.

I stopped at Suzi Q's Pay 'n Pak on my way to encounter this vagabond, Fiddler, at Reilly Wash. I opened the door to my truck but I'd parked too close to the pump to open it all the way, and had to inhale mightily in order to squeeze myself out. I filled my gas tank, which gave me a chance to find out about something that should have occurred to me in the first place had I been thinking straight. I left my truck parked next to the pump and went inside, where I grabbed a packaged ham sandwich and a cup of coffee and waited until I was the only customer before heading to the cash register.

"Hey, Lindsie."

"Hey." We were good buddies by now.

"You remember when I asked you this morning about how you first heard that Merle Tuttle's place burned down?"

"Sure do," said the teenager. "And I told you that everyone knew about it."

73

"If I recall, it was more like, 'everyone who came into the store was talking about it.' "

"Same difference."

"Well, think real hard for a minute, and try to remember who exactly was the first one to tell you."

I waited while the young lady scrunched up her face and looked skyward. I took my last five-dollar bill out of my wallet and handed it to her.

"I remember now. It was Brittney Nearing."

"Tell me what Brittney said."

"She said, like, 'You know what I just heard? Like, I heard that Sheriff Tuttle's place burned down.' "

Meaning Brittney must have heard it from someone else, since for certain it was too soon to be in the *Public Pinyon*.

"She say where she heard?"

"No. She didn't say. Sorry."

Another dead end. My turn to scrunch up my face, which Lindsie couldn't fail to notice.

"Maybe from her boyfriend?" she offered. I suppose Lindsie felt guilty she hadn't earned her reward yet.

"Her boyfriend. And who might that be?" I asked.

"Jalen."

"Jalen Taggert?"

"Yeah. You know him?"

Maybe my five dollars was going farther than I bargained for.

"We've met," I said. "Thank you, young lady. You've been a big help."

I got a smile in return that Ashlee Vega would envy.

In my truck, I took a bite of my sandwich, then called Gimpy Okleberry.

"What can you tell me about Jalen Ray Taggert?"

"Jalen?" Just in the way he said the name I could tell Gimpy was about to become diplomatic.

"Not a bad kid," he continued. "Couple of arrests for stupid teenager stuff. Joy riding, egging cars, stealing a pizza. That kind of thing. His father pays the fines and he's let off with the usual warnings. Why?"

"His name just came up in a conversation. And this morning he tried to intimidate me and Poot."

Okleberry had a good chuckle over that.

"Jalen acts tough, but he's never been in real trouble."

"All bark and no bite?"

"That's about right."

"Enough bite to burn down Merle's place?"

"Jeez! No, I don't think he'd do that."

"Okay, thanks." I almost hung up. "Wait," I said. "Who's the father that bails him out?"

"Sloan Taggert. Owner of Culvert Operations."

I had seen a business by that name on the edge of town. It was a name that jostled some cobwebs out of my past.

"That the outfit that sells irrigation and drainage equipment?"

"That's the one. Everyone here calls it CO_2. One of the oldest businesses in Loomis City still standing."

"What's the two for in CO_2?"

"Back in the day it was originally called County Outdoor Services and folks called it plain CO. Rolls off the tongue better than having to say County Outdoor Services. When Sloan inherited the business from his daddy, he changed it to Culvert Operations and kept the initials but added the 2 since it's the second generation. As long as we have farmers, ranchers, and desert, we'll have CO_2."

I thanked Gimpy, then chewed on that information along with my ham sandwich. After I visited Fiddler it would make sense, time-wise to drop by Culvert Operations on my way back into town. Getting ready to squeeze back into my truck, I opened the door, which banged against the gas pump. That gave me a thought. I closed the door and went back inside Suzi Q's.

The radiant face on the cover of the issue of *People* magazine that Lindsie was reading was Ashlee Vega's.

"Sorry to interrupt," I said, "but do you sell kerosene here?"

"Uh-huh. Out back. How much do you need?"

"I don't need any right now, but do you recall if anyone's bought any in large quantities lately?"

"Uh-huh."

Seems I was getting the shakedown treatment again.

"I'm all out of cash, Lindsie. Can you take a rain check and tell me who and when?"

"Sure. About a week ago. It was Fiddler. He bought three gallons."

"Thank you kindly."

Before I turned on the engine, my phone rang again. I figured it would be Gimpy with more to say about Jalen Taggert, but it was Poot.

"I checked out the Winnebago," he said. "Everything packed away neat and tidy. Bed made, military style. Even the cracks between the car seats were clean," Poot said.

"In other words, the worst conditions to find a clue."

"Yep. But I finally got a lead on Harold Wohlmer."

"I thought you just said—"

"I didn't get the lead from the Winnebago. I went to all the stores in town, showing Wohlmer's photo to anyone I could get to look at it. The guy at Knead The Dough remembered him, but that was when he'd been with his wife. *Before* he disappeared. I finally got a hit *after* he went missing at Outside Influence. You know that outfit?"

"Nope."

"New camping and hiking retailer on Main and 300 East. Sells to affluent recreational adventurers."

There's a contradiction in terms somewhere in there, I thought, but refrained from comment.

"The owner, a fellow named Matt Jarvis, said he saw Wohlmer walking with another guy in front of his store. Wohlmer appeared excited or agitated. Jarvis couldn't say which for sure. The other guy kept patting him on the back."

"Who was the other guy?"

"He says he's seen him around, but because Jarvis is relatively new in town, he didn't know his name, and since he had no idea it would become a serious issue, he didn't ask."

"What time?"

"Around nine, nine-thirty."

"Shortly after Wohlmer left his Missus."

"Yeah."

"Description of the guy he was with?"

"Caucasian. About five-ten, five-eleven. Mid-fifties. Thin. Muscular maybe. Closely cropped hair. No facial hair. Heavy-duty overalls, well-worn, not for show."

"So more likely a local than 'Roundtree' cast."

"Could be."

"What direction did Wohlmer head after his conversation?"

"Jarvis didn't know. He had to attend to a customer."

It wasn't much, but it was something. The first thing we had to go on, really. Problem was, the description of the man Wohlmer was talking to fit about half the locals. In other words, all the adult males. I gave some thought to how we might narrow down the field as I drove out to Reilly Wash. In the meantime, I told Poot to grab as many volunteers as he could muster and span them out from Outside Influence to try to determine what direction Harold Wohlmer's wandering mind took him to.

CONRAD MICHENER

After the horseshoe competition, I was back in my room with Ashlee, trying not to think about Madsie. I had almost gotten through judging it without falling asleep until Cade McClellan, chairman of the Traditional Games Competition Committee informed me that this year there had been a record number of dead ringers. Dead was not a term I needed to hear in any context.

It's not that Maddison Hadcock and I were close. That might have been the public perception because of our stage personas. The backstory was that Alexis and Vernon had been "married" for twenty-four years and had raised our daughter, Jordan, together. We had been deeply in love, but as time passed my preoccupation with the pressures of my job as sheriff, combined with Alexis's innate haughtiness and her arrogant father's constant interference in my work, pushed us further and further apart. Her affair with a young environmentalist, DeWitt Cheney, was the last straw. We separated, though deep down inside our love would endure. In other words, it was like every other Western series that's being produced these days. But who knows, maybe in a season or two the scriptwriters would have brought us back together.

In real life, Madsie and I had detested each other. She thought I thought she was a lousy actress, and she was right. I had heard rumors that Alfie wasn't going to renew her contract after the current season, and I did nothing to derail them, which she didn't appreciate. In fact, she thought I was the instigator, which I wasn't. Now that she was dead, it was one less headache for Alfie and me, and I know that it's very mean-spirited to think that way, but there you go. The worst of it was, if people realized I had that thought, it could make me a suspect. That, I didn't need.

Now, as per Inez's instructions, I was back in detective mode, investigating *The Mysterious Case of Arson* at the Tuttle ranch, hoping to shove away the dreary thoughts of Madsie's murder.

"Where were you between five and seven this morning?" I asked Ashlee.

She seemed incredulous, maybe because I was in the process of unbuttoning her blouse as I popped the question.

"Where do you think I was?" Ashlee asked, unkindly pushing me away. "I was in bed. With you!"

"Aha! But I didn't come to your room until *after* seven. You could have been out to Tuttle's ranch, burned the place down, and been back here by seven. You wouldn't be the first to pull a stunt like that, you know."

"Are you out of your effing mind?"

"So you don't deny it! You admit it's possible. You then engaged in sex with me to throw me off the track and *pretended* to enjoy it."

"You got that last part right. And I've got to go. Ladies' knitting hour at the library."

"I'm not doing so well with this detective stuff. Am I?"

"No. In fact, you suck at it."

"Thanks. I'm supposed to interview Alfie next. Any advice?"

"Yeah. Stick to acting."

She shut the door behind her. Hard.

I met Alfie in the lobby. He had just finished his talk about movie cowboys. It was the same talk he'd been doing for years, burnishing it from time to time with tasty new yarns he made up as he went. Like how he once beat James Garner at an all-night poker game. He never even met James Garner and couldn't tell the difference between a pair of fives and a royal flush even when he was sober. I had asked Alfie to come to my room because every time I looked at my "Roundtree" outfit I wanted to heave. He declined, as he only had a few minutes before running off to a coordinating meeting with the directors of the big parade tonight. As long as they gave me a semi-comatose horse that didn't give me a hard time, that's all I cared about. I'd bring two Xanax just in case: One for me and one for the horse.

I took the elevator down to the lobby, and by the time I found Alfie, I'd gotten two "Howdy, pardners," three "Good day, Sheriffs," and one "My man!"

"I'm in a hurry, Michener," Alfie said. "You've got questions for me? Ask." He sounded irritated.

"You sound irritated," I said. That was probably not the best way to have started my interview, because he began to walk away.

"Wait. Hold on. This will only take a minute."

"Go on, then."

"Where were you between five and seven this morning?"

"As I just told the other clown also pretending to be a sheriff, I was engaged in boudoir gymnastics with Madsie."

"You were?" My mouth must have dropped open. Number one, I thought they hated each other. Number two, that was only a couple of hours before she was killed. Yet Alfie didn't seem to even know it yet.

"Yes, I was. And if you have greater success contacting her than I have had, she will corroborate it."

"Oh."

"Any more questions?"

"Not at the moment."

"Good. And let me just add a parting comment, Michener. A little birdie told me you're trying to get out of your 'Roundtree' contract. Don't even think about it. Like it or not, you'll be a bloody cowboy for as long as I say you will."

Alfie walked off before I had a chance to warn him not to leave town. My investigation had not gotten off to a very promising start. I was ready to take a break and asked the concierge where I could get a decent cup of coffee, if such a thing were possible in Loomis City. I hoped he wouldn't say Knead The Dough, because I'd been there once before and what they called a cappuccino tasted more like the three-day-old Special Blend at the gas station.

"Knead The Dough," he said. "Best coffee in town."

Some days you just can't win. When I got there, I ordered a mocha chai latte and retreated to a dark corner where I could at least seek refuge from the heat and bothersome tourists.

I wasn't there for more than a minute when I started getting the sideways glances and hearing the whispers. "Roundtree's here!" "What's he drinking?" "Is that a chai latte? Ooh, let's get one." A few courageous and/or desperate souls sought my autograph. My intentionally illegible scrawl could be deciphered either as Roundtree or Michener, depending on who one wanted to brag to his friends about. Probably Roundtree. Just after I finished signing, "To Ella, from squiggle" on the bill of her "Roundtree" visor, I saw the sheriff's trusty sidekick with the handlebar moustache enter the café. I raised my menu close to my face so he wouldn't see me. He approached the barista, showed him a photo, asked a few questions, and left.

That gave me an idea. As I got up, a pair of drooling cougars in "Roundtree" T-shirts approached me, their eyes bulging like on Bugs Bunny cartoons. Before they could dig their fangs in, I said, "No time now, gals. Talk to my publicist. Her name is Inez," and left them to figure out how they'd find Inez.

I went up to the barista, cutting to the front of the line by saying, "'Scuse me, folks. Got some urgent business to attend to." I was Roundtree. No one batted an eyelash. It's good to be king.

"Yes, sir!" the barista said. "What can I do for you?"

"That short guy with the moustache. What did he want?"

"There's an old man who's been missing all day. They're out looking for him and wanted to know if I'd seen him."

"And?"

"He was in here this morning with his wife. Then he disappeared, I guess."

Bingo. Just the direction my moribund investigation needed.

"Hmm. Maybe I can help find him," I said. "What's he look like?"

"Big guy. Rough-looking, a little. But friendly at the same time. You know what I mean?"

"Name?"

"Wohlmer. Harry Wohlmer."

"Thanks, pardner." I even tipped my hat like I did on TV.

"Any time, Sheriff."

Could it be a mere coincidence that this big, rough guy just happened to disappear only hours after Merle Tuttle's stable was burned down and Madsie was killed? I think not. As my scriptwriter often has Roundtree say, "I don't believe in coincidences." Low cellos in the background and maybe some contemplative piano arpeggios. I think if I can find this guy Wohlmer and have him thrown in jail, it will be one more feather in the cap of Vernon Roundtree. Nielsen Ratings, hold on to your hats. Who said this sheriff stuff was difficult?

Chapter Eight

2:00 p.m.

JEFFERSON DANCE

Loomis City's recent celebrity notwithstanding, it was still a frontier town surviving precariously in the midst of a desert wilderness, where all evidence of human habitation quickly tapers into nothingness; where all roads end in stone and dust, and the inaccessible takes over.

I put my foot on the gas pedal where the speed limit notches up out past Suzi Q's, the last outpost within the town's incorporated boundaries. It was approaching midafternoon and I had made no progress to speak of. Who had killed Maddison Hadcock? Who had burned down Merle Tuttle's stable? How had Harold Wohlmer disappeared into thin air? I had no idea what the answers were to any of those questions. Maybe I'd gotten a little smug over past successes. All I knew was, with the way things were going, I deserved a kick in the rump more than a pat on the back.

I glimpsed the Navajo souvenir stand on my right as I passed it. They seemed to be doing a brisk business. I drove faster, and maybe I was going too fast, because out of the corner of my eye I thought I saw ostriches to my left. I needed to convince myself I wasn't hallucinating from dehydration, so I stopped and backed up to take a closer look, and sure enough that's what it was. A flock? A herd? Whatever it's called, a bunch of ostriches grazed on an acre or so of surprisingly green grass within a chicken wire fence. Maybe it should be called ostrich wire.

After the ostrich farm and then the cutoff to Tuttle's ranch, the only sign of humanity was the asphalt under my tires. Rolling desert extended as far as the eye could see, and at this time of year, it was bone dry. That's why I had no reservations about pulling off onto Reilly Wash. The chance of a flash flood coming through the wash was as remote as my current chance of bagging a bighorn sheep.

Reilly Wash ranged in width from ten to fifty feet. For the most part, it was more or less flat-bottomed with gently sloping banks. The exceptions to that description were the S-curves created by infrequent but powerful flash floods, where the water cut deeper into the bank, making them so steep that I couldn't see above them. Some people call such intense gullying an arroyo but around here we just use the term *wash*. Or sometimes, dry wash. When I was a kid, I recall wandering on my own through the washes, collecting arrowheads and ancient Native American potsherds by the bagful. They used to be a dime a dozen, but over the years so many had been taken that, like the rain, they'd all but disappeared. Plus, it was now illegal to gather artifacts, and rightly so.

The bed of the wash had a sandy base covered in stones, from pebble-sized on up, that had become round and smooth from being rattled against each other through millennia of flood cycles. Though my truck had good clearance, I had to maneuver around occasional boulders and tree limbs that had been washed downstream by previous floods and been laid down whenever and wherever the current had slowed.

I passed the cottonwood grove that Linda Benallie said was my landmark and began to look for indications I was nearing Fiddler's shack. Since it hadn't rained for a long time, I kept my head out the window looking for the usual signs: tire tracks and footprints. Or discarded cigarette butts and beer cans, which last a lot longer than prints. At first, there were plenty of tracks, and where they appeared relatively fresh and led out of the wash I stopped the truck and followed them on foot, hoping either for a sign of Fiddler's shack or better yet of Harold Wohlmer.

Those hopes were not to be satisfied. All the tracks just trailed off to the horizon and were likely the product of recent backpackers or pubescent teenagers escaping their parents for some rapturous alone time. The tracks could have been a day old or a week old. To have followed each one of them would have taken months and I didn't have the luxury of time. I should have brought Linda Benallie with me, who was familiar with the terrain.

After a while, there were fewer tracks, partly because the farther upstream I went the rockier the wash became. Around each curve, I hoped to see the shack Linda had said was the abode of this Fiddler character, but after twenty minutes and about two miles, I was on the verge of giving up.

Finally, I saw something promising. A bicycle tire tread and, nearby, footprints etched in a steep, sandy bank, heading up to a ridge about fifteen feet above me. When I brought my truck to a stop to get a closer look, the noise of the engine and the crunching of the stones under the tires ceased, and I was rewarded with the gift of silence. In the same way that it sometimes requires circumstances to be forced upon us before we realize how deafened we've become to the din of the human rat race, it took my ears a few seconds to adjust to the silence and to appreciate the new reality; but when they finally did, I heard the faint but captivating sound of a strummed guitar that must have been there all along.

I considered approaching with stealth, which my training had made me highly capable of, but then thought better of it. If it was indeed Fiddler, and if he was armed, he might react to such a surprise with undue alarm and put a bullet through me without asking questions first. Also, he may well have heard my truck for miles, which would have rendered stealth meaningless.

"Fiddler?" I called out from outside my truck. The strumming stopped.

"Fiddler? Sheriff's office."

Not even an echo.

It was slow going following the prints up the steep bank. My boots slid on loose red sand, and I had to grab on to erosion-exposed juniper roots to pull myself up. It was a noisy effort and more than once I lost my footing. When I finally got to the top, I was on the relatively flat desert plain. Ten yards away from the edge of the bank was the shack I had been searching for, though even calling it a shack was a compliment it hardly deserved.

It was constructed of weathered boards of random sizes that had been collected over time from down in the wash, the flotsam of old cabins and mine timbers. How it held together was as much an architectural wonder as the pyramids, though I suspected it wouldn't last as long. It was more of a tepee shape than a traditional house structure, with a low entrance that one would have to crawl through. If I tried to do so, I would be a sitting duck from anyone inside if their intent was less than hospitable.

Next to the shack lay a mountain bike. The frame was old and rusty but sported an unlikely pair of new tires. I took a cursory glance at the treads, and determined they were not caked with clay. I heard a soft, metallic clattering sound from within, as if someone was preparing lunch.

I patted my gun, just in case.

"Okay, Fiddler," I called one more time. "Come on out."

The clanking stopped for a moment, then resumed. I picked up a broken pinyon bough next to me, perched my hat on top of it, and approached the shack. When I was close enough, I thrust the branch through the door opening, expecting a loud reaction. There was none. No sound at all.

"Do I have to burn this place down, Fiddler?"

Still nothing.

Well, I can't waste a whole afternoon hoping he'll come out, I thought, and I was not inclined to be the second arsonist of the day, so I got down on my hands and knees and crawled through the door.

A guitar lay on the packed dirt floor. Cans of food and beer, some empty, some not, were scattered randomly about. An open can of baked beans that was about to boil over sat on a lit, single-burner kerosene stove, which I turned off. The whole place smelled of neglect, and if I wasn't mistaken, of marijuana. That aroused my curiosity. It didn't take long to discover a substantial cache of weed and paraphernalia, including a bong and cigar casings. On a wooden plank supported by sandstone blocks, a small stash of newly rolled joints fitted neatly in an empty sardine can. I pocketed those, not for future use but for future reference.

The only thing missing was Fiddler, unless he had transmogrified in a manner embraced by Native American tradition. Because in his stead was a cagey blue-black raven, which must have entered the shack as soon as Fiddler fled, having awaited its opportunity for a free lunch. Among the most adept survivors in the desert Southwest, it seemed less frightened than irritated by my presence. I seem to have interrupted it helping itself to whatever morsels were available for consumption. It sidled up to an almost empty can of fruit salad and, carrying it in its massive beak, calmly strolled to the opposite side of the shack. From there it turned its head to the side to keep a wary, intelligent eye on me, while it downed a coveted maraschino cherry.

"You're obviously smarter than I am," I said to the bird, and left it to its good fortune. I backed out of the shack and looked around. There were jumbles of footprints leading in all directions. Where Fiddler could have gone to hide while I was scrambling up the bank was a mystery I didn't have time to solve. There didn't seem to be any good hiding places, but there didn't seem to be any bad ones, either. Tucked away in the endless hills that rolled to the horizon were thousands of warrens of millennia-old ancient Pueblo Indian cliff and cave dwellings, and of silver mines much more recently abandoned by white men. Somewhere among those countless stands of pinyon pine and juniper, the occasional broad cottonwoods, and the expanding thickets of invasive Russian olive and tamarisk along the banks of the wash, he was there.

The raven might be smarter than me, but next time I'd at least be smarter than Fiddler.

CONRAD MICHENER

What is it they say? Work interfering with life? That's something I try to avoid at all costs. But how about pretending interfering with pretending? This geezer, Harold Wohlmer, was now on my radar and I was gung-ho to move ahead with my investigation, but my festival schedule told me I had to go over to the high school to be MC for the *Roundtree Days Up 'n Comers* talent show. I couldn't think of anything I'd rather do, except for anything else. Last year I walked out of the 4-H animal husbandry competition because watching a two-ton swine giving birth was the most disgusting thing I'd ever seen. Go figure. But Stewie had chastised me in no uncertain terms about my obligation to stick to the word, if not the spirit, of my contract with my producers.

I was not alone hosting the talent show. My "daughter," Jordan, aka Ashlee Vega, was my cohost. The makeup folks brushed on a little gray around my temples and whatever other magic they do so I'd look older than a brother. The techies wired us up on the floor of the gymnasium and handed us microphones, the list of contestants with their fifty-word bios, and perky thirty-second scripts to start and end the show. It was kind of like the Thanksgiving Day Parade for losers.

Ashlee, dressed like Dale Evans on steroids, would have made Roy Rogers forget Trigger in a hurry. She wore a tight-fitting denim shirt, fastened with imitation ruby snaps undone from the top just far enough down to show a tease of cleavage without upsetting the mothers of young children, but giving the fathers something to think about during the hula hoop routine. In a more private setting, I would have attempted to rip her blouse open, and Ashlee must have seen the look in my eyes because she whispered, "Don't even think about it," just as the mics went live.

She and I were all smiles introducing the acts, with Inez snapping one photo after another for the social media world, waiting with bated breath for the next installment of Vern and Jordan.

Well, I'll tell you, I've heard some barbershop quartets in my day, but didn't Four Boys From Blanding, in their novel arrangement of "Sweet Adeline," just beat all? (I'm being sarcastic.) And the baton twirling team, the Emery Emeralds of Emery County, whose drum major seemed to blow his whistle at random intervals or whenever he could catch his breath, whichever came first? And the pudgy little girl, June Frolich, paralyzed from the waist down from a car accident, who aspired to become an opera star, singing a stirring rendition of "Climb Ev'ry Mountain," the only problem being she sang in a key heretofore unknown to four hundred years of Western music? And the jump rope team from up north in Oakley, who switched seamlessly from Double Dutch to rodeo lariat demons, roping a half dozen calves, strategically prodded onto the gym floor by able assistants, in thirty seconds flat? There was even a Roundtree imitator named Garrison Reardon whose day job was a car mechanic. Dressed in a reasonably poor imitation of my iconic cowboy outfit, he mimicked the way I talked in the role, along with every gesture I'd come to be associated with: the thoughtful head scratch; the squinted eyes looking off into the horizon, searching for meaning in life; the jutting chin when I was about to tell off the bad guy; the subtle gesture of rubbing the toe of my boot into the dirt just before making an endearingly self-deprecating comment. Reardon was a frighteningly good amateur pretender imitating a highly paid professional pretender. He and I could've easily ended up in each other's shoes but for luck of the draw. That thought sent shivers down my spine. I'd rather be dead than a car mechanic. I would have voted for Reardon to win the prize, but it was not to be. The audience members were the judges. Ashlee and I were just the MCs. They went for "Climb Ev'ry Mountain." Sympathy vote, no doubt.

But it wasn't all fun and games, if you can believe that. As riveting as the acts were—I'm being sarcastic again—all the while I kept my eye out for Harold Wohlmer. He could be anywhere. And if he committed arson once, who knew when he might strike again? "A big guy. Rough, but friendly," the barista had said. There were plenty of old farts in the bleachers who fit that description. Even some of the women.

The show finally ended, and we did our thirty second "Thank you. Good-bye. We love you, Loomis City." Wave. Wave. I gave Ashlee a fatherly hug around the shoulders and a peck on the cheek, much to the delight of the departing crowd. As we handed in our microphones, the production folks removed the wires they'd snaked through our clothing. My offer to help remove Ashlee's went unrequited. Inez continued snapping photos of us to post wherever she posts. That gave me an idea.

"See you later," I said, and headed off to my hotel room, where no one would bother me.

Chapter Nine

3:00 p.m.

JEFFERSON DANCE

Whoever first said, "Mad dogs and Englishmen go out in the noonday sun," created a powerful image. However, he was wrong to suggest that noon is the hottest time of day, at least here in the desert. It would have been more accurate, if not as poetic, to say, "Mad dogs and Englishmen go out in late afternoon when the temperature has reached its maximum." Which must mean I'm part mad dog, as I'm fairly certain there's no English blood in my family's lineage.

Since my truck's air conditioning gave up the ghost after it surpassed a quarter-million miles long ago, I drove over to Merle Tuttle's place with the windows open. Tuttle was out, which I was glad of. The questions I had were better answered by the landscape, whose honesty I could depend on. I walked around the ruins of his stable like a paleontologist, except instead of hunting for fossilized dinosaur tracks, it was boot, bicycle, and truck tracks. Not quite as ancient, perhaps, but just as informative. The water from the dousing of Merle's house and fields had made a muck of things in some areas, but in others it wetted the earth just enough to preserve a few identifiable tire tracks before drying hard as concrete in the arid sun. Set in stone, as it were.

The results were mixed. There were some truck tire tracks that bore promising signature patterns but, thinking about Fiddler, no bicycle tracks that I could find. Next, I searched for the sprinkler irrigation controls, which the arsonist had considerately turned on in order to set a perimeter, preserving Merle's house and the thousands of acres that could otherwise have burned. I ultimately found the irrigation valve box well beyond the corral behind the stable. The automatic timer was set for 10 p.m.

The day was turning even hotter, as if to impress (and oppress) even the most stoic among us who might have pretended it was no bother. The morning's light cloud cover was a distant memory and had long burned off. One wouldn't think a brilliant blue sky would be oppressive, but as I left the ranch behind me and churned up a cloud of dust, I tried to imagine the ingenuity of earlier cultures in this part of the world who had made the land habitable, long before people like Sloan Taggert bestowed upon it the miracle of modern irrigation.

I pulled up in front of the Culvert Operations warehouse about a hundred yards down 1100 West, just south of Route 12. It was surrounded by a large area of hard-packed dirt, cordoned off by a chain-link fence. Parked within the fenced area were about a dozen vehicles. The smallest was a pickup truck and the largest a fourteen-wheeler, and in between were backhoes and other earth-moving apparatus. Emblazoned on the doors was a logo, to varying degrees covered with dust, of the initials CO_2 encircled by a field of green. All the vehicles showed a good amount of wear and tear. They'd been around a long time. Might that mean business was suffering? Surrounding the warehouse were organized stacks of pipes ranging from half-inch galvanized up to monsters I could've just about driven my truck through.

At one end of the warehouse were a few wooden steps that led up to a door with the word OFFICE hand-painted above it. The gate in the fence had a padlock, but instinctively I shook it anyway to see if it would open. That was a mistake. Three impressively large and aggressive growling canines bounded from around the corner of the warehouse and lunged at the fence. I had just enough time to jump back before my hand would have been turned into lunch. It was far from the cordial welcome I had been hoping for.

I took another precautionary step back and continued along the outside of the fence, though my prolonged presence did little to please the dogs, which followed my every step with murderous intent. At least that's what their growling seemed to imply.

It was my mistake not to have called first. Chances were that on the final day of *Roundtree Days,* Taggert wasn't even there. So, I tried to phone him, but the cell service out there was predictably spotty. I called his name aloud, but my voice was no match for the dogs' barking.

I started to head back to my truck, but apparently the dogs had done me a service by providing an alarm, because the office door opened, and a man emerged. The dogs immediately swirled around him, begging for affection or meat, or both. The man approached the fence but made no effort to let me through. That was fine with me.

"What do you want?" he said. Now I wasn't so sure what to say and stood there like an idiot because I had planned on asking him about Merle Tuttle. But I now found myself face to face with the person who fit Poot's description as being the last person to have seen Harold Wohlmer before he disappeared. Like a good country-western singer, I changed from one tune to another without skipping a beat.

"Sloan Taggert?" I asked.

"Could be."

"I'm from the sheriff"s office."

"I can see that." He looked at me a little more carefully. "Do I know you?"

"I don't think so. You know a man named Harold Wohlmer?"

Taggert's eyes narrowed. He seemed confused, as if he had been anticipating an entirely different question.

"Nope," he said. "Never heard of him. Anything else?"

"You were seen talking to him this morning on Main Street."

"I talk to a lot of people on Main Street. That's why they call it Main Street."

"Harold is an older man. Take a look." I showed him the photo on my phone. "Big, open face. Stocky. Clean-shaven, straight part in his hair. He's got dementia. He's missing and his wife is desperate to find him."

Taggert had been looking straight into my eyes. Staring, really. I noticed that he never blinked. He took a quick look at the photo, then returned his gaze to me.

"Dementia, huh? Yeah, now I remember him. I didn't know his name. He just came up to me on the street and we had a conversation."

"About what?"

"He was talking some gibberish about 'Roundtree'. 'Roundtree' this. 'Roundtree' that. Who has time to watch that junk? Only thing I know is that it's ruined this town."

Like father, like son. Or vice versa.

"So you weren't able to help him?"

"I had no idea what he was talking about."

"Do you know where he went after talking to you?"

"Am I my brother's keeper?"

"That's your answer?"

His eyes remained locked on mine.

"Am I my brother's keeper?" he repeated.

"One last thing. Where were you before seven o'clock this morning?"

"Sleeping."

"Can anyone confirm that?"

He looked at his dogs, which were swimming around his legs.

"Was I here sleeping, dogs?" he asked them.

There being no commands in his question, they ignored his words.

"See?" he said. "They confirmed it. Just like I said. You don't believe them, come on in and ask them."

"Thank you for your time."

He turned his back on me and headed back to the office. His dogs followed him inside, which I appreciated.

Before I left, I made a closer inspection of Taggert's trucks. The bed of the pickup, a Ford F-150, was loaded with gear. I got into my truck, fished the business card out of my pocket that Linda Benallie had given me, and began to give her a call. Then I remembered there was no cell service, so I drove back to Suzi Q's and called again.

"Is there a history between Sloan Taggert and Merle Tuttle?" I asked Linda.

"I remember the names from my childhood, but that's about all."

"You mean like, 'I can't quit you, Merle,' kind of history?"

I laughed. "No. More like animosities, business dealings, who runs the town. Things like that."

"There's some of that, but I can't talk now. Deadlines. Meet me in an hour at Chuck's Wagon. Root Beer's on me."

CONRAD MICHENER

It took me almost an hour, but finally I got it just the way I wanted it: "*H.W., I know who u r & what u did. Meet me in Vermillion Arms Lobby @ 7PM. No questions asked. Reward for info leading to arrest. $$$! R.T.*" I reread it, and since I wasn't limited to a hundred-forty characters anymore, I added "*&* *conviction*" after "*arrest*" to make it look more official. Then I clicked on Tweet, and for good measure repeated the message on Facebook. Blast off! Launched into cyberspace.

What I'd realized at the talent show when I scanned the bleachers for a single individual, was that I couldn't do a full-blown investigation on my own. Without a cop's resources like staff, assistants, squad cars, and doughnuts, how was I going to make progress? When Inez clicked her camera, my brain clicked. I saw all those "Roundtree" fans, who went to that dinky talent show only because a big star like me was there. Multiply them by a million and you'd have the approximate number of fans and followers I had on social media. They, the huddled masses of couch potatoes yearning to be relevant, would be my eyes and ears. They would spread my message. Sooner or later Harold Wohlmer would receive it. I was confident that at seven o'clock I'd have my man in custody. Stop the presses!

Within a minute after sending out the Tweet, I heard the ping of a text message. It was from Inez. I expected she'd be congratulating me on my brilliant idea. Then I opened it: "*R U some kind of idiot?*" it read.

I was stunned.

"*Pls elaborate*," I jabbed back. Clearly, she didn't get it.

Rather than text me back, she called, using language I hadn't heard since season five of *The Wire*. The gist was, she felt that not only had I put myself in a no-win situation, I had come close to crossing a line of legality in about a half dozen ways, if not obliterating it entirely. I shot back with the classic male response—I blamed it on her.

"Well, you put me up to it!" I said. "It was your idea. Remember? 'Solve the mystery,' you said."

"Beyond making no sense and being self-contradictory—"

"What do you mean, 'self-contradictory'?"

"You think this Harold Wohlmer is going to show up, turn himself in, make a full confession, and then collect a reward for himself when he's sent to prison?"

"That's not—"

"And your little message could get this guy in serious trouble. There's no proof he did anything wrong. He's just missing. But some social media loony could take your message the wrong way and you could get him killed. We could even be sued. Don't you see that?"

I really couldn't, so I did what I usually did when I was confused. Changed the subject.

"So what do we do now?" I asked.

"How about putting you in witness protection?"

"Okay, I'm sorry. As they say on 'The Sopranos,' fuggetaboutit."

I could sense Inez mulling in the ensuing silence. Whenever Inez mulled it was a crapshoot. Would her pragmatism overrule her holier-than-thou-ness? Sometimes it did, sometimes it didn't. My fate hung in the balance.

"I had arranged for a photo op at Tuttle's ranch," she said.

"I don't want to go there. As I said, Sheriff Tuttle and I aren't on the best of terms."

"I understand that," Inez said. "He was screwing Ashlee and you're worried he might challenge you to mortal combat over her."

"He's thirty years older than me. I'd be gentle."

"He could lift you with one arm and tie you up before you could say uncle. But you don't have to worry. I checked. He's not around. He's been at the insurance company all afternoon."

"What do we have to go to his ranch for?"

"To make it *look* like you're investigating without putting anything in writing."

I was starting to feel guilty. And a little paranoid. Time for another Xanax.

"Can I write a retraction of my Tweet?"

"Once it's out there, honey, it's out there. Meet me in five minutes at the curb."

Chapter Ten

4:00 p.m.

JEFFERSON DANCE

Twiddling my thumbs for an hour while waiting to meet Linda Benallie was not going to help me resolve any of my three dilemmas, so I headed back to Reilly Wash. It was approaching the hottest time of the day, and I'd be surprised if the temperature hadn't reached triple digits. As I drove down Route 12, I shielded my eyes from the sun that was now hovering in front of me, teasing me with a mirage reflecting off the road surface. It wasn't hard to picture parched pioneers driven crazy by the illusory prospect of water, which looked so real and so close but which turned out to be yet another bitter disappointment, sometimes the final one.

I slowed down as I approached the Navajo souvenir stand. The trinkets didn't interest me—as colorful as they were—as much as the lemonade and a possible lead.

"Fifty cents, mister!" a little girl shouted out. She was about seven or eight and had apparently been appointed the spokesperson for the enterprise. Her younger brother was the bartender. The adults at the souvenir stand looked straight ahead but kept a wary eye on me.

I knelt down to the little girl's level.

"*Ya te'eh,*" I said in greeting.

The girl's eyes opened wide. She probably couldn't believe an Anglo, a *belagana*, could speak Navajo. I just hoped she didn't try to engage me in conversation, because I could count the number of Navajo words I knew on one hand.

"*Ya teh*," she replied, giggling.

"That lemonade looks real good and I'm pretty thirsty today, so how about we make it a double?" I said and handed her a dollar bill. Her eyes opened even wider at the sight of so much money. She tried to hide her delight, but a couple of other siblings behind her started jumping up and down, hooting and hollering at their good fortune. Somehow, they didn't seem to be suffering from the heat nearly as much as I was.

"How's business been?" I asked.

"We've made twelve dollars and seventy-five cents today," the girl said with pride.

"Seventy-five cents? How do you get seventy-five cents if you charge fifty cents a cup?"

"One man gave us a tip."

The little brother piped up, "He was from New York!"

"How many days have you been here?" I asked the girl.

"Since Wednesday."

Before I could ask another question, a shadow crossed over the girl. Not a figurative one. A real one. I looked over my shoulder, and a Navajo woman who was the right age to have been the girl's mother, asked me, "Can I help you?"

"The little girl reminds me of my daughter when she was that age. It must be the smile."

"They're having fun and making some money. We have a permit."

"No doubt. And I'm grateful for the service they're providing. I was just wondering if any of you might have seen a truck go by this morning."

Perhaps if she weren't Navajo and speaking to a stranger, she would have laughed at such a dumb comment. But she answered politely.

"Probably three-quarters of the vehicles that go by here are trucks, so the answer is yes a hundred times."

"This would have been between five and seven this morning. In either direction. It would have been a Ford F-150, and it would have had the insignia CO_2 on the side."

"Let me go ask," she said. "In the meantime, I think you need to buy more lemonade."

"No doubt," I said. It wasn't a bad idea, either.

She returned a few minutes later.

"My husband says the truck you described did pass here a little before six this morning. Going toward the sunrise."

"Much obliged," I said. On my way back to my truck I handed the girl an extra dollar. Her smile brightened my day. I wasn't going to be outdone by some New Yorker.

Now that I knew the terrain of Reilly Wash and the location of Fiddler's shack, I made much better time. I parked my truck out of Fiddler's ability to hear the grinding of the engine and crunching of the tires, and under a steep bank where it couldn't be seen from any angle around the bend. The rest of the way I made on foot along the wash, treading only on areas of fine sand to avoid detection. Approaching the shack, I concealed myself alongside a grove of ten-foot-high browning tamarisk, which had grown so thick that no plant other than a half-strangled scrub oak had enough space, light, soil, or moisture to compete.

When I was a boy, which I like to think wasn't that long ago, stream beds were bordered by an impressive variety of native grasses and foliage. With the invasion of tamarisk, the entire riparian landscape of the West had been altered. There were no local herbivores that could tame this tenacious predator, which crowded out almost all the other species that had been here since the last Ice Age. Some would say that's just the nature of nature. Things change. If tamarisk were a verb, it would describe what had happened to the people of Loomis City, overrun by progress. They'd been tamarisked. Was it for the better? Depended on who you asked, the tamarisk or the scrub oak.

My hiding spot was as good as a hunter's blind. In a way, I suppose I was now a hunter. Though there was little danger of being seen through such density, by practice I hunched down anyway, finding a minuscule clearing next to a flat boulder. Then I waited, hoping that Fiddler was either inside his lair or, if he was still in hiding, was hungry for his lunch and would soon make his appearance. Since I didn't hear any guitar music, I guessed the latter. I would not be fooled by the raven again, because he was perched on top of the shack. This time he was joined by a partner who lit atop a juniper ten feet away. It flapped its wings once and settled down to watch the entrance as intently as I did. The three of us had Fiddler covered. We all waited.

Something moved out of the shadow of the boulder next to me. I looked down and found I had a tarantula as a neighbor. He was a large one, about six inches in diameter, but I didn't expect much trouble from him as long as I didn't move precipitously, which was my plan anyway. I was not encouraged when he lifted his forelegs in my direction. I gathered he was sending me a message that this was his territory and I was trespassing on his land. It's been said tarantulas are friendly, but I have yet to meet one I can trust. I sympathized with his desire not to be tamarisked, so I moved a foot or two to my left, upon which the tarantula returned to his lair.

A small herd of antelope, which had been grazing about thirty yards upwind from me, lifted their heads, suddenly alert. I didn't think I had done anything to spook them. Then I heard the unmistakable bounce of an old mountain bike. The antelope bounded off toward the horizon.

Fiddler eventually came into the restricted field of vision afforded by my hideout. He was medium height, scrawny, long hair and heavily bearded, tattered jeans, a UCLA sweatshirt in serious need of washing, and a purple and green wool Sherpa hat. Not that I needed further confirmation, but unlike Sloan Taggert, he did not fit the description Jarvis had provided as the person who met Harold Wohlmer in front of his store. He appeared unarmed, so I kept my gun holstered. The birds gave Fiddler the once-over and decided there would be no easy pickings. Spreading their wings in leisurely fashion, they lofted themselves into the air, searching for greener pastures.

I, on the other hand, had been rewarded for my patience. Fiddler clearly had no idea I had returned to the vicinity because he was crooning the strains of "Light My Fire," singing in unrestrained full voice. He was no Jim

Morrison, but I had to admit his singing wasn't too bad.

Fiddler looked like he had taken the lyrics to heart and was about as high as a kite on a blustery day in March. When he was within fifteen feet, I stepped out from my makeshift blind.

"We need to talk," I said.

His first instinct was to run, which would have been fine because I knew I could catch him. His second instinct, which was even better, was that he realized he couldn't outrun me.

"What do you want?" he asked. He spoke in an unnaturally loud voice. Hard of hearing? Maybe he didn't talk to people very often.

"You always singing 'Light My Fire'?"

"It's a song. I like it. What's it to you?"

"Merle Tuttle's stable was burned down this morning. We'd like to find out who lit his fire."

Fiddler shrugged.

"None of my affair," he said. Again, it was almost a shout. I would have thought someone this reclusive would be more inclined to whisper. I'd known some folks who conversed loudly in restaurants, as if they needed extra attention to feed their self-esteem, when feeding their bellies was insufficient. I'd known others whose same tendency was the result of being high. Or who were somehow mentally afflicted. With Fiddler, it seemed it could be a combination of any or all of them.

"I understand you've had more than one run-in with him."

"So? I'm not the only one."

"Where were you this morning?"

"Here. And as you can guess, there wasn't no one else here who can say yes or no to that."

In anticipation of his reaction to my next statement, I readied myself for Fiddler to bolt.

"I understand you bought three gallons of kerosene at Suzi Q's last week."

He surprised me.

"So what?" he said. He scratched at the L on his sweatshirt.

"Tuttle's stable was burned down with kerosene."

"Hey, mister. I buy kerosene at Suzi Q's every month. Along with pickled eggs and beef jerky and highly caffeinated beverages and Zig-Zag rolling papers and all the other miraculous wonders of western civilization that esteemed establishment has to offer. I use kerosene to cook with and I still got two gallons, three-and-a-half quarts left in my container. You think I burned down Merle Tuttle's stable with a pint of kerosene?"

I hesitated.

"Want to see for yourself?" he added.

"I'll take your word for it. For now. But I've got to keep an eye on you. You'll have to come into town with me."

"You charging me? For what?"

"Possession of a controlled substance."

"So you're the one who stole my jays!" he cried.

"Think of it as saving you from yourself."

He whined louder than a hound baying at a full moon. I let him finish his beans and take his guitar. He sat next to me in my truck, strumming, on the way back to town. It wasn't bad playing, either.

"Tell me about you and Tuttle," I said, in between renditions of "Like a Rolling Stone" and "Blowin' in the Wind."

"Nothing to tell."

"Remind me how come you called him the Antichrist."

"You heard about that?"

"How would I be asking if I hadn't?"

"It was all a misunderstanding."

"Was it a misunderstanding you threw a rock through a restaurant window?"

"See? That's what I mean. I was aiming for someone's head and missed. My aim was errant. I can't help it if I have a bad aim."

"He locked you up for it. You must've resented that."

"I've been arrested and locked up so many times, if I resented each one of them there'd be no place in my heart for love."

"So now you love Tuttle?"

"Have to. Got no choice."

We passed a dirt road that had a small sign with an arrow that said, BEAUVILLE LUXURY ESTATE. MODEL FOR VIEWING. 0.5 MILES. I stopped my truck and made a U-turn.

"Slight detour, Fiddler."

"Is this really necessary?" He seemed suddenly anxious.

"Why?"

"No reason. Just getting hot. That's all."

"We'll find out if it's necessary once we're there."

An open gate set in a totally useless and unnecessary, four-foot-high sandstone wall, which any eight-year-old could climb over, encircled the development. What was the wall keeping out? The desert?

I must have been thinking aloud, because Fiddler said, "The hoi polloi. The great unwashed. The undeserving proletariat. People like you and me."

I let him vent about the inherent unfairness of the capitalist system. It seemed to make him feel better.

Beside the gate was a sign that read: HALF-ACRE LOTS STARTING AT $1.2. Since it was unlikely they'd sell properties for a dollar-twenty, presumably the developers decided it would've been gauche to have added the word *million* for those who had enough cash to buy. At the bottom of the sign was a phone number.

I drove into the development of about twenty homes, all of which were gray-brown stucco, low-slung but sprawling. Most of them were still under construction, a few were barely more than a foundation. Though it was a Sunday and a day off from work, the place had more of a feel of abandonment than of a weekend respite from construction. Only two or three of the houses appeared fully functional. Around them, someone had made the poor judgment of planting trees that would grow better on an English hillside than in the Western desert. They were dead, not surprisingly. Of the finished homes, only one, the model, had a swimming pool with water in it.

"You stay here," I said. "I'm getting out to look around."

"How do you know I'm not going to take off?"

"Because you're going to keep playing your guitar and singing your songs, and if I hear the music stop, I'm going to find you and break your arm."

"Fair enough, brother."

There was no car in the driveway nor in the garage, so I assumed Alfie Moran was out and about. I approached the house and went around to the pool where I expected to find, and did find, sliding glass doors that entered into a den or sunroom. The pool was the shape of a large lima bean, suggesting it was intended more for socializing than exercising. That particular pool shape is usually referred to as kidney-shaped, but the color of the water, a murky yellow-green, brought the lima bean image to mind and also suggested the water, in serious need of cleaning, hadn't been swum in for some time. The sense that construction was in a state of limbo was reinforced by piles of dried coyote scat that I cautiously side-stepped.

I had no intention of going inside the house without permission and no specific objective other than to get more of a sense of who Moran was. The fact that he was out here alone in this surreal nowhere land shouted volumes about his personality, though exactly what the lyrics were remained to be seen.

I looked in through the glass doors, not touching anything. The house was decorated with modern, expensive, and—to some people's tastes—tasteful furniture. A long white leather couch inexplicably faced inside, literally turning its back on the reason for the picture window glass door. Almost everything was white except for some colorful things hanging on the walls, which much more discriminating people than me might refer to as art. Everything was in order. No trash or clothing or bodies strewn around. Actually, it looked as if Moran had hardly spent any time there at all. That wouldn't be surprising, given the round-the-clock schedule of the weekend, and with the oppressive seclusion, I couldn't blame him. Other than the location, there was nothing suspicious to take away from my reconnoitering.

Fiddler was still singing when I got back to the truck. He must have been nearing the bottom of his personal playlist because he was down to "Wild Thing." But there was little that was making my heart sing.

I started up the truck, stopping on the way out of Beauville to call the phone number on the sign. I was perplexed by the suspension of activity, and with Moran seemingly the only occupant I wondered if there might be some connection.

Surprisingly, there was cell reception. I considered myself lucky until I received a recorded message telling me the number I had dialed was no longer in service and there was no further information. Vaguely recalling the column on the page in the *Public Pinyon* that had the supposedly humorous ad for the new steakhouse, I called Linda Benallie.

"Do you keep records of the town meetings?" I asked.

"When I attend them, I take notes. But since those meetings are generally as exciting as a wake during the Black Death, I don't go that often, in which case they just send me summaries. If you want the details, Loomis City has a website that has the official minutes. Why?"

I could feel her journalistic antennae shoot right up.

"Just curious about a few things. Thanks."

I didn't give her time to ask further. I called Gimpy next, while I was still getting a connection, and told him to download the minutes of the past few town meetings, print them out, and highlight anything that had to do with Beauville Luxury Estates, Alfie Moran et al, and any connections with Tuttle. I kept an eye on Fiddler to see if he'd squirm, but he didn't bat an eyelash.

"When do you want it?" Gimpy asked.

"Fifteen minutes."

I started driving. My next question was for Fiddler.

"How come you call yourself Fiddler if you play the guitar?"

Out of the corner of my eye, I caught him smiling, as if he was a math whiz who was asked to add two plus two when the question he had been expecting was an explanation of the causes of the Spanish American War. In other words, he had a secret and I just needed to ask the right questions to find out what it was.

"Used to play the violin when I was a student," he replied. "You know, Bach and Mozart types. Don't get me wrong, that was good stuff. But you ever try to sing while you're playing the violin? Can't be done. Sounds like someone's strangling you. Besides, playing antiwar songs on the violin at Vietnam protests just didn't cut it. So, I traded it in for a guitar, but kept the name. I like the sound of it. Fiddler. Beats Guitarist."

"That when you started getting arrested? At antiwar rallies?"

"Arrested and beaten up. Those were the good old days."

"Where're you from? Originally."

"You know, I've been so many places. Can't really remember. Before I came here, I was in San Francisco. Before that? Only Jesus knows."

"You remember your real name?"

"I think so. No one's asked in a long time. Leon."

"Leon what?"

"Leon Something."

I gave him a look that he interpreted correctly. He clutched his arm protectively and leaned away.

"What's it to you?" he asked. "Why do you have to know?"

I was getting tired of playing games. I stopped the truck, leaned over him, and opened his door.

"You're free to go," I said.

"Really?"

"Yeah. Just leave your shoes here."

"If I do that, my feet'll burn before I get ten yards."

"Your choice. Your feet or your last name."

"All right. Snipes. Yeah, that's it. Leon Snipes. Fiddler sounds a lot better, though. Leon Snipes. Huh."

I let it go at that. Leon Snipes was quiet the rest of the way.

CONRAD MICHENER

Go ahead and envy me. I was a passenger in Inez's blood-red Miata convertible with the top down as she sped along Route 12, her lustrous tresses blowing in the wind. Just like a dark-haired Ingrid Bergman. And I was Cary Grant. If I too had a dimpled chin, I would have shown it off, thrown my head back, and laughed, *"Ha-ha-ha-ha-ha!"*

We had taken her car because cast members like yours truly were required to stay in character for the whole damn weekend, even down to the vehicles we drove. Alfie tried to strong-arm me into driving a pickup. That's where

I'd drawn the line. I grudgingly compromised on a Toyota Land Cruiser, but I kept it parked in the hotel lot except for dire emergencies, like trying to find a drink after nine o'clock. So it was fine with me to be in the passenger seat of Inez's perky roadster.

We were on our way to meet up with the camera crew, which had already trucked up to Tuttle's ranch to get ready for the shoot of the "investigation." Once we found Wohlmer and had him arrested, they could re-edit the chronology, and with a little lighting adjustment in post-production, they'd make it seem like I had been there in the morning. The wonders of modern technology.

So why did she suddenly pull off the road into this dumpy Indian souvenir stand? Could it be she hadn't appreciated the radio stations I'd been scanning: NFL football and the Lord's salvation? Sunday afternoon in rural America. *Geeeeeeeee-zuz!*

"What are you stopping here for?" I asked. "You can get better souvenirs in town."

"Photo op. Look at those adorable children selling lemonade. It's perfect. Go buy some lemonade and I'll get their parents to sign the release forms."

"But it's hot as hell out here."

"All in the name of ratings, Connie dear," she said, and slid out the door.

I replaced the cowboy hat on my head, which I had taken off so it wouldn't blow away in the wind, and got out of the car. I walked up to the Indian kids, who looked like they hadn't bathed since the last time it rained and were wearing tattered T-shirts with holes in them. The smallest one wasn't even wearing anything below his waist. Some photo op. Maybe for *National Geographic*. They didn't seem to recognize who I was, which was kind of a relief, but still pissed me off a little.

I pointed at the pitcher of yellow beverage and asked the girl, really slowly so she'd understand, "Lemonade real? Is this lemonade real?" She was about six or seven and had her arm around a boy, who was younger.

She nodded. Not very talkative.

"You have change of dollar?"

Another nod.

"Okay," I said, and gave her a dollar.

"C'mon. We're going," Inez said, walking quickly up to me.

"But she hasn't given me my lemonade."

"The parents won't sign the release form. Let's go."

"Let me get my dollar back."

"Put it on my account. Come on."

"Wait," I said. "I have an idea."

"I'll wait in the car," Inez said. "Hurry up."

There were a good number of tourists at the souvenir stand. Maybe Harold Wohlmer had been there. I looked down at the kids.

"Have you seen a big, creepy old man wandering around the desert?"

For some reason, they all ran away.

As I got back in the comfort of Inez's car, I thought I saw the one-eyed sheriff drive by in a pickup truck going in the other direction. There was another guy sitting in the passenger seat, but Dance blocked my view of him. I hoped it was Wohlmer so I could end this ridiculous charade.

The camera crew, having arrived at Tuttle's ranch long before us, had all the cameras and lighting in place. I had one cameraman with a handheld next to me at all times so as I walked around, the camera saw what I saw.

"So, what am I supposed to be looking for?" I asked.

"Just look like you know what you're doing," Inez says. "Stop and kneel down every once in a while and sort through the rubble like you're looking for something in particular. Pick up some charred junk, inspect it carefully, then gaze out on the horizon as if you're thinking about things."

"Maybe I'll even find a real clue."

"Doesn't matter. We'll get good footage either way."

"Do I have someone doing makeup?"

"In the van."

"Good."

I spent the next half hour wandering around the property, acting sheriff-like, with the cameras rolling. It was still hot as hell, and I was getting tired of horizon gazing. I began to think that maybe the Japanese show in British

Columbia might not be such a bad idea. Maybe the masseuse who caters to the Kobe cows could find a slot in her schedule for me.

I knew the sun was starting to get to me, because I found myself wondering about this guy, Wohlmer. About how it could have been possible for him to burn down the stable in the early morning, get back to town, have coffee with his wife, and then go murder Madsie. Hadn't the barista said the guy was friendly in addition to being big and rough? I guess it would've been easy enough to fake the friendly part. I do that. A lot. Yes, it was possible. But the big question was, did I have the slightest inclination to do anything about finding out the truth? I still had hours of Roundtree commitments to go, and experience had taught me that Alfie easily got hot under the collar if I tried to beg off.

I had barely finished asking myself the big question when it was answered for me in two ways. First, I stepped in the one damn place on the whole property where a tire track had created a puddle, which required me to scrape mud out of the soles of my boots with a stick. Second, Inez said, "We're good to go. I'll send this footage to my media contacts."

"Scraping mud off my boot?"

"Connie, there's very little that you can screw up that our editors can't fix. We'll have you up on multiple platforms in hours. Your fans will see you solving the mystery of the torched stable."

"But we haven't found out who did it? Right?"

"No, but we'll just say that we have a person of interest and hope to apprehend him shortly."

"Should we mention names? That guy Wohlmer?"

"Probably not. We don't want to get sued."

"So, the investigation's over?"

"Investigation over."

"Free at last! Free at last! I need a drink."

"Just make sure you clean your boots before you get in my car."

As I was acceding to the lady's request, one of the cameramen came over to me. A big, bearded hulky guy with his gut hanging out of a "Roundtree" T-shirt whose name was probably Olaf. I had seen him on various sets before but never had occasion to interact, and I had hoped to keep it that way, so I started walking away.

"Mr. Michener," he said, in a surprisingly high voice. Not as high as Tiny Tim, but higher than Mike Tyson. I kept walking, pretending I didn't hear him.

"Mr. Michener!"

"What is it?" I made sure that he sensed the irritation in my voice.

"I've got something for you."

He handed me a paper bag.

"It's from some guy who came here on a bike. Kind of a Woodstock relic."

I knew what was in the bag but didn't know how to ask the next question. I got the feeling, but wasn't sure, that The Hulk was familiar with the situation.

"Uh, he said you can pay him later."

I didn't want to give away too much, so I offered a cursory "thank you" nod and headed to the car. Inez was waiting in the driver's seat.

"All clean," I said, showing her my boots. "You got any matches?"

"In the glove compartment. Next to the roach clip. What did you get, Indica or Sativa?"

"What do you think? A half of Sativa."

"Nice."

I rolled us two jays and passed one to Inez.

I was soon feeling pretty good on the drive back into town. I didn't even need that drink anymore, though I wouldn't have refused it.

"Wohlmer is the key, man," I said. "He's the one killed Alexis. I know it."

"Alexis killed?" Inez laughed. "Sheriff Roundtree, I do believe you're stoned."

"Got that one right, honey."

Chapter Eleven

5:00 p.m.

JEFFERSON DANCE

We arrived at the jail, and I told Gimpy to make Fiddler comfortable in his cell. Gimpy knew Fiddler from his previous visits and handed Fiddler the keys to lock himself up.

"Got those town meetings for me?" I asked Gimpy.

"I got them on the computer, but I couldn't print them out."

"How come?"

"Copier's out of toner."

"Well, then go get some damn toner. I'm going over to Chuck's Wagon. When I get back, they better be on my desk."

"Whatever you say. But you might want to stop by Little Saigon on your way."

"And why is that?"

"Seems someone broke in around lunchtime. No one took anything. I didn't want to bother you with it, what with all you've got on your hands."

My first thought was wondering why someone would break into a restaurant at lunchtime. My second thought, which answered the first, was that Jalen Taggert was behind the mischief.

I was already late for my meeting with Linda at Chuck's Wagon, and now I had another thing I had to deal with. But first, I needed to call Tuttle, not about the Beauville business per se, because I wanted to chew on that for a while.

"Merle, I've got Fiddler locked up here."

"Fiddler?" Tuttle coughed up a somewhat artificial laugh. "What did he do now?"

"Maybe burn down your stable?"

"Nah. You think so? You got proof?"

"Maybe. Maybe not. We'll see."

Another thought occurred to me.

"Merle, what time of day do you usually do your watering in the summer?"

"Like everyone else does, at night. Lessens the evaporation rate. Saves water. Saves money."

"That's what I figured."

"I would've thought you'd know that without asking."

"Slipped my mind. When you found your stable burned, did you turn on the sprinkler system?"

"Didn't have to. Like I said, someone did it for me. Any more dumb questions?"

"Maybe. Tell me, who does the irrigation work for your land?"

"CO_2. They do everyone's. Why?"

"Thanks."

When I stopped at Little Saigon it smelled so good, I would have stayed if I didn't already have another engagement. The place was so busy I couldn't find anyone working there who was not in constant motion. The hostess was an older woman elegantly dressed in a colorful traditional Vietnamese costume. I corralled her the moment she returned from seating a customer.

"I understand you had a break-in earlier today," I said.

"Yah. No problem. Not really a break-in. He came through back door. Then he run away when he sees my sons. No damage."

I asked whether the intruder fit the description of Jalen Taggert. If it turned out to be him, he'd have some explaining to do.

"No. Not that person. Old person. Big man. Red face."

I showed her Harold Wohlmer's photo on my phone.

"This man?" I asked.

"Yes. That's the person."

"And you said he ran away?"

"Not really run. Just like go away. We let him go."

"Did you see which way he went?"

"No. My sons closed the door."

"And you're sure there was no damage? Nothing stolen?"

"Maybe he's little bit crazy man," she said.

"Why do you say that?"

"Only thing he took was box of matches."

"Was there anything special about those matches?"

She smiled.

"Had our address. Maybe he wants to come back for dinner."

I thanked her for her time. I didn't know what Harold Wohlmer needed with matches from a Vietnamese restaurant, but I'm pretty sure it wasn't to melt s'mores over a campfire. Whatever the reason, I had to call Mrs. Wohlmer with the obvious question. But considering the stress she was under I also had to be tactful.

"I was wondering if you or Mr. Wohlmer might have noticed anyone suspicious around your Winnebago between five and seven this morning?" I asked.

Mrs. Wohlmer paused before answering.

"Sheriff Dance, I've heard about Sheriff Tuttle's stable being burned down, so I think what you're wanting to find out is if Harold was here at that time. I can assure you that he was because I could hear his snoring even through my earplugs. But thank you for your thoughtfulness. Now, is there anything else I can help you with?"

"No, that will do for now," I said. "Thank you kindly."

Chuck's Wagon was patterned after an Old West saloon with doors that flapped in and out. An out-of-tune honky-tonk Player Piano clanked away Stephen Foster's greatest hits. An enlarged, framed photo of Butch Cassidy and the Sundance Kid, aka Paul Newman and Robert Redford, overhung the bar. Bowls of free peanuts adorned each table and patrons were invited to discard the shells on the floor. I'm not certain that was a tradition that Butch and Sundance ever indulged in, but if they had, it would at least have ensured that no one could sneak up on them unheard.

Even from her back, it wasn't hard to spot Linda. Sitting in a booth, she was a head taller than anyone else. I crunched my way over the floor to her. She had an ice-filled, thirty-two-ounce root beer waiting for me. I have to admit, after having been out in the hot desert, anything cold and liquid was appealing. She had also ordered me the Ground Chuck special, a half-pound bison burger with bacon and grilled onions.

"Sorry I'm late," I said. "Thanks for the soda."

I couldn't be sure, but she might have put on some makeup. Or it just might have been the dim lighting.

"Free refills, too," she said.

"And the burger. How'd you know I was hungry?"

"You look like a man who likes his meat," she said.

I let that one pass.

"Tell me about Tuttle and Taggert," I said. I lifted the burger to my lips.

"Tell me about Maddison Hadcock," Linda said, looking me straight in the eye.

I looked straight back and returned the burger back to the plate, deciding quickly how I was going to play this hand.

"What do you know?" I asked.

"Some, but not enough. And it's not good."

"Who told you?"

"A little birdie."

She saw the look on my face that indicated I didn't like that answer. She laughed.

"I'm a reporter and I protect my sources," she said. "Wild horses couldn't drag it out of me. And you're not even that wild."

I took a deep breath.

"This can't get out," I said. "We've got a killer on the loose, who may well still be here in Loomis City. If the news spreads, the town'll be spooked, he'll be spooked, and we'll lose him. Not that we have anything to lose yet. Worse, he could kill someone else."

"I understand that and I want to help," Linda said. "But this is not local news. This is 'Roundtree.' It's a national story, and I want to be the one to break it."

"You can help by giving me some history on Merle and Taggert. You do that, you'll be the first one to hear from me when we've got something."

"Promise?"

"It's what I said, isn't it?"

Linda held out her hand.

"Deal," she said.

Her handshake was strong and firm, and she held it for a good long time.

"Where are you staying, by the way?" she asked.

"Out by Getzler Ridge, south of town."

"There aren't any accommodations there."

"In my truck. I'd figured I'd be leaving by tomorrow morning, but I hadn't planned on an arson, a missing person, and a murder to deal with."

"Getzler Ridge once belonged to us, you know," she said. I understood "us" to mean her Navajo side of the family. "It's a sacred site. Had a different name, of course. Why are you staying out there?"

"Nostalgia maybe," I said. "I happened to have been born in its shadow."

I had opened my big trap when I should've known better.

"You'd mentioned you'd grown up here in Loomis City," Linda said. "But Getzler Ridge? In those days? There's nothing out there now. Back then there would've been less than nothing. That means your family would've either been Navajo or loners, and you sure don't look Navajo."

"Close enough." I knew this wouldn't be nearly a sufficient answer for a reporter, and she gave me a look to indicate as much.

"You putting on your Woodward and Bernstein hat?" I asked.

"Let's say Brenda Starr, star reporter."

"All right. I lived here only until I was four. My father, Lincoln, was a ranch hand. Long before they invented the term *horse whisperer* he had a knack for breaking in horses without breaking their spirit. If he'd stuck with that, he probably would've been successful."

"But?"

"But Pappy was cursed with natural good looks and an easy manner with folks."

"Like father, like son. But where's the curse?"

"He convinced himself he could be a rodeo star. He hitched himself to that wagon and the rest of us along with it, and he dragged us along the old rodeo circuit the next nine years. I think we must have been through every town in the West that had a road going through it. It hardly seemed we were more than a month in any one place."

"How did you go to school?"

"Our schooling—that means my older sister and me—was not part of my father's plan, except as far as teaching me to ride and rope and shoot by the time I was eight. Which he did a good job of."

"Did your mother home school you?"

"Ma probably would have if she hadn't always been packing and unpacking and getting chores done. And if she had been able to read."

"So how did you get your education?"

"Most towns had public libraries. They were cool and dark, and you weren't allowed to talk, so Ma figured it was the best place for us. She'd drop us off there while my father went off to seek his fortune and she'd tend to the housework. There was never a shortage of Dickens and Twain and Fenimore Cooper. There was an old maid librarian named Sue Giddings out in Winnemucca, Nevada, who gave me *The Bear* by William Faulkner to read when I was ten. Enjoyed that. You might say Miss Giddings changed my life."

"And did he become a star?"

"Faulkner?"

"Your father."

"Pappy was never as good as he thought he was, but not bad enough to discourage him sufficiently to quit."

"So what happened?"

"We were up at the Three Forks Rodeo in Montana. In the bull riding competition, the bull got the better of him and flipped him off his back like a ragdoll. Before the clowns could distract the bull, he spun around and trampled him. Pappy wasn't killed, but he did lose the use of his right arm."

"He was lucky to have survived."

"Luckier if he hadn't. He became alcoholic and abusive to my mother. One day he wandered off and that was the last I saw him. We scraped by for a while. Then my sister married a soybean farmer in Iowa and took my mother with her."

"Have you heard from your father since?"

"I heard he died at a shelter in Bismarck some years ago."

"And you never came back to Loomis City until now?"

"No reason to. I had a ranch up in Cache County and was doing pretty well with that, but when they started surrounding it with suburbs I sold. I can't complain about the price they paid me, but looking back, maybe I shouldn't have."

"You didn't like being hemmed in."

"Didn't and don't."

"And how did you get involved with helping law enforcement?"

"That's a story for another time, Miss Benallie. Right now, I'm supposed to actually be law enforcement and not twiddling my thumbs, so if you could tell me about the Tuttles and the Taggerts I'd be much obliged. I was too young to remember anything but their names."

"Fair enough. You answered my question. I'll answer yours. The Tuttles and Taggerts both go back a long ways in Loomis City," she said. "Since the late nineteenth century, both families held prominent positions in the town. Sometimes business, sometimes politics. In this town, those are harder to separate than Siamese twins. And they most always saw eye to eye. I'll scratch your back, you scratch mine, sort of arrangement. The Taggerts saved the town, or what was left of it, during the Dust Bowl. They dug drains and swales and culverts, and laid irrigation pipes and let their customers pay whenever they could, or not at all if they couldn't. There wasn't much water, but because of the Taggerts, there was enough for the town to make it through. Meanwhile, the Tuttles kept the town's institutions from falling apart. Everything from the selectmen to the Rotary to the PTA to the Boy Scouts. Kept the fabric of the town intact. Without those two families, there'd be nothing here today but tumbleweed and jackrabbits. That's why the people in town listened to what those two families had to say."

"But things changed when 'Roundtree' came."

"You bet. The Taggerts have always had a strong self-reliance streak. Traditional Western mentality. They don't want anyone telling them what to do or how to do it. When the 'Roundtree' folks came into town, the Taggerts felt that none of what they'd done for Loomis City counted for anything anymore. That they were becoming marginalized. They turned bitter in a real hurry."

"And the Tuttles didn't share their point of view?"

"Some actually did, but Merle was one of those who felt the town was just withering on the vine and was going to be swallowed up by the desert sooner rather than later. He got the chamber of commerce and all the service organizations to back the 'Roundtree' idea, first the show, then the festival. It saved the town, but it also split it."

"You think that'd be enough reason for Sloan Taggert to burn down Merle's stable? And why now?"

"The second question's for you to solve. The answer to the first one is 'partly.' Because there's more. You see, Merle Tuttle was married to Sloan's sister, Selma, until six years ago."

"They got divorced?"

"She died."

Linda noticed my eyes narrow.

"No, there was nothing fishy about it," she said. "Selma had been ill a long time with cancer. But the split over 'Roundtree' I think had created such hard feelings that Sloan maybe thought Merle was responsible for Selma's illness. I don't know. It's just a feeling."

"Is Sloan married?"

"Divorced. Back in 1990, he served in the first Gulf War, Desert Storm. When he came back, he and Marlene had a child who didn't survive infancy.

Years later they had Jalen. She left shortly thereafter for parts unknown. Not sure why, but ever since he got back from Kuwait, he's had an anger management issue."

"Angry enough to kill?"

"Selma?"

"No. Hadcock."

Linda almost choked on the ice she was chewing. Clearly, the thought had never crossed her mind.

"No," she said. "I can't imagine that. He didn't want to have anything to do with the 'Roundtree' people. He'd cross the sidewalk sooner than he'd talk to them."

I finished my root beer.

"Could you find out more about Maddison Hadcock?" I asked. "I don't know anything about her except her name and the role she played on the TV show. I need to know who she was, what she was into, who might have wanted to harm her."

"I'll get Sonny Boy on it right away."

"Who's that, your stuffed lizard?"

"No, my little brother."

"Here in Loomis City?"

"Anywhere but. He's my eyes and ears around the world. Right now, he's in Southern Cal."

"Hollywood?"

"Close enough. He started out as an amateur computer hacker in Silicon Valley. Now he's got an aerospace startup in Anaheim. But he knows everyone. You know the type. Natural schmoozer. And I figure since Hadcock and the 'Roundtree' crew are based around there, he could nose around, no problemo."

"Let me know as soon as you can, okay? And before I forget, I need to know more about Leon Snipes."

"Who?"

"Fiddler."

Linda gave me a salute.

"Aye, aye, captain," she said.

"Thanks," I said. "You've been a help."

As I turned to leave, she said, "You don't have to sleep in your truck, you know. You can stay at my place." Adding, "No charge."

She saw the look on my face and laughed again.

"That's not the way it sounded," she said. "I own a B&B outside of town. You notice the ostrich farm on the way out to Reilly Wash?"

"I did."

"That's mine. Head In The Sand. Ostrich farm and bed and breakfast. Nothing like ostrich steak and eggs for breakfast. High in protein, low in fat. And their poop is rich in nitrogen. Makes great fertilizer. Some folks are leaving Loomis City right after the fireworks tonight. I'll have rooms to spare."

"I'll consider it," I said. "You certainly are versatile."

"I'm good at a lot of things."

CONRAD MICHENER

"You can't act your way out of a paper bag, and you never could."

That was nice to hear. That's why Alfie had invited me to this dive called the Can Festival. To tell me I couldn't act. What made matters worse was, the beer was as insipid as the clientele. Even when I pointed out to him that the bar's claim to fame was a big screen that aired "Roundtree" episodes around the clock during festival weekend, it didn't shut him up.

It wasn't the first time, and it wouldn't be the last that Alfie told me what he thought of me. I knew it wasn't personal. Actually, it was personal, but what I mean is that he gave everyone the same treatment when he was in an anxious mood, which was almost always. Plus, I was still high as a kite, so most of his barbs flew right past me. Thank God for drugs, right? At least, for once, he was keeping his voice down. The customers would be thinking the two big "Roundtree" *machers* were having a brotherly heart-to-heart.

I gathered his current anxiety was about Madsie being missing. No one had told him she was d-e-a-d, and I had promised to keep my lips zipped.

So all I could do was commiserate, and that didn't seem to be going so well.

"Where the hell has she been?" he asked.

"I know. I know. I've been trying to get hold of her."

Of course, I hadn't. But even if I was about to be decapitated by Freddy Krueger and she had been a 911 dispatcher, I wouldn't have called her. There was something about her that was toxic. Not that I am a particularly upstanding soul, but I'd never met anyone who was so self-centered and backstabbing, and considering my given profession, that's quite an endorsement.

"I can't tell you how many times I've called her," Alfie said. "Where the hell is she? You must know."

And on and on it went. Once again, he warned me about trying to weasel out of my contract. I was tempted to say, "If you think I'm such a bad actor, why the hell do you want to keep me?" But I kept my mouth shut and let him rant.

When he realized that his wrath would go unrequited by my Gandhi-like passive resistance, he gave me a parting shot about how I was starting to look old. Totally below the belt. He left me with his beer only partially drunk, but fully unpaid.

As soon as he was out of earshot, I called Stewie. Not surprisingly, he didn't answer. I really didn't expect him to. It would have been after hours on a Sunday night, and it was hard enough to get hold of him during business hours. His voice message cheerily stated, *"If this is one of my clients, be assured I'm out there making you a great deal. If you're not one of my clients, you should be. In either case, please leave a message and I'll get back to you one of these days."*

I left a message. "I hope you're out there making me a great deal to be a Japanese cowboy."

Chapter Twelve

6:00 p.m.

JEFFERSON DANCE

When I got back to the sheriff's office, Gimpy was gone. He'd left a neat pile of town meeting minutes on the desk. I sat down to read, but before I could start, Poot arrived to give me his progress report. He was worried we were giving Alfie too long a leash when he was currently the only person that we could connect, however tenuously, to Hadcock's murder. I expressed appreciation for his concern, but I reasoned that if Alfie were the murderer, the smartest thing he could do would be to pretend ignorance and go about his business. Fleeing would simply give him away and in the meantime, we could easily keep a wary eye on him. So far, given Alfie's tight schedule, it had not been a problem to keep him under surveillance. He had been everywhere he was supposed to be.

Poot also relayed the festival organizers' growing concern regarding Maddison Hadcock's unexplained absence, and he felt it would lessen their unease if we quietly let them in on the situation. I thought he made a good point regarding the importance of assuaging their anxiety, but I didn't want to go as far as telling them she had been murdered. I asked Poot to come up with a plausible cover story of why she was unavailable and to keep the number of informed people at an absolute minimum. When the truth finally came out, which would have to be soon, there would be enough of an uproar as it was. I also suggested Poot have another talk with Conrad Michener to find out if someone else might have had a lethal ax to grind with Maddison Hadcock.

"Any progress on Harold Wohlmer?" I asked.

"Nope. The only sightings were Jarvis's and the Vietnamese restaurant. After that, nothing. Seems it's almost easier to become invisible surrounded by crowds than when no one's around."

"Anything else?"

"I saw Sheriff Roundtree himself at Knead The Dough a few hours ago."

"Michener?"

"Yep, Michener."

"Anything interesting?"

"Maybe. He was holding his menu two inches from his nose, so I figured either he's in serious need of reading glasses or he was trying to make sure I didn't notice him. I guessed it was the latter, so after I'd asked the barista a few questions about Wohlmer and left the café, I kept an eye on Michener through the window. He went up to the barista, asked some questions of his own, then hightailed it."

"Any idea why?"

"I think so. After he left, I went back in and asked what got Michener so riled up. The barista said that Michener gave the impression he thinks Harold Wohlmer burned down Merle's stable."

I didn't know whether I should laugh or bang my head against the wall.

"Lord, save me."

"Yep."

After Poot headed out, I read the note that Gimpy had left on top of the pile of the town meeting minutes: *Goes back a year. Two a month. Hope you're happy.*

The pile was formidable. I glanced quickly through all of it to see what might be of value. There were regular reports of the budget committee, the school committee, the parks, and recreation committee. It was hard to believe Loomis City had enough people for so many committees.

Only when I got to the zoning board reports did I slow down. Extrapolating from references to minutes in prior meetings, it seemed the developers of Beauville Luxury Estates, a firm called LMNt Corp., had requested permits to build their development a year or so before the minutes of the first meeting that Gimpy had compiled. Where I picked the story up, there had been some concern that the construction was going to be on land that had until then been open range, but the issue that really stuck in everyone's craw came down to one word: water.

According to the calculations the town commissioned from an independent hydrological consultant, it was determined that the quantity of water the development would need, both potable and for purposes like landscaping, washing, sanitation, and swimming pools, was off the charts, especially considering the paucity that nature bestowed upon this region. LMNt was asked where they proposed getting so much water. Their answer was from a pipeline that diverted water from the San Juan River. The only hang-up: The pipeline didn't exist.

The pipeline was only in the planning phase, and even at that modest stage its construction was being contested in court by the Sierra Club, Southern Utah Wilderness Alliance, and other environmental groups who argued that such a diversion would not only cause irreparable harm to the delicate ecology of the desert, it would favor a few wealthy individuals over the vital interests of the vast majority of stakeholders: ranchers, farmers, and common citizens.

The meeting's minutes didn't go into details of the arguments, but clearly LMNt was desperate for a solution, to the extent that they went before the town's zoning board of appeals and guaranteed they would find the water for their needs if only Loomis City would grant them the permits.

There was a lot of back and forth. Having the new development would mean local jobs and more tax revenue. On the other hand, what if the pipeline never became reality? Would the guarantee mean that the town would then be compelled to divert water to LMNt that had historically been provided to everyone else?

Ultimately, the vote was close, but the permits were denied. LMNt, thus hogtied, was unable to seal the deal after having sunk millions of dollars into the project. Shortly and predictably thereafter they went belly-up. The model home which Alfie Moran was using for the weekend was the only house completed, a sad testament to an ill-considered and risky gambit.

What was more interesting for my purposes, though, was that Merle Tuttle, who tended to argue on behalf of the modernization of Loomis City, was against LMNt's plan because of his fear he'd lose water for his ranch. On the other hand, Sloan Taggert, the traditionalist, had been provisionally contracted to do all the land-moving and pipe-laying for the development, and had argued that the permits should be granted. He probably lost out on years of revenue from that single decision. Coming out on the short end of the public squabble could not have enhanced his relationship with Tuttle, especially after having already lost the battle for the future vision of Loomis City.

It could have been pure coincidence that Taggert was connected both to Harold Wohlmer's disappearance and to Merle Tuttle's burned stable, but with evening approaching and Wohlmer's life possibly hanging in the balance I decided that if I made an error, I'd rather it be of commission than omission. Something had to be done, even if it was rash, but I needed Tuttle's input.

It was only a hop, skip, and jump from the office to the All America Insurance building on 300 West, where I hoped to find Tuttle. In preparation for the midnight grand parade, town volunteers were beginning to cordon off the street with temporary barriers, restricting pedestrians to the sidewalk. A tour bus from Kanab in the process of unloading dozens of additional eager and elderly Roundtree fans increased the pedestrian traffic even more, making my hopping, skipping, and jumping more like an Olympic slalom event.

At least I was right about finding Tuttle. I wouldn't normally expect an insurance company to be open at six o'clock on a Sunday, but with the beehive of activity surrounding *Roundtree Days* weekend, these weren't normal times. Every business was open late, like booths at a carnival huckstering Kewpie dolls, and All America Insurance was no exception.

Merle was sitting across a desk from his agent, who looked like the cat who ate the canary. Merle looked like the canary. The agent, strategically positioned to see anyone coming in the door, was the first to notice me and immediately leapt from his seat.

"Welcome to Loomis City," he said. "Les Henderson. New in town?"

Merle turned. The look on his face turned from anguish to hope, as if I'd arrived in the nick of time to save him from drowning in a sea of effluence.

"Pleased to meet you," Henderson continued, extending his hand. Except instead of wanting to shake mine, he handed me his business card. "What can I do for you today?"

I began to explain I was there to speak to Merle, but Merle interrupted me.

"It seems Les and I have run into a bit of a logjam here," he said. "Seems that if the stable burning down had been an accident, Les here could cut me a check right away, no problem."

Merle was looking at me in a peculiar way, doing strange things with his eyes, as if he wanted to send me a message by brain waves without the benefit of words.

"But if there is an ongoing criminal investigation," Les continued, "we would, by company policy, have to wait until its conclusion to determine liability. And also, well, as I was trying to explain to Merle—"

"He was trying to explain that if it was somehow proved I was involved in setting the fire, I wouldn't get any check and I'd be in a heap of trouble. Is that right, Les? That you don't trust me after all these years?"

"It's not a matter of trust, Merle," Les complained. "It's just standard policy, like I said. That's all."

"But it was an accident. Wasn't it?" Tuttle was asking me. He gave me that look again. It was like a dog that you forgot to walk for a whole day and was having a hard time holding it in.

The problem now confronting me was a head-scratcher. Tuttle and I well knew the answer to his question—the first thing he had told me that morning was that someone definitely started the fire—but I saw where he was going. He needed money, whether it was to rebuild his stable or for some other purpose, and didn't want to have to wait until they checked him into assisted living to get it. Unfortunately, the facts, as I so far knew them, spoke otherwise. And though Tuttle and I were friendly acquaintances, I did not cotton to being manipulated into the position of being on the wrong side of them. While I was trying to figure if there might be another way to expedite his claim, I noticed that Henderson had a big old grandfather clock in the corner, ticking away almost silently. It felt like a countdown telling me I was running out of time. I made a decision. Maybe it was hasty. Time would tell.

"Merle," I asked, "do I have authority to make arrests?"

"Shoot, yeah. As acting sheriff, you have the authority to act like a sheriff."

"Fair enough. In that case, I'll put my neck on the line and say that the stable burning was assuredly no accident."

Merle glared at me like I'd just eaten his firstborn alive.

"And that an arrest is imminent," I added.

"How soon?" Merle asked, realizing I might not be the cannibal he thought.

"Before the sun sets, if I can help it. I hope to have a confession by the end of the day and complete the paperwork within twenty-four hours."

"You'd best be sure," Les cautioned me. He kept the smile, but there was nothing behind it.

"I'm sure enough."

To be honest, I wasn't sure. But if I waited until I was, Tuttle's check might never come in. Even worse, Harold Wohlmer might check out.

"You need me to be there?" Merle asked.

I considered the potential of the situation going from bad to worse if he were there.

"I think I'll be okay," I said, and nodded in the direction of Les Henderson. "You've got enough to handle as it is."

"Thanks," Merle said. "Call me at the house if you need me."

CONRAD MICHENER

My handy-dandy activity schedule told me I was supposed to have made an appearance at the lassoing competition at the fairgrounds. Oops! Too late for that. I could blame that on Alfie for having spewed all over me for most of the hour. A desperately needed vodka martini after that. Make that two desperately needed vodka martinis. Or three. I headed back to the Vermillion Arms with just enough time to spare for a well-deserved nap after a long day of intense inertia before my seven o'clock rendezvous with destiny in the lobby. Turning the corner from the Can Festival, I was walking past the swimming pool at the Rustler's Motel—who exactly were the rustlers, the owners or the guests?—when I hit pay dirt.

There, standing in the middle of the motel pool, surrounded by two scrawny little boys and one scrawny little girl in water wings throwing around a beach ball, was Harold Wohlmer! *Big guy. Rough-looking a little. But friendly at the same time*, was what the barista said. It was him, exactly. He was a little rounder and had less hair, at least on his head, than I had pictured him, but I had no doubt. It had to be Wohlmer.

When I stopped, he looked me straight in the eye. I could tell he knew I'd outed him. He was at my mercy.

"Hey, kiddos!" Wohlmer said. "Look who's here. It's Sheriff Roundtree!"

"Who's Chef Rountree?" the smallest one of them said. Assuming the show was past his bedtime, I let the kid's comment pass.

"Mr. Wohlmer, I presume," I said, playing it nice and cool. I wanted to avoid violence at all costs, especially with the kids around. I also didn't want to have to jump into the pool, which the kids had most likely peed in.

"Nope," he responded. "Not me."

"What is your name, sir?"

"Schwartz. Stanley Schwartz. Why?"

"I'll ask the questions, if you don't mind. Where are you from?"

His look suggested he was losing his cool. Just what I would have expected from a desperate man on the run.

"Westbury, Long Island. What's this all about?"

The kids stopped throwing the ball and started to watch us.

"May I see some ID, Mr. Schwartz?"

"I'm standing in a swimming pool in my swimming trunks. I don't have any ID on me. It's in the room."

"Let's go to your room, then," I said. I wasn't going to let Wohlmer off the hook so easily.

"I don't have the key. My wife has it, and she took my daughter for some retail therapy on Main Street while I take care of the grandkids."

"A likely excuse, Wohlmer."

"Wohlmer? Who's this Wohlmer?"

"I might have to take you into custody if you don't come clean."

"Custody? Who do you think you are? You're an actor. You're not a sheriff. Is this 'Candid Camera' or something?"

It was a standoff. He was right, I couldn't really arrest him. But I did have one more card up my sleeve.

"Okay, Mr. Stanley Schwartz from Westbury, Long Island," I said. "I'll let it go this time. But you better. Not. Leave. Town."

In any event, it was time for me to head to the Vermillion and find out if someone responded to my Tweet. I turned on my heel before his mouth had a chance to close. As I walked away, I felt a splash of water against the back of my pants. I refrained from turning around, so as not to exacerbate an already tense situation. Then the beach ball hit my head.

Chapter Thirteen

7:00 p.m.

JEFFERSON DANCE

It was a short ride, but long enough to appreciate the sun start to set and begin to cast its rose glow over the desertscape with colors so implausible that artists hesitate to duplicate them. Dusk brought a stillness to the land as if the animals, plants, and the rocks themselves paused for a moment of reflection before the nocturnal hunting began and the patterns of life and death, kill or be killed, resumed. It was a pattern from which we humans would not be excluded.

There were four gentlemen I'd been considering as suspects in the arson of Merle Tuttle's stable, including Tuttle himself. Conrad Michener had provided me a photo of his paramour's posterior to substantiate his alibi. But he had taken the photo at 7:38, and it was well within his ability to have gone from Tuttle's ranch and return to the comfort of Vega's embrace after the time the stable fire was set. Michener also had a tried-and-true motive: jealousy. Unlikely though it seemed, Tuttle and Vega sounded like they had genuine feelings for each other. It was not impossible, as Quasimodo and Esmeralda from *The Hunchback of Notre Dame* had so poignantly demonstrated. What was lacking in Michener's case were the means and the evidence. He didn't appear to have the mental wherewithal to plan the arson or the skills to manipulate the irrigation system.

My second suspect was Leon Snipes, aka Fiddler. He, too, could not account for his early morning whereabouts, and his run-ins with Tuttle were well documented. He was not the most savory character on the planet, or in Loomis City for that matter, but he seemed relatively harmless and his explanation of the kerosene purchase sounded genuine. Of course, it was possible he had stashed extra fuel, but then again, I had no evidence. And, since he had been around for so many years, why now?

Tuttle had admittedly been in the vicinity of his ranch when the stable was burned down, but then again, he lived there. Yes, he could have been the one who dampened down the perimeter to keep the fire from spreading to his house and rangeland. And he clearly seemed to be in a big hurry to settle his claim for the insurance. What dissuaded me from concluding he was the culprit was that I didn't think he could be such a good actor; first, the anger in his eyes when Poot and I showed up at his ranch. Second, when I said I was about to arrest someone, he didn't flinch. If he had a notion I was about to arrest an innocent man in his stead, he would've shown it.

That left only one other person.

I hadn't arrested anyone for a long time, since my law enforcement days. As I drove back to Culvert Operations I went through the procedure, practicing the Miranda rights out loud to be certain I got it right so that Sloan Taggert couldn't later claim I hadn't done everything by the book.

This is what I had to go on. Motive: revenge. Bad blood had long existed between Tuttle and Taggert. They had been on opposite sides of the argument about Beauville. Taggert came out on the losing end of it, taking a major hit both to his reputation and to his pocketbook. Beyond that, Taggert considered Tuttle to be a turncoat who had sold out the town for his own advancement, and indirectly bore responsibility for his sister's death. Evidence: The tracks by Tuttle's stable matched Taggert's Ford F-150, both in the tread and with telltale cupping in the right rear passenger-side tire. The tires were caked with red clay soil. None of the tires in his other trucks had any. And the only place that had similar wet soil in recent history was at Tuttle's. The fifteen-gallon plastic drum in the truck bed could've contained kerosene, which I would confirm with or without Taggert's cooperation.

I also guessed Taggert, intimately familiar with Tuttle's sprinkler system because he had installed it, had turned it on manually in order to mitigate the possibility of burning down the house and starting a brushfire. I hoped his fingerprints would be found on the irrigation system timer and handle, but that would take days to determine, at least. The damning evidence was that he had been driving east on Route 12 before dawn and he had lied about it.

From what Linda Benallie told me, it seemed evident that the enmity between the two had gone past the point of no return, and that the burden of ending the feud before someone got hurt had fallen on my shoulders. And I needed to end it now, not because of Merle's insurance money, but because I still had a murder to deal with. And if I could twist Taggert's arm to get him to cooperate, I might find out more about what happened to Harold Wohlmer.

When I got out of my truck with all these details running through my head, I realized I had left my hat, which was supposed to be setting on it, on the passenger seat. As I turned back to retrieve it, I bent slightly to reach the door handle. This was a good thing because otherwise the bullet would not have missed my head.

I forgot about my hat for the moment, it being less of a priority to me than my head. I hunkered down on the driver's side of my truck, away from the line of fire, near as I could tell. If nothing else, at least it tended to confirm my belief that it was Taggert, not Snipes, Michener, or Tuttle, who was responsible for the stable fire.

"Sloan Taggert," I hollered, "you're under arrest."

Another shot rang out, from an entirely different direction. The two shots couldn't have both come from Taggert. I was pinned down in a crossfire. If I tried to get back into my truck, I wouldn't make it past opening the door. If I stayed where I was, I wouldn't even make it to the door. That prescient grin on the bighorn ram at the Vermillion Arms seemed wider than ever.

"That you, Jalen?" I shouted. "You better put down your gun or you'll be in just as much trouble as your daddy."

"Says who?"

If there had been any doubt, I was now certain that it was indeed Jalen Taggert with Sloan. I didn't want to have to shoot either of them, but if it came to it, I might have no other choice.

"Speaking of daddies"—it was Sloan this time—"I remembered who you are. You're Linc Dance's son, aren't you?"

"What of it?"

"Yep, you're his spittin' image. He thought he was too good for this town, and you're no different."

Before I had a chance to debate the point, another shot shattered the side-view mirror. If I didn't want to end up like a steer at an abattoir, there was only one place for me to go. I slid underneath the truck and unholstered my gun. If there was anything positive to be said about my predicament, it was that my truck was parked outside the chain-link fence and their vehicles were inside it. If they tried to make off, they'd have to manage to get through the gate and then past me, in which case I'd have the advantage. Or they could just try to wait me out. We were at a stalemate.

Or so I thought. Another shot blew out my front left tire. And then a second tire. Two more tires, and I'd be crushed by my own truck. As plans go, theirs seemed to be gaining the upper hand.

A third tire blew out, leaving only a small wedge of daylight between the bottom of my truck and the ground. My gun might never forgive me, but I decided that if I wanted to avoid ending up flat as a flapjack, I had to convert it into a more utilitarian tool. Fortunately, my firearm of choice is a Colt .45-70 Peacemaker, which has an overall length of thirteen inches and is solidly constructed. I managed to wedge it between a flat rock on the ground and the underside of the chassis, giving me an inch or two of breathing room. How long it would retain its balance was another question, one which I tried to refrain from thinking about.

A bullet blew out the fourth tire. With a groan, the truck sagged down to the wheels. Lying on my stomach, I had enough room to breathe as long as it didn't involve a lot of inhaling. But I couldn't move effectively, and obviously my gun was no longer available for self-defense.

Contemplating mortality from the undercarriage of a pickup truck was discomfiting in more ways than one, but that was the unlikely situation in which I found myself. My only advantage—and it was a stretch to call it that—was that the Taggerts could not be sure if I was dead or alive, so I played possum and hoped they'd come within range for me to make a fight out of it. Things became pretty quiet, but not for long. The deliberate grind of the Taggerts' boots on dry earth communicated their cautious but determined approach. It was time to come up with an impromptu Plan B. I quietly clawed at the ground to get some dirt that maybe I could throw in their eyes when they looked under the truck. After that, it was anyone's guess, and I was trying not to guess.

Plan B was disrupted by my canine friends, and it wasn't because they needed a walk. They arrived at the party ahead of their masters, snarling in frustration that they couldn't fit under the truck to keep me company. Shoving their snouts in sideways, they snapped at my legs and arms and didn't miss by much.

Amidst the dogs, there came a pair of knees, then a pair of hands, then Sloan Taggert's pugnacious countenance.

"Hey, son," he called to Jalen. "Look what we've caught. A trespasser."

The boy's face joined the man's. Their grins were no more benign than the dogs'. Like father, like son, like household pets.

"Look what he's got propping up his truck, Pops. Mighty clever, lawman!"

I took exception at Jalen's mocking, drawn-out inflection of the word lawman, but I was not in an ideal position to do much about it.

"Tell you what," Sloan said to me. He lay down on the ground, much like I had. "I'll give you ten seconds to reach for your gun and shoot. After the ten seconds, I shoot the gun away. Either way, fair fight."

Either way, I was a dead man, compressed by two tons of steel on top of me. Jalen started laughing.

"Ten," he said, still giggling. "Nine. Eight. Seven."

I threw the dirt in their eyes. While their sniggering changed to curses, I tried to squirm out from under the truck, but my pant leg found favor with one of the dogs. Plan B was looking precarious. I managed to give the dog a kick in the side of its head, which drove him off for a moment. At least Jalen wasn't laughing anymore, but he was still counting.

"Three. Two. One."

Sloan Taggert pointed his gun at mine. I'd be crushed the moment he shot it out from supporting the truck. As he was about to pull the trigger, a shot rang out, and then another.

"Sloan Taggert. Jalen Taggert. Call off your dogs and stand with your hands held high, and I better not see any sign of a firearm in them. You're under arrest."

Poot's voice was always welcome, but on this occasion, it sounded pretty as Pavarotti.

Jalen quickly moved to obey. Sloan hesitated, which won him a bullet spitting dust close enough to his ear to make him holler. That ended his hesitation. I heard a dog make a run at Poot, only to cry out, ending in a whimper.

Shortly thereafter, Poot's face replaced the Taggerts' in the narrow strip of darkening sky visible from under the truck.

"Shoot the dog?" I asked.

"Nah. Just a well-aimed poke in the snout. Guess he didn't realize I'm am-by-dextriss. You okay?"

"Yeah. How'd you know I'd be in trouble?"

"You hadn't arrested anyone in such a long time, I figured you'd screw it up."

Under Poot's direction and with his gun trained at all times, the Taggert men placed their own hydraulic jacks underneath the four sides of my truck and lifted it enough for me to slide out. I apologized to my .45, which showed no ill effects, and I wasn't too much the worse for wear, either, except for a few scratches and being covered in red dirt. It felt good to see the whole sky again.

"I was hoping you'd show up sooner or later," I said to Poot, dusting myself off with my hat. "I didn't hear you drive up."

"Didn't drive," Poot said. "Rode out here on Sally and tethered her yonder." He nodded in the direction of the far side of the warehouse, where his mare waited tranquilly in the shade. "Had a feeling surprise might be the order of the day."

Sloan Taggert interrupted.

"You know we were just kidding. Right?"

Poot and I stared at him. That was a pretty audacious claim, especially with Poot's gun still aimed at him.

"Y'see, we were just trying to scare you off. We don't like no busybodies. No way we were meaning to cause you bodily harm. Isn't that right, son?"

"Shoot, yeah. It was all a practical joke. We just cherish our privacy." He had that dumb grin on his face again.

"You mean having a truck lying on top of you is your idea of a joke?" I asked.

"Dang," said Taggert, "there's more'n enough clearance on those trucks when it's resting on its wheels. Even if it was a dinky Toyota."

Taggert chuckled and was imitated by Jalen Ray. It was the phoniest damn laugh I'd ever heard.

"Pretty funny," I said.

"Yeah. All a joke."

He might've been right about the clearance. And maybe it was indeed all a big joke. But whether he was right or wrong, or whether it was a joke or not, my right fist on his left jaw provided a clear signal I had not been amused. Though I seriously bruised my hand in the effort, I was not remorseful to see Sloan Taggert on his back, writhing in the dust. And it wiped the grin right off Jalen Ray's face, too.

I helped Taggert to his feet. Poot picked up his hat, which had flown off with the impact of my blow, dusted it off, and pressed it back on Taggert's head. Poot and I bound the Taggerts, hand and foot, and loaded them onto the bed of their Ford to haul them into town, but not before taking photos of its tires for future reference as evidence.

"Where are the keys?" I asked Sloan.

"Find them yourself."

I considered another fist to the jaw, but I wouldn't do that to a man who was tied up.

"Never mind," Poot said to me. "We'll just leave these two gentlemen where they lie and come back in a couple of days. With this weather, they'll be dried out like beef jerky."

I looked up at the sky and saw my old cawing friends. Or at least their relatives.

"You're wrong there, friend," I said. "They won't last that long. Crows will get to them before that. You know how they like to poke out the eyes first."

"They're on a hook in the office," Sloan Taggert said.

"Thank you kindly," I said.

As I got into the truck, I asked Poot, "By the way, how'd you know I was here?

"Your number one fan. Came looking for me."

I gave Poot an inquisitive look.

"You know," he said, "the big gal with the glasses."

"I know damn well who you're talking about. But I didn't tell her I was coming here. I hadn't even decided yet."

"She said after talking to you, she felt something was brewing with the Taggerts. Said she had a premonition and that I'd better get out there. I generally make it a policy not to act rashly upon premonitions, but it was easier to acquiesce to the lady than to suffer the consequences she threatened me with."

I had a premonition to thank for my life.

CONRAD MICHENER

It was so damn hot that by the time I got to the Vermillion Arms my pants were already dry. I gave serious consideration to having Schwartz's grandchildren arrested for elder abuse, but since the evidence had evaporated it would be a matter of he said/she, he, he, and he said. The odds were not in my favor.

A crowd had gathered outside the hotel, but that was nothing compared to the mob that had congregated in the lobby.

"There he is!" people started to shout as I entered the hotel. There was a

136

lot of finger-pointing in my direction as well. I couldn't tell whether they were happy to see me or getting ready for a lynching, but with all the jostling and cursing, I gathered it was the latter. The amazon reporter from the local paper was standing off in a corner with a pen and pad. What was she writing? My obit?

Okay, I said to myself. *I'm Vernon Roundtree. I'm the one in charge. What would Roundtree say?*

A shrimp who looked like Danny DeVito with an attitude stepped forward. He seemed to be the spokesman for the mob.

"We read your Tweet," he said. "We're here to collect our reward."

I couldn't think of a damn thing Roundtree would say. Responding to an uppity peewee had never been in my script.

"You're telling me you're Harold Wohlmer?" was the only thing I could think of. Looking down at shorty, he obviously didn't come close to fitting Wohlmer's description. I tried to keep a straight face, but the more I looked at him the funnier it seemed. I burst out laughing, which might not have been the most tactful thing to do. Maybe I shouldn't have had that last drink.

"Who the hell is Harold Wohlmer?" a lady behind the guy shouted.

"You didn't say anything about a Harold Wohlmer," Little Guy said. "You said, 'H.W.' I'm Herb Warren."

"And I'm Hillary Williams," said the obnoxious lady.

"And I'm Harvey Weinstein!" a geeky-looking guy in the back shouted out. That got a laugh, though it wasn't a very friendly one. But at least it was a little levity.

I took the opportunity to exert my persona.

"Okay, folks. Let's all calm down a mite." *Mite* was one of those folksy words Roundtree was scripted to use a lot, like *reckon* and *gumption* and *hiatus*. A mite too often for my taste, but, hey, the ratings were good. Might as well try it here.

"Don't you worry. I reckon we'll sort this all out. You see, what we have here is simply a little confusion, created by those east coast PR folks. We know what kind of folks *they* are. Sometimes they've got the gumption to think they reckon they know a mite more than we do." Things were moving too fast for me to get *hiatus* in there.

I got some nods of assent. The mob was quieting down. Though I had no idea where I was going from here, maybe I'd get out of this with my head still on.

"Let's have a show of hands. How many of you have the initials H.W.?"

A good two dozen hands shot up. About half the crowd.

"And what about the rest of you? What are you here for?"

There was a lot of shouting back, but the gist was they all had information assuredly leading to the arrest and conviction of H.W. and they wanted their reward. Maybe we could have a lottery, I proposed. Or I could hand out chits or chads or whatever they were called. Or vouchers. Fortunately, I hadn't specified any particular amount in my Tweet. Unfortunately, I think I had disturbed the hornet's nest again.

"Calm down, folks," I said. But they were making such a racket, I don't think too many people heard me, so I had to shout too. "Hey! Shut your goddam mouths already!"

Oops. Out of character. Surprisingly, it did achieve the desired effect. But I had this queasy sensation that from what I'd just said, the mob was starting to realize that Sheriff Vernon Roundtree was a fictional character and that I wasn't him. After five seconds of stunned silence, I perceived a distinctly angry undercurrent. Things could get ugly, as Vern would say. It was time for a hiatus of some sort. I took a quick look at possible escape routes. I had an advantage of about thirty years on most of them and could probably outrun them for as long as it took, even with my cowboy boots on.

As they started to advance on me, who should arrive but Inez. She's a smart cookie, and I could see her evaluating the situation instantly. She worked her way toward me and quickly whispered something in my ear. The last word was *idiot*, but what came before it was worth repeating.

I raised both of my hands up high so everyone could see. That stopped them for a second, which was all I needed.

"Hey, folks. Good news. My posse is bringing in the varmints who burned down Merle Tuttle's stable. Let's head over to the jail and cheer my boys on as they throw them into the hoosegow!"

Chapter Fourteen

8:00 p.m.

JEFFERSON DANCE

I swerved to hit every pothole on Route 12 between Culvert Operations and the jail. Poot rode to the side on Sally in case the Taggerts got bounced so hard they tumbled out of the truck bed. Along the way, my phone rang. I saw that it was from Gimpy Okleberry but the reception was bad and I couldn't make head or tail of it. Anyway, I was only a few minutes from town and figured it could wait.

Which turned out to be a bad decision, because when we arrived at the sheriff's office there was a scene I would like to have avoided. Standing in front of the building were Conrad Michener and Ashlee Vega in their "Roundtree" getups. Michener had his arm around "his daughter's" shoulders. Their determined expressions bore equal doses of concern and pride. In what? I wondered, but I could take a good guess. As if that wasn't bad enough, they were surrounded by a mob of overage groupies. When they saw me pull up in Taggert's truck with father and son tied up in back and Poot following on his mare, they let out a cheer. Michener and Vega approached me as I got out of the truck. The crowd quieted, hanging on every word.

"Good work, Deputy," Michener proclaimed in a stentorian voice for all to hear. "You've done our little town proud."

He patted me on the back. I looked at him for a long moment, considered my options, and decided rather than break his jaw, I'd best get back to my job booking the Taggerts. Besides, my fist was still sore. We untied the Taggerts' feet and hauled them out of the truck. Poot had Jalen. I took Sloan, who made life even more difficult by suddenly becoming passively resistant, going limp, and playing dead as a possum. I almost had to drag him into the office. I saw Linda Benallie on the perimeter of the crowd, camera in hand. I caught her eye, and she gave me a smile as wide as the Cheshire cat's as she took a snapshot of me covered in dirt from head to foot, holding Taggert by the collar.

Inside the jail, Snipes was strumming his guitar and crooning "The Thrill Is Gone." Gimpy apologized a blue streak for not being able to give me advance warning of the welcoming party.

"Just go get Michener and Vega and tell them I want to see them."

"When?"

"Now. And hogtie them if you have to." I didn't have to ask twice.

Poot and I locked up father and son in the cell next to Snipes. When Snipes saw the Taggerts he segued seamlessly to "The Ballad of the Green Beret."

"Knock it off," Sloan Taggert said.

Fiddler stopped singing the lyrics, but kept humming the tune.

"I said, knock it off."

This time he stopped singing altogether but started whistling.

Like his dogs, Taggert lunged aggressively, if futilely, at Snipes. The bars separating the cells insured that his attack would be ineffectual, which I suppose is what Snipes was banking on. Taggert's arm could only reach so far through the bars. Snipes continued to taunt, holding his guitar tantalizingly close but just out of range of Taggert's fingertips. I'm confident Snipes's cackle would not have sounded as arrogant but for the safety of his steel surroundings.

"Oh, the poor little military industrial complex," he taunted. "All locked up with the flower child pacifist."

"That's enough," I said.

"But, Sheriff—"

"I said that's enough."

Snipes got the hint. He shut up and sat on a bench in the far corner of his cell to mope. I hadn't expected to find myself on the same side of an issue as Sloan Taggert, but sometimes circumstances produce strange bedfellows.

Poot must have caught my chagrin. He was smiling at me.

"What's your problem?" I snapped.

"Maybe I'll just go back to the hotel and give Room 12 a closer look to see if we missed anything."

"You do that."

I was confident Taggert had been responsible for burning down Merle Tuttle's stable but was more than confused at how violently he'd resisted arrest. And he continued to vehemently deny having anything to do either with the arson or with Harold Wohlmer's disappearance, other than their chance encounter outside of Jarvis's store.

"You was trespassing on our property!" Jalen yelled at me, which was not only beside the point, it was untrue. "We have a right to stand our ground from federal intrusion."

"I'm sure you do," I said. I had more pressing things at the moment than getting into a tautological battle with nitwits like Jalen Ray Taggert over whether the U.S. was a democracy or a republic, and returned to the office to try to get an update on the Wohlmer situation.

There was a knock on the door.

"You wanted to see us?" It was Conrad Michener. He sounded contrite, and Vega, by his side, looked contrite, but I was in no mood to grant absolution. The day might be cooling off, but I was only getting hotter.

"What kind of lame stunt do you think you were pulling? You think this is some damn TV show?"

"It wasn't our idea." He sounded like he was going to go on, but he stopped sudden as a galloping horse at an eight-foot fence.

"Alfie's doing?" I surmised.

"Uh-huh."

"And you bought it?"

"It wasn't for us to turn down. It's in our contract. They literally own us for this weekend. If we'd refused, you can be sure their lawyers would've had a field day."

I put it on my mental list to have another conversation with Moran. Whether it was time to inform him of Maddison Hadcock's death twisted in my mind. Before I could decide on that, another question entered my mind.

"How did Alfie find out I was arresting the Taggerts?"

They both looked at the ground.

"If you keep acting like little kids that denied raiding the cookie jar, you'll spend the night in the cell with them." I chinned in the direction of the Taggerts.

They could tell I meant it, because I did.

"It was Merle," Vega said.

"What was Merle?"

"Merle called me. He told me you were going to arrest someone, but he didn't know it was going to be the Taggerts."

"Why would he be doing that?"

"I don't know. He asked me to tell Alfie. That maybe it would cause some excitement for the tourists. He thought it would help persuade Alfie to buy one of his scripts or something."

"That's the truth," Michener said.

"Well, here's for the two of you to decide," I said. "If you interfere one more time with anything even remotely connected with my work here, you'll be calling your own lawyers, not for legal advice, but to post bail. Understood?"

"Look, it wasn't our—"

"Understood?"

"Yeah. Okay. I got it."

"Good. Get out. And on your way out the door," I said to Michener, "take off that damn badge."

I asked Gimpy whether anyone had called in about spotting Harold Wohlmer or a man using a walker. The answer was no to both.

I looked in on Snipes in his cell. Frankly, I had little of substance to hold him on, he was low on my priority list, and his drug-enhanced imitation of Jerry Lee Lewis singing "Great Balls of Fire" was getting on my nerves, along with a lot of other things.

"You're free to go," I said to him, and opened his cell door.

"Actually, it's pretty comfortable here, if those Taggerts would just mind their manners. Food's good. Bed's comfy. Mind if stay a while?"

"Go."

"Can I stay if I give you an idea?"

"Depends on the idea."

"Well, what if this Harold fellow and the fellow with the walker are one and the same fellow?"

I dialed Harriet Wohlmer's number and put the call on Speaker.

"Mrs. Wohlmer, does Harold ever use a walker?"

"Hardly ever. Usually at home."

Snipes mouthed the word "Bingo."

"Why usually at home?"

"Oh, my Lord. He says he doesn't need it, but I think it's because he feels so ashamed that his balance isn't what it used to be, and it makes him look weak. It's not that he isn't strong enough. He still chops wood in winter."

"Understood. Did you happen to bring his walker to Loomis City?"

"Yes. We keep it in the Winnebago. In case of emergencies."

"Are you in the Winnebago now?"

"No. I'm with the Muscvardsens. They're doing their best to keep my spirits up. I don't want them to think they're not doing a good job, so I keep smiling."

"God bless them, and you too, Harriet. Might I ask you, when you're back at the Winnebago, to give me a call and let me know if Harold's walker is there?"

"I don't know whatever for, but yes, I'll call you."

"Thank you, and I just want you to know, we're doing all we can."

"Yes, I know you are. Thank you so much."

Little by little, I told myself. Be patient. But how much longer could Harold Wohlmer last, wherever he was?

I called Poot.

"By any chance, did you see a walker when you inspected the Wohlmer's Winnebago?"

"He use one?"

"Might," I said.

"Are you trying to make my day even harder than it already is, or are you just taking Conrad Michener out on me?"

"Just asking. So just answer."

"I don't recall seeing a walker. If I'd been looking for one, I might've found one."

"Fair enough. Speak to you later."

A cooling off period, as it were, was in order.

CONRAD MICHENER

What a difference a few short blocks can make!

I felt a little guilty, in fact, marching over to the jailhouse at the head of a mob. It reminded me of the scene in *Frankenstein* when they went to kill the monster. The only things missing here were the torches. But I was not about to complain. No longer being the focus of their wrath was a relief. Thank you, Jesus, for delivering Inez unto me.

By the time we reached the jailhouse, the crowd had swelled even more with gawkers. This was going to be a ratings bonanza, except that the old guy with the limp from the sheriff"s office was frantically trying to shoo everyone away. Fortunately, no one paid any attention. Once blood is in the air, there's no turning back.

Ashlee was already there waiting for me, all decked out in her best Jordan outfit. When she saw me, she reached out and gave me a big, daughterly hug, with a big, daughterly smile. So proud of her dad! I reciprocated in kind, trying to keep the lust out of my eyes. I just hoped we could keep up the act until Dance showed up with Wohlmer.

Luckily, we didn't have long to wait. Dance drove up in a pickup truck with Shorty following on a horse. I didn't see anyone in the truck with him, and for a moment I had an anxiety attack that Inez had been the recipient of bad gossip.

Dance brought the truck to a stop, and he and Shorty manhandled two

144

men out of the back. I didn't get it. Neither of them looked at all like the description I'd gotten of Harold Wohlmer. Even the man who claimed to be Stan Schwartz was a closer fit. Both of these guys were too young, neither of them was heavy, and they certainly didn't look friendly. But I was not about to quibble.

Nor was the crowd, and when they saw the two men tied up, they let out a cheer. Ashlee and I followed the script Inez had hastily laid out for us. We approached Dance, who was covered in dirt. I didn't even want to know what that was about.

"Good work, Deputy," I said, loud enough for everyone to hear. "You've done our little town proud."

I didn't want to shake his filthy hand, so I patted him on the back and the dust went flying. I wasn't sure if he appreciated my gesture or not, but at least the crowd knew who was boss.

After Dance and Shorty hustled the two crooks into the jail, Ashlee and I thanked all the "townsfolk" for their support and told them not to forget that the stores were open late and not to miss the parade. As I was about to remind them about the fireworks, Limpy came up to me.

"Sheriff wants to see you."

"I'm busy," I said. "Show biz."

"He said he wants to see you now."

"Look, I'll be there as soon as I can."

I kind of had an idea what was about to come down and needed a minute to mentally prepare. After I got lots of slaps on the back for a job well done and Ashlee got more than her share of hugs, the crowd started to disperse. We waved good-bye as we headed into the sheriff's office. "Night now!" "Have a good one!" There was a lot of commotion coming from one of the jail cells and some familiar guitar playing in the background. I knocked on the office door.

"You wanted to see us?" I asked. Inez had told us our best option with Dance would be to sound contrite. I could do that when I had to.

"What kind of lame stunt do you think you were pulling?" Dance said. "You think this is some damn TV show?"

We were not off to a good start, but when One Eye intimated that it might have been Alfie who was the mastermind, I decided that a little white lie wouldn't hurt. Inez had been the savior. Alfie had been the pain in the rectum. And with Alfie being our boss, it would make sense.

"Uh-huh," I said. Why not? I explained that our contract obligated us to do whatever they asked of us.

Dance seemed to consider that, but then caught me by surprise, and asked how Alfie knew he was going to arrest the Taggerts. I had to think fast. Should we give out information from Inez that was probably said in confidence? Or should we make up a lie and get caught? This guy seemed too good at catching people in lies, so I got ready to throw someone under the bus. Ashlee beat me to it.

"It was Merle," she said and explained how Merle called her to tell Alfie, all in the hope of getting his script produced. It sounded a little cockamamie, to be honest, so I piped up.

"That's the truth," I said. Well, at least most of it was, except for substituting the name Alfie for Inez.

Dance gave us a slap on the wrist with a warning and threatened to jail us if we got in his way again. I thought that was a little below the belt.

As we left, he told me to take off my badge in a pretty nasty tone of voice. Some people have a lot of chutzpah, if you ask me. He hadn't even given me a chance to ask if either of the guys he arrested was Harold Wohlmer.

Chapter Fifteen

9:00 p.m.

JEFFERSON DANCE

I told Gimpy to keep an eye on Snipes and the Taggerts and headed over to a swanky new microbrewery called the Can Festival on 100 South and 200 East. That's where my *Roundtree Days* guidebook informed me the finals of the team cribbage competition were taking place.

Surrounded by a mob of kibitzing seniors, Bob and Dot were engaged in a tense duel of wits with their opponents, a couple in matching Hawaiian shirts of similar age as the Melansons. The four combatants alternated slapping cards down on the table and shouting out seemingly random numbers, like "fifteen for two, fifteen for four, a run for three, a pair for two, and a go for ten." Then, like manic acupuncturists, they gleefully poked little toothpick-like markers into holes in the cribbage board and started over again.

I approached the Melansons during a lull in the action, while Dot shuffled the deck for the next hand.

"Sorry to break your concentration," I said. "But I have a quick question."

"Can't it wait?" Bob asked. Dot dealt everyone six cards. I could see Bob's mental calculations clicking almost before he'd looked at all his cards.

"Is this the person you saw with the walker?" I blocked the view of his cards with my cellphone photo of Harold Wohlmer.

He and Dot both looked.

"Yes, that's him," Dot said.

Bob, suddenly excited, whispered into my ear, "He's the one? He's the one who killed Alexis?"

"Honestly, I don't think so," I said. "It's just that he's missing and we're trying to figure out where he might have gone."

"Oh," Bob said, losing interest.

"Thanks," I said, "and good luck." I don't think either of them heard me.

On my way to the Vermillion Arms, I pondered a slew of questions. Why had Harold Wohlmer used a walker when his wife said he didn't really need one and didn't like to be seen with it in public? Why was it no one had spotted him with his walker in the Vermillion Arms after the Melansons had? Even amidst a crowd, a big man using a walker would stand out. Was his presence at the hotel at the time of Maddison Hadcock's murder purely coincidental, or was it conceivable he was somehow involved? Could it be he discarded the walker somewhere? If Wohlmer was wandering aimlessly, wouldn't it be likely he would've been easily spotted? Could it be he went somewhere with a purpose? And what were matches from a Vietnamese restaurant all about?

I made a quick detour to Outside Influence. Behind the cash register was a young man, tanned and athletic-looking with a carefully trimmed beard. He wore a heavy, lumberjack-style shirt, which might not have made much sense in the hot summer sun, but since the evening was cooling off, it was not inappropriate. He was in the process of finalizing the purchase of an expensive, combination propane/wood/charcoal camping stove. I suppose if you didn't have three logs and a match but had a lot of money to burn, it was an adequate though cumbersome substitute.

"Matt Jarvis?" I asked, after he had finished his sale.

"Sorry. We just closed."

I showed him my badge and produced photos of Sloan Taggert and Harold Wohlmer.

"You recall seeing the old man having a heated conversation with this person this morning?"

"That's them. But I can't say for sure it was heated. I couldn't hear a word."

"Fair enough. Was the older gentleman using a walker?"

"Nope."

"You sure?"

"Yep."

"Thank you. How's business this weekend?"

"Making a killing."

I reminded myself it was just a figure of speech.

I went to the Vermillion Arms and up to Room 12. Rusty was gone but had pinned another note to the door. *Gone fishing.* Poot was inside and gave me a summary.

"Since there was no forced entry, it could be Hadcock knew the person who killed her and had invited him in. On the other hand, there's no sign that that person spent any time here other than to attack her. No second coffee cups, no cigarette butts, no extra newspapers. Nothing that would have belonged to anyone but her."

"You believe Moran?" I asked.

"Yes and no. Could've done it. Doesn't seem the type."

"Who ever does?"

"And he did make all those phone calls to her after she was dead."

"Could've done that to throw us off. Find her cellphone?"

"Nope."

"Whoever it was had quite a tussle," I said, scanning the swath of destruction.

"Suggests they were about equal strength."

"For a while, anyway."

One thing that was still sticking in my craw was the Taggerts' excessively violent resistance to my efforts to arrest them. If Sloan Taggert hated Tuttle enough to burn down his stable because Tuttle cozied up to the "Roundtree" folks …

"You think the Taggerts could've been up to more than burning down Merle's stable?" I asked Poot.

"You mean like murder?"

"Yeah. Or like kidnapping Harold Wohlmer."

"Don't know why they'd do that. Ask the Taggerts."

"I have."

They'd been as believable as ostriches in Utah. But then again, there were ostriches in Utah.

I suggested we take the elevator and leave out the back door by way of the Vermillion Arms basement. If Hadcock's murderer had wanted to escape detection, that would have been the best route. I should have thought of that when Doc Albers spirited Hadcock's body out of the hotel.

The elevator was one of those antique contraptions with polished woodwork and a metal grate for an inner door. And it was frustratingly slow. Arriving in the basement, we turned left and followed the exit sign along a semi-lit corridor. We inspected the furnace room, then a laundry room, beyond which another corridor intersected. A few employees came and went, but none said they'd been around on the morning shift, and in any event, no one had noticed anything out of the ordinary. There were storerooms for packaged food and for supplies, and a utility room with mops and buckets. Nothing. We went back through them again. In a dark corner of the laundry room, surrounded by trolleys of stained table linens, was the one thing I hoped I would not find. An old person's walker. I expected I would not need a call back from Mrs. Wohlmer.

Poot went to the desk clerk and got a big ring holding about fifty pounds' worth of room keys, a relic of old-fashioned hotels that was appreciated as a quaint throwback feature of the Vermillion Arms. As heavy as they were, somehow I trusted them more than new-fangled plastic cards, which shows you how desperate I was to trust anything. I called Gimpy to bring as many volunteers as he could muster and go through every room in the hotel. Wohlmer could be disoriented or could have locked himself in some room. That's what we were hoping for. The alternative was he was still out in the desert, where even a healthy person would be fast running out of time. We didn't want to think about that yet. Whether he was dangerous or simply a victim was anyone's guess.

CONRAD MICHENER

My investigation was collapsing around my feet. Now that arrests had been made for burning down Merle Tuttle's stable, I concluded that meant Harold Wohlmer was home free, wherever he was. Maybe he really *was* missing. Now, that was a novel thought. But that also meant Inez was right about my Tweet being a royal screw-up. I'd gotten a lot of people convinced he was a felon, and now I suppose we had to un-convince them. I'd leave that part to Inez. She'd know how to spin it. This whole business was taking up more than its share of my psychic energy, and I was about to ask Ashlee, around whose well-conditioned shoulders I still rested a paternal arm, if she wanted to screw, and then it hit me.

If Wohlmer hadn't burned down the stable, but he was still missing, maybe he was Madsie's killer. What other logical explanation could there be? I hadn't yet asked Inez to handle damage control, ergo I didn't have to ask her to undo damage control. It was all getting way too confusing.

"You want to go screw?" I asked Ashlee.

"I'd rather eat dinner," she answered. "I'm hungry."

She saw my hangdog reaction.

"No offense," she said, and walked off without me.

No offense, my ass. So much for filial affection.

I headed over to the Vermillion Arms bar to drown my sorrows in a sea of eighty-proof. Halfway through my second Long Island Iced Tea, I called Stewie.

"Do you realize what time it is?" he asked.

"Nine-thirty. *Ish*," I said.

"I mean here. It's almost midnight."

"Yeah, but that means it's noon in Tokyo. I want that deal. I gotta get out of here."

"Connie, boychik"—he always calls me boychik when he's about to try to convince me that what he's about to tell me is going to be for my own good—"you only have a couple hours left of that *mishigas*. Then you're home free. Hang in there. We'll get the Japan deal. Don't worry. What I'm telling you is for your own good."

I wanted to tell him all about the Wohlmer investigation, and how it had followed me throughout the day like a plague of locusts.

"And by the way," Stewie continued, "tell Inez she did a great job with your so-called Harold Wohlmer investigation. Almost seemed real. Mazel tov."

He hung up. I finished my drink and ordered a third. Above the bar mirror was this ridiculous statue of a naked woman with clammy-looking skin. Nineteenth-century porn. They certainly liked 'em plump and pale in those days. Only a medical examiner would think it was lifelike. Her face gave me the creeps. It never changed from this weird smile, like it was saying, "You, Conrad Michener, are a total jerk and if you don't change your life you're screwed." I told the bartender to cover it up with a tablecloth or something. He said, "No can do, pal. Roaring Meg's our patron saint." I gave Meg the finger and left.

Chapter Sixteen

10:00 p.m.

JEFFERSON DANCE

I met Harriet Wohlmer at her Winnebago. We sat at a foldout Formica table. On it was a vase of plastic flowers next to a photo of a much younger Harriet and Harold. She was trim, wearing a modest dress, buttoned to the collar, with short sleeves that puffed out. He was in an army uniform, sporting a Bronze Star. From his current age, I gathered he must have been a Vietnam vet. They had been a handsome couple, and you could see in their smiles and in their eyes their optimism for the future.

Harriet served us iced tea in plastic cups with the Vermillion Arms logo. I informed her that, so far, the room search for Harold at the hotel had come up empty.

"I just don't know why Harold would have taken his walker with him," she fretted. "And then just left it there. Hidden? Why? I just don't understand. Is it possible someone took it from him?"

"It's a possibility. Do you and Harold have friends staying at the hotel?"

"No! That's the thing. We don't know anyone there. It's so expensive. And too fancy. It's never been our style."

She continuously squeezed and un-squeezed the fingers of her folded hands.

"And it's been such a hot day," she said. She pulled a tissue from a box on

153

the table and wiped her eyes.

"We have to assume he couldn't have gone far," I said. "You just keep being strong."

"I'll be fine. I'll be fine. I just don't understand what's happening."

Time to ease back. Framed, autographed photos of the "Roundtree" cast were screwed into storage compartments above our heads. On the dashboard were bobblehead dolls of Vernon and Jordan Roundtree, but not of Alexis, the wife and mother who had abandoned them.

"Tell me about your fondness for 'Roundtree'," I said. "I've never seen it."

That elicited a small smile.

"You haven't? Well, I'll just have to tell you all about it. We just love that show. I believe we've seen each episode of each season at least three times. We've probably watched our favorite ones ten times. We've memorized all the lines."

I noticed a TV monitor anchored up in a corner, like in a hospital room, opposite a bench seat. She saw the path of my eyes.

"Oh, yes. And we watch it when we're traveling, too."

"You have your favorite characters?"

"Vernon Roundtree, of course. He's everyone's favorite, I would imagine. So thoughtful, but he's also strong. And so good at figuring out little clues that no one else can see."

Harriet was rallying, which I was glad to see. I was also glad she didn't know the personality of Conrad Michener, the real human being behind the Vern Roundtree facade. The last thing she needed was another bubble burst.

"Harold says that he wouldn't mind seeing Vernon pop someone in the mouth a little more often, but he likes him too. What we can't understand is how Alexis would run off with DeWitt Cheney. It's not that we don't approve of environmentalists, though Harold says they're the ruin of our economy. It's that I think she's just doing it to spite her father, Lyman, even though it's costing her her marriage to a good man. She doesn't realize how much it's hurting Vern. I don't care for Lyman Honeycut. He's too cutthroat. Do you suppose they named him Honeycut because it sounds like cutthroat and he uses sweet talk, like honey, to take advantage of people? With Lyman it's all about power, even more than wealth, I think. Harold is a little more sympathetic to Lyman than I am. He thinks Lyman has every right to his wealth. 'It's every American's right,' Harold says. But look at the pain it's caused. Lyman lords it over Vern. He and Alexis, his own daughter, don't speak to each other. Alexis and Vern end up separating, and Lyman is out to ruin DeWitt. He might even try to have him killed next season. Right or not, I'm just not sure it's all worth it."

It was good to hear Harriet talk animatedly, even if it was only about the fiction of a TV show. She must have noticed the look of bemusement on my face.

"But we love the show, anyway!" she said, with a smile. It was a beautiful smile.

At least it took her mind off things, for the moment, anyway.

"Thank you, Mrs. Wohlmer."

"Harriet."

"Thank you, Harriet. Don't give up hope. We'll find Harold."

"I know you will," she said. But that's not what her eyes said.

While I was with Harriet Wohlmer, volunteers had started to shut down motorized traffic on Main Street in preparation for the parade. Returning to the office took even longer as street vendors set up their booths and pedestrians swarmed over sidewalks and streets alike. The parade would start on the west end of Main Street, move eastward, and finish at the base of Larson's Bluff, when the fireworks would begin. I don't know what Poot had done to mollify the folks who were waiting for Maddison Hadcock to show up, but that wasn't my priority at the moment.

The jail was a relative oasis of tranquility compared to the hubbub outside. I opened the Taggerts' cell door and told them to accompany me into the office, because what I had to say was none of Snipes's business. The door wasn't particularly soundproof, so I turned on the radio to a country music station, and reluctantly closed the windows. Even the commotion coming in from the street might not be enough to cover what I anticipated was going to be a heated conversation.

"Why'd you burn down Merle Tuttle's stable?" I asked Sloan Taggert.

"I didn't. But I should've."

"Why?"

"He's a traitor, that's why. Like your father."

"Let's leave my father out of it and stick to the matter at hand. On what account is Tuttle a traitor?"

"On the account he conspired with the enemy."

"What enemy?"

"The Hollywood homosexuals and harlots. He conspired with them to destroy the moral fabric of the incorporated town of Loomis City and turned his back on his neighbors, the good people who have lived and died here."

Taggert sounded piteous as a beaver with a toothache, and I wasn't going to argue with him about his reasoning, which was of dubious merit, in particular how it was possible for dead people to feel slighted by Tuttle turning his back on them.

Taggert had a point that the character of the town had indeed changed, and changed forever, though I wondered if he'd ever considered how Native Americans felt when his ancestors arrived and changed the character of the land that they had lived on for the previous thousand years. Somehow, I didn't think that line of reasoning would mitigate Taggert's sense of injustice. Yes, it was true: Loomis City was no longer an "authentic" Western town, self-sufficiently relying on traditional means of survival—ranching, farming, mining. On the other hand, before "Roundtree" arrived, Loomis City was a sunset away from becoming an authentic Western ghost town. What Loomis City had recently turned into might not be my cup of tea, but then again, I don't live here and I don't drink tea.

"Lots of local folks like what's happened to Loomis City," I said. "You've got to admit that. Why pick on the sheriff of the county? Sounds like a damn fool thing to do."

Jalen, who until now had been sitting quiet in a corner, jumped up.

"Because the real reason Merle turned his back on us was for pussy, that's why! I seen the two of them. Hell, it had nothing to do with making Loomis City prosperous."

156

The two of us looked at Jalen. It dawned on us at the same time, but between us I think it was Sloan who was the more shocked.

"What are you saying, boy?" he asked.

"Nuthin'."

"Don't say another word," Sloan said.

He was protecting his son now. But I wasn't Jalen's father and was not about to be so obliging.

"You're bitter because of your aunt?" I asked Jalen. It was more a realization than a question.

"What do you know about my Aunt Selma?"

"Only that she died too young, and maybe it pained you that Merle befriended Ashlee Vega not too long after he became a widower."

Sloan Taggert intervened.

"Everyone in town knew what Merle was getting from that Jezebel. And why. He just wanted to be part of that crowd. We weren't good enough for him anymore. And to get in, he went and sold us out."

"And so, Jalen," I said, "you figured you'd send a message that anyone who sold out the town would have a price to pay. That's why you burned down Tuttle's stable."

"I call it a deterrent."

"You do that. I don't think that's what the judge is going to call it."

Sloan stepped up again.

"The United States court system is bogus. They have no jurisdiction over our natural sovereignty."

I wasn't going to get into that, either. I addressed both Taggerts.

"You also wanted to send a deterrent to Maddison Hadcock?"

"Don't know who you're talking about," Sloan Taggert said. But the color drained from his face.

"Isn't she one of the Hollywood harlots who've ruined the town?" I reminded him.

"Never heard of her."

"Then tell me about Harold Wohlmer, the old man you had a conversation with, in front of Outside Influence?"

"What old man?"

"You've already told me that you had a conversation with an old man who was talking gibberish. Do you recall that?"

"Nope. Don't recall no old man, gibberish or not."

I was tired of being played. I've been called a redneck more than once in my life by people who didn't know better, and it never much bothered me. But if it meant I'd been lumped together with this sorry excuse for a Westerner, I'd make sure in the future to lather up with sunscreen and keep my neck a pale shade of white.

"Mr. Taggert, if some harm has come to Mr. Wohlmer that's of your doing, I give you my word you'll pay a heavy price, your natural sovereignty be damned."

There was a knock at the door.

"Who the hell is it?" I barked.

Linda Benallie came through the door.

"This a bad time?" she asked, but with a smile on her face.

I took a look at the Taggerts and decided I'd had enough of them for a while.

"Let's go," I said to Linda.

"Where to?"

"Anywhere but here would do just fine."

I escorted the two of them back to their cell. Snipes started singing "The Battle of New Orleans," and I didn't tell him to stop.

The only place in town that wasn't overcrowded and where we could talk without being overheard was back at the *Public Pinyon* office. Linda opened the mini-fridge and pulled out a pair of Rolling Rocks.

"Cheers," she said. "Hope this will cool you off."

I raised my bottle, took one swig, and was reminded of the remedial effect of a cold beer on a hot temper. I sat on one side of her desk and she on the other. A pile of papers lay between us and on top of the pile was Little Zeke, purring on his back, his fangs protruding, next to the stuffed Gila monster.

"You arrived just in time," I said. "I was running low on patience. You have something for me? I'm running low on time, too."

"Maddison Hadcock. My little brother, Sonny Boy's been nosing around. Checked out some back issues of *Variety*, then made a few calls. She was a piece of work. She started out as Roberta Hanson. Her first employment was as a backup in a punk rock band in Gary, Indiana, whacking a tambourine against her thigh. Then went out to L.A. where she graduated to soft porn and changed her name to Jazmyn Starr. After a few years, she decided to be Maddison Hadcock and transition into "serious" acting, getting freelance spots as an extra. Then some bit parts. Tried the cabaret route. Career didn't seem to be going anywhere until Alfie Moran discovered her and signed her up to be Alexis on 'Roundtree.' Since then, it's been all gravy train. Lots of money, lots of magazine covers. Two husbands, three divorces."

"How does that figure?"

"She married one guy twice."

"How come this isn't common knowledge?"

"She's got a great publicist, Inez Lopez. She created a new identity for Hadcock, combining fact and fiction, with emphasis on the latter. Lopez was the real brains behind Michener and Vega showing up when you brought in the Taggerts. Not Moran."

So, Michener lied to me again. I put that in the back of my mind for now.

"Enemies?" I asked.

"Sounds like there were a lot. Some from her dark past, maybe. Folks on the set considered her a pain in the derrière. Always demanding to be treated like the Queen of Sheba."

"But bad enough to be murdered?"

Linda shrugged. The information might be helpful but opened more cans of worms than I had fishhooks for. I thought about Rusty Carlisle camping out by some stream, away from all this, and envied his solitude.

"What's with these?" I asked, pointing to the clutter of papers and photos that formed Little Zeke's desktop mattress.

"Trying to put together a story about the weekend. The presses must roll, good news or bad."

She pulled the stack of photos from under the cat, who didn't appreciate the disturbance, and flopped off the desk with a thud and a grunt.

"Take a look at these," she said, handing them to me. "There are a few of a big, handsome galoot, a little worse for wear, covered in dust. Which d'you like the best?"

A sequence of about a dozen shots showed me hustling Sloan Taggert into the jail, snapped one after the other. Linda probably hadn't even taken her finger off the shutter button. I looked like the Abominable Dirtman and was about to tell Linda nix on publishing any of them, when I noticed something interesting.

"Tell me what you see here," I said to Linda, "and I don't mean the big, handsome galoot."

I handed her the photos. She took a good, long time scrutinizing them, adjusting her horn rims.

"Wow!" she said. "I see what you mean. The change on Sloan Taggert's face. At first, he's being his usual defiant self, all sneer and spittle. Then all of a sudden something's come over him. It looks like he's seen a ghost."

"Follow his gaze, Linda. Where's it leading?"

"Ashlee Vega! What do you suppose? Is this about Merle replacing her for Selma?"

"I'd think if it were that, he would've tried to attack her, not collapse. And he's known about the two of them for some time. But the moment he saw her, he went limp on me. I thought he was just trying to resist arrest."

Vega had made Sloan Taggert's knees buckle like she had made mine, but this time it wasn't because of her smile. She hadn't even been looking in his direction. She had been smiling up at Michener's kisser. I put it on my mental list to have another talk with her.

"Can I keep these photos?" I asked.

"Sure. I can make copies if I need to. But that's not all."

"Really? What else?"

"Our friend, Leon Snipes. Once you told me his real name, it was easy enough to get some background. He's not the harmless innocent pothead we took him for. Back in the late sixties, Leon Snipes was a member of the Students for a Democratic Society."

"Along with thousands of other college kids who joined the SDS," I argued. "I don't see a problem there. They might've been anti-war, anti-establishment, but I can't say they didn't have a point."

"But our friend Leon didn't stop there. He apparently got bored with peace rallies and theoretical manifestos and craved some real action. He joined the Weather Underground that branched off from the SDS and was involved in planning the bombings of banks and government buildings, including the U.S. Capitol. The Weathermen essentially declared war against the United States for us being in Vietnam. Snipes was arrested several times, but never convicted. When he was drafted, he dodged off into Canada. And then he disappeared."

"To remake himself into the sweet vagabond we know and love."

"Or so he wants us to think."

I finished the rest of my beer and thanked Linda. We both stood up.

"Thanks again," I said. "Let me know if you find out anything else."

She replied by bending her neck down and kissing me flush on the lips. I can't deny it did a good job taking my mind off my troubles.

There was a knock at the door.

"To be continued," Linda said.

It was Gimpy.

"Sorry to interrupt," he said.

"Interrupt what?" I snapped.

"Oh, nothing. I didn't see anything."

"What do you want?"

"Just that Fiddler and the Taggerts are causing a ruckus again. I thought maybe I should just release Fiddler like you said."

"Who said anything about releasing him?"

Gimpy's mouth dropped open so far, his lower jaw almost unhinged.

"Never mind," I said. "I've got some more questions for him."

CONRAD MICHENER

In a few more hours, the parade would be a mere distasteful memory and I'd be on a plane wending my way for a week of Cabo hedonism. But for the moment, I was content. Or at least, I should have been. That naked statue smirking at me at the bar had threatened to puncture my inflated ego. But, after a highly stressful and tiring day, I was finally getting what I deserved—and more, if it must be told. If anything could rid me of that disagreeable image it was cleansing my pores in a hot tub with my two lovelies, Ashlee and Inez, both vying for my affection. At least that's what I told myself they were doing. In reality, they didn't seem particularly interested in me. When I suggested we all get naked, Inez put her index finger down her throat and Ashlee told me to keep Wee Willy buttoned. But the night was young, and as Sir Winston said, "Nevah, nevah give up." Maybe there were supposed to be three nevahs, but I only had two babes.

Inez had discovered the Shangri-La of Loomis City through one of her media contacts. It was a hilltop mansion that belonged to a millionaire who had the good judgment to get out of town and go to Vegas during *Roundtree Days* weekend. Which proved beyond a shadow of a doubt there was one intelligent person who lived in Loomis City. (Now that he was gone; well, you do the subtraction.) As a result, the house, which had a grand view of the town, was vacant. And the three of us had the hot tub, perched on the edge of the property and surrounded by a well-irrigated tropical garden, all to ourselves. With no other houses in sight, we had total privacy. Ashlee had brought all the ingredients for cold margaritas, which put the "hot" in hot tub. We toasted each other more than once but fewer than ten times. Life was getting better by the moment and any disquiet I had had about Harold Wohlmer was fading nicely into a not unpleasant fog.

Just when I had built up a good sweat and as all the tensions of stardom were draining out of me, Inez said, "Gotta get going."

"What?" I asked. "Why?"

"Parade. Gotta get ready."

"Me, too," Ashlee said.

162

The two of them stood up together in their skimpy bikinis, and I almost fainted. Wee Willy rides again!

"Coming?" Inez asked.

"In a manner of speaking."

"Hurry up," Ashlee said, and I watched their two pairs of oh-so-grabable buns recede into the darkness. Just like that, they were gone, vanishing into the house to change. But as we had all driven crammed together in Inez's Miata, they would have to wait for me, regardless. I knew I had to get ready, too, but I lingered on, soaking up what good vibes remained.

My phone rang. The girls must be getting antsy waiting for me, I thought, but I wasn't going to let them rush me. They'll have to come out and get me.

I looked at the caller ID and then I almost fainted for real. It was from Madsie. It couldn't be. Could it? Was she alive? I jabbed Accept.

"Madsie?" I asked.

"*Smithereens!*" a man hollered into my ear.

"What the hell?"

"*Smithereens*, I say! Blow it up! Don't try to stop me!"

"Stop you from what?"

"You know! You all know!"

"No. I don't know. Who is this?"

"I don't know! I don't know!"

"What do you mean, you don't know?"

"You don't know Harold?"

Harold Wohlmer! Was it him? Did he know I'd been after him? Where was he? He could be watching me here in the hot tub. I looked around. All I could see was dark. This guy was a loony. He really was Madsie's killer!

"Where are you?" I asked.

He hung up.

I got the hell out of the hot tub and ran inside, just as Ashlee's phone rang.

Chapter Seventeen

11:00 p.m.

JEFFERSON DANCE

Gimpy escorted Snipes into the office and sat him down opposite me at the desk. He brought his guitar, as per my instructions. Snipes looked everywhere but at me. I suppose he sensed something was up.

"You like Bob Dylan, Leon?" I asked Snipes.

"He the man, bro," Snipes said, looking at the ceiling. "Nobel Prize, man."

"What are your favorite Dylan hits?"

He took off his Sherpa hat and started twisting it.

"Aw, man, that's like choosing which of your children you love the most."

"Fair enough. You know 'Subterranean Homesick Blues'?"

"I've heard it."

"Sing it for me."

"Man, that's a long one."

"Give it a try."

Snipes dawdled as he tuned the guitar, and it wasn't any more in tune after five minutes than when he had started.

"Sing it," I repeated.

He half-heartedly strummed the opening chords, then stopped. "The rest of it escapes me. As I said —"

"Yeah, it's a long song. But maybe you remember the line about needing a weatherman to know which way the wind is blowing. That ring a bell?"

"Just what are you getting at, Sheriff?"

"Only this, Leon. Your flower child act is over. I have an idea what you were up to when you joined the Weathermen, and it wasn't about clouds and beautiful balloons."

"That was another lifetime ago, Sheriff."

"Seems to me that throwing rocks at people's heads, accusing Merle Tuttle of being the Antichrist, and provoking the Taggerts into violence are not exactly what I'd call turning over a new leaf. Now, whether you like it or not, you're going to stay in jail until I say otherwise and you're going to shut up, or I'll find enough charges to keep you behind bars for a long time. Is that understood?"

He sulked like a hound that had to stay home on the first day of hunting season, but I wasn't having any of it.

"Is that understood?" I repeated.

"Yes."

"Yes, what?"

"Yes, Sheriff."

Snipes clearly thought the interview was over, which is what I was hoping, and had begun to relax. Until a few minutes ago, it had been my belief that, other than the drugs and paraphernalia I had found in his shack, there was no law that he'd broken. But Snipes had proved to be such a nuisance that I'd hoped there would eventually be something bigger I could pin on him, since unfortunately there was no law against being annoying. And now, I thought I'd made the connection.

"How long have you been selling weed to Alfie Moran?"

The way I posed the question made it sound as if Moran had admitted this to me, as if it were fact, and it made Snipes squirm trying to figure out how to answer it without getting caught in a lie.

"Now and then."

I considered what Linda had told me about Snipes's past history in the town.

"If 'now and then' means for five or six years, I might believe you."

"That's about right."

"What's been on the menu?"

"The usual."

"Spit it out."

"Bud, hash, blunts, spliffs, kifs. Like I said, the usual."

"Who else have you sold to?"

"One or two others, maybe."

"Names, or I'll be inclined to introduce you to Sloan Taggert's mongrels."

"Are you threatening me, sir?"

"I don't know. Possible they'd like you. Shall we give it a try?"

"Okay. Whatever. Michener. Vega. You know, the cast. The crew."

That would explain why he'd tended to show up during festival weekends. It wasn't to rail at the tourists for having his avowed "stasis" disturbed, as Linda had thought. It was to peddle dope and who knows what else to people who had ready cash.

I escorted Snipes back to his cell. Sloan and Jalen Taggert stood up in theirs and moved away.

"Question for you, Jalen," I said. "This man here, ever sell you drugs?"

Jalen looked down.

"I'll answer for him," Sloan said. "He did. Once. And I found out about it. And I told the scum if he ever did it again, I'd put a bullet through his skull."

That cleared up another mystery for me—why Snipes and the Taggerts had such a passionate hatred for each other. Unfortunately, there were other more pressing mysteries that I was still far from solving.

Now, I have nothing against Disneyland, but when it takes over a town, even for a weekend, I can't help but stop and reflect: Is this the new West? Is this real? And if it isn't, how much does it matter as long as people are enjoying themselves? And making enough money to keep the town going?

And enjoying themselves they were, in droves on Main Street. The parade began to take shape. Caparisoned show horses for the "Roundtree" celebrities were lined up in front by their trainers. Under the glare of floodlights, local kids in marching band uniforms warmed up on their horns and drums. The

Miss Vermillion float, made to resemble an old silver mine, was graced by none other than Lindsie, looking much more womanly in a pink gown than in her Suzi Q's uniform, surrounded by waving maids of honor. They were followed by another row of horses, more mundanely appointed than the first set, upon which were mounted the board of selectmen and other local dignitaries. With the crowd's excitement level rising at the gathering extravaganza, so did sidewalk sales of hot dogs, burgers, fries, pizza, popcorn, cotton candy, Navajo fry bread, tacos, pulled pork sandwiches, and beverages both alcoholic and nonalcoholic alike, as if consumption was the essential fuel that powered the engine of the celebration.

I was glad I'd appointed Poot to be in charge of crowd control. He was nowhere to be seen but had done an efficient job cordoning off Main Street to clear the parade route. At each corner, helpers wearing ROUNDTREE VOLUNTEER T-shirts directed the street crossings at intervals timed to coordinate with breaks in the parade. There was inevitable crowd jostling to get the best view, especially of the celebrities, who were beginning to emerge, accoutered in their TV outfits, from some hidden sanctuary within the Vermillion Arms.

Actors who played minor but regular roles came out first, waving their hats, putting on whatever stage face they were supposed to. If they were good guys, a cheer went up. If they were bad guys, they bore the brunt of good-natured booing. When robber baron Lyman Honeycut stepped out, there was a mix of both. When DeWitt Cheney, the environmentalist, and Alexis Honeycut Roundtree's illicit lover, made his appearance, he became the recipient of less cordial verbal abuse from one bunch of onlookers. "Tree hugger!" "Wife stealer!" "We don't need you here. Get out of town!"

The angry words stirred others to come to his defense, and some pushing and shoving ensued. I waded through the crowd and approached the impromptu jury hotly debating Cheney's right to life and liberty.

"Okay, folks," I said. "That's enough. Let's not forget this is a make-believe TV show and we're all here to have some good, clean fun."

That's all it took to defuse the situation. I saw Poot forcing his way through the revelers toward me, evidently intending to relay the same message.

"It's okay here," I said. "Just a few folks a little hot under the collar."

"That's not why I've been looking for you. We've got a hostage situation. It's Harold Wohlmer."

"Who's holding him hostage?"

"Other way around. For the past hour, Harold has been calling everyone connected with 'Roundtree' from New York to L.A. He's been ranting. Talking about some conspiracy between Alexis and DeWitt. Telling everyone not to interfere. That he's got a hostage and will blow everything to smithereens."

"Don't interfere with what?"

"I think we've got that figured out. There's a shed at the top of Larson's Bluff. It's filled to the brim with fireworks for tonight. The company handling the event is this California outfit called Sparktacular. We called them after Harold called. They sent their best technician, a guy named Dinesh Rao, to do the honors. We think he's in the shed with Harold. They tried calling Rao, but there hasn't been any answer."

"How do you know Harold's in the shed? And how did he get the phone numbers for the 'Roundtree' people?"

"He's got Maddison Hadcock's cellphone, the one we couldn't find. He just went right down her contact list and punched their numbers. We traced his location from its GPS. That's how we figured to call Sparktacular."

"What does he want?"

"Doesn't say. Not sure if he even knows, from the sound of it. Should we send in a SWAT team?"

I thought about those matches he stole.

"There's no cover up there. It's just barren. If Wohlmer sees them coming up the hill like an armed assault, he'll get spooked and we'll have at least one more corpse on our hands, and if he blows the place up, it'll be a lot worse."

"You're the boss."

"Thanks."

I told Poot to inform the parade directors to change their route. Rather than end up by the bluff they should turn right on 300 East, head south, circle around and finish back on Main Street. Make up any excuse they wanted. Tell them to keep circling if need be. We didn't want a panic on our hands, or tourists getting caught in a crossfire. Call the Granstaff County fire department to bring their trucks. Tell them to join the parade until we need them.

Before I decided how I was going to confront Harold Wohlmer, I called Harriet. I told her I hoped I hadn't awakened her, but that I had some news and needed to see her right away at their Winnebago.

A few moth-attracting streetlights, glowing orange-yellow, illuminated the encampment of RVs parked at the high school lot. Disembodied band music, floating on the night from three blocks away on Main Street, lent an ominous gaiety to the conversation I was about to have. Harriet was waiting for me, backlit by the open door of her Winnebago. I think we were the only two people in Loomis City who were not at the parade. And Harold.

Fatigue and worry were etched on Harriet's face. Twisting her handkerchief in her hands, she tried to joke that I needn't have worried about waking her up because she'd never be able to sleep until she found out what happened to her husband. At first, she was overjoyed when I told her we had found Harold and he was alive. But when she heard that he was holding a hostage, her worst fears materialized. She pleaded with me not to harm him, and I told her we'd do everything we could. I asked her what he might have meant by "not to interfere."

"I have no idea."

"Harriet, is there any reason you can think of that Harold chose to go up a hill?"

"What hill?"

"Larson's Bluff. Outside town, where the fireworks are supposed to be."

I glanced again at the old photo of the Wohlmers on the Formica table next to the artificial flowers and felt so sorry that their lives, once so full of hope and youthful energy, were turning out to be so fraught with pain and turmoil. And then it struck me. In the photo. Harold's uniform.

"Harriet," I asked, "did Harold serve in combat?"

She looked at me as if I was totally off subject, and then she understood. "Oh, dear. Oh, dear."

"Tell me."

"Well, I don't know if it matters."

"Everything matters now."

"Hill 875."

"What's Hill 875?"

"Vietnam. Harold was a lieutenant in Alpha Company. There was a battle. They called it the Battle of Hill 875. Our boys suffered terrible, terrible losses. They gave him a Bronze Star, which Harold appreciates, but he's never gotten over that battle. He never wants to talk about it. What little he says is that they were just pinned down and couldn't tell where the enemy was coming from, so they just shot and shot and shot until they were out of ammunition. I found a book about it because Harold wouldn't talk, and I needed to know. I'm his wife. It said they were under withering crossfire for days. Withering crossfire. Harold could never recall when he stopped shooting. The doctors said his PTSD might have contributed to his dementia."

"Why didn't you mention this to me before, Harriet? His PTSD?"

"Harold is just so proud, Sheriff. And, at the same time, he is so ashamed. He says he feels like he let me down. That he's weak. So, I've had to try and hold up my end of the bargain. I've tried to convince him that he's worthy, and I guess I've tried to convince myself as well. And of course, they—the doctors—don't know for sure, and who knows whether they'd admit it even if they did? And all for one little hill in the jungle that didn't even have a name."

While Harriet was talking, my phone lit up. I saw that Linda Benallie had been trying to reach me. Before calling her back, I helped Harriet back into her RV and told her to try to get some rest. Then I called Gimpy and told him not to let Leon Snipes out of jail under any circumstances. It might be a coincidence that Vietnam was an intersection between him and Wohlmer, and maybe even Sloan Taggert, but if there was more to it, I wasn't going to take any chances.

I dialed Linda's number.

"Sonny Boy's called me with some dirt on Hadcock," she said.

"No time for that now." I explained where I was going.

170

"I'm coming with you. I'll tell you on the way."

At first, I was going to say no, then changed my mind.

"Okay, I'm leaving in thirty seconds. Come with Poot. You'll get your exclusive. I just hope it's not an obituary."

CONRAD MICHENER

I was still dripping wet when we got the hell away from the mansion, looking over our shoulders, scared to death we were being pursued by Harold Wohlmer. When we arrived at the Vermillion Arms, Inez parked her car in the lot, and we went into the hotel through the back entrance. That was the right call because it made it easier for us to avoid the mob lined up for the parade, who might have questioned our out-of-character garb: Ashlee in a sarong and me in a Speedo. And who knew if Wohlmer was in the crowd?

We ran up to our rooms and quickly became our television selves, though we were still shell-shocked from the phone calls all three of us had received. We were soon to find out that we were not the only ones, either. Just about everyone in the cast, plus members of the production team, had received a threatening call from Wohlmer. This guy was bonkers. He was on the loose and he was dangerous. I knew it all along.

The cast congregated in the lobby as instructed, in order to get ready for the parade, but you can believe that no one wanted to go through with it. Even with the parade directors informing us that we were changing the route and assuring us that everyone would be safe, they were so hush-hush that it was hard to believe. On the other hand, the cast seemed to be the only people who were spooked. The crowds seemed totally oblivious, as crowds often are, and were as mindlessly excited about the *Roundtree Days* parade as ever.

"What the hell's going on?" I asked Alfie. He had also been the recipient of a phone call from Wohlmer, and now that there was impending doom we were all suddenly bosom buddies.

"Damned if I know," he replied. "This bloke is off his nut, but I've been led to believe the authorities have it under control."

"What I don't get is, if he's not the one who burned down Tuttle's stable, what's he up to?"

"Could it be he was involved in Madsie's murder?" Alfie asked.

That thought had entered my own mind and gave me a shiver. Of course, with my luck I'd been picked to be the parade's official grand marshal. I'd be at the head of the whole damn thing.

"And we're just supposed to sit on our horses and be sitting ducks?"

"Ours is not to reason why, dear Connie."

"Yeah, maybe. But don't forget how the noble six hundred ended up. Dead."

Chapter Eighteen

12:00 Midnight

JEFFERSON DANCE

The parade began, marching eastward along Main Street, the revelers blissfully unaware of the imminent danger. Poot, Linda, and I raced toward Larson's Bluff. I had no idea how Harold Wohlmer had avoided detection and made it up that hillside on his own, or what he had done to that technician, Rao. All I knew was that Wohlmer had been a decorated soldier who had survived hell. He had been well-trained to do what soldiers do.

I drove off the road and up the hill as far as I could, parking the truck ten yards directly below the shed and keeping the headlights on so Wohlmer could easily see us. No subterfuge. The last thing I wanted was for him to be startled by an ill-considered surprise and respond with an ill-considered reaction. I told Linda to stay in the truck. Poot and I went the rest of the way on foot. To our backs and down below was Loomis City celebrating the climax of *Roundtree Days*. We could hear the cheering, faintly, in the night air.

I looked up at the sky, wondering whether it would be for the last time. City dwellers don't understand the magic of a night sky—how dark the night could, should, be; the ocean of stars dwarfing the puny points of light the town below had to offer. I had always felt the intense blackness of the desert night sky to be a comforting blanket for the soul. But on this night, it felt like an extension of the blackness that lived within Harold Wohlmer, and the price many might have to pay for it. The yipping cry of not-so-distant coyotes, emerging out of the darkness, lent a plaintive voice to the sense of impending doom.

If Wohlmer set off the fireworks, they could kill the five of us. But that wasn't the worst of it. With the grass under our feet dry as tinder, it would touch off a range fire that could race down the hillside and engulf the town. He wouldn't even need fireworks for that. A single match would do it. There was no irrigation up here, either from Culvert Operations or anyone else, and a nocturnal breeze was blowing briskly from the top of the bluff, straight down toward Loomis City. I shuddered at the image of the entire hillside covered in flame, illuminating the night, with nothing in its path to stop it.

The shed door was open, but the light was so dim it took a while for our eyes to adjust before we saw a man, a shadow within a shadow. My flashlight was on, but only to find our way. I wasn't going to point it at Harold, sitting on the floor, his back against the wall, his legs outstretched. Next to him lay what at first I thought was a duffel bag of some sort, but when it moved I realized it was something living, and when it moaned I realized it was Dinesh Rao. What appeared to be a large rock lay between them.

"Harold," I said. I spoke slowly and clearly, but not aggressively. "We're here to take you home."

"*Smithereens!*" Wohlmer yelled. "I've got matches!"

To prove it, he lit one. For a moment, I saw his face. He was flushed, his eyes fearful and roaming. And then it was dark again.

"It's okay, Harold. Are you okay?"

"Okay, okay."

"And the man with you?"

"The enemy. I couldn't help it. Had no choice."

"Of course not. Is he hurt bad?"

"Who?"

I tried another tack.

"Your wife is looking forward to seeing you."

"Wife?"

"Harriet. Mrs. Wohlmer."

"Harriet. Harriet. Harriet Wohlmer? What episode is she in?"

I looked at Poot for help. "How am I supposed to answer that?"

Poot cupped his hand by his mouth.

"Same episode that Alexis Honeycut Roundtree is murdered," he said matter-of-factly to Wohlmer. It sure wasn't the response I would've given, considering the circumstances, but I'd never second-guessed my partner and I wouldn't now.

"She deserved it!" Wohlmer insisted. "She had an affair with a tree hugger! Turned her back on her own family! Had to be punished. Had to."

"Someone tell you she had to be punished?" I asked.

"She had to be punished."

"Yes, she had to be punished, Harold. Who was it that told you that?"

"Well, it was that nice fella."

"You remember his name?"

"That nice fella in overalls. Military man, like me. I told him what Alexis was doing behind Vernon's and her father's backs. It wasn't right, I said. And he said, 'You're a smart man, Harold. But you know who's worse?' He said, 'It's the daughter. The daughter, Jordan. She's a hussy. A harlot. It's 'cause of her Alexis left.' Well, I couldn't believe it, she's so sweet. But you know, he said he had proof. Proof she was sharing a bed with the sheriff, her own father! 'That's an abomination,' he said. And that's why Alexis ran off with the tree hugger. Made sense. 'But someone's got to do something about it,' he said. 'Someone's got to save Vernon's honor. Honor's number one. It's up to you to punish her.' He was a nice fella. Saw I was a military man, too. Said it was my duty. I suppose it was. I called him back and told him, mission accomplished."

"And he congratulated you on a job well done?"

"You would've thought, right? Strange. Said he didn't remember who I was. Hung up on me. Strange. I'm Harold."

"You completed your mission, Lieutenant Wohlmer. You've done your job. Now come on out and let's go home to your wife."

I took a step forward. That was a mistake.

"Smithereens!" Wohlmer shouted. *"Vermillion a million!* Don't take another step. *Million Vermillion! Death!"*

I stopped in my tracks.

Harold lit another match and held it above his head. When it burned down to his fingertips, he threw it at a box of fireworks. There was nothing to do but wait. It didn't catch.

"What now, Dr. Freud?" Poot asked quietly. "Should we get Mrs. Wohlmer up here?"

"I've been thinking of that, but I don't think so. I don't want her to have to see this. Worse, she might inadvertently say something that'll set him off."

I heard Linda open and close the truck door behind us, then her long strides.

"I told you to stay in the car," I said.

"Stay here and keep talking to him," she replied. "Give me your keys. I've got an idea."

"Beer run?" Poot asked.

"Better. Just make sure Wohlmer doesn't light another match."

We stalled for time by getting Wohlmer to talk about some of his favorite "Roundtree" episodes, keeping it light. Anything to prevent his thoughts from turning totally inward, which was not a safe place. One errant match would be all it took to turn this hillside into an inferno. The only thing left of Loomis City would be a headline.

Not sure how much time passed, but our ride down memory lane was running on fumes when I finally heard someone approach behind me. I dared not turn around for fear of breaking the connection with Wohlmer, who had taken to almost incoherent rambling.

"That you?"

"Yeah," Linda said.

"This better be good. Wohlmer's getting tired of listening and I'm getting tired of talking. We might have to risk moving in."

"Lieutenant Wohlmer," Linda said in a loud, clear voice, "I've brought someone who wants to meet you."

I heard the sound of horse hooves. Trotting up to us, dressed in his sheriff's outfit, mounted on a golden palomino, rode Conrad Michener.

CONRAD MICHENER

One by one, we exited the hotel, greeted by the cheering throngs. We waved back, pretending all along we were having a grand time. If there's one thing actors can do well, it's pretend. Maybe it's the only thing we can do well.

We waited for the announcements to the crowd. First, that Maddison Hadcock would not be at the parade, having to attend to urgent family matters, but she sends her love to all her fans. Second, because of the record-breaking numbers on hand, we would be making a detour in the planned parade route, circling around to make sure that everyone had a chance to enjoy the entertainment before heading to Larson's Bluff. I understood the backstory to the first announcement but had no idea what was behind the second.

I mounted my horse. They told me his name was Gooch. As stipulated in my contract, he was docile and compliant. I'd developed enough equestrian prowess to convince the crowd that I knew what the hell I was doing. Though I'm sure the local ranchers were snickering at my expense, most of the out-of-towners had probably never been closer to a horse than watching reruns of "Mister Ed."

Ashlee hopped on her nag with a little boost from her horse trainer, who managed to "accidentally" place his hand on her ass as he administered his professional assistance. I don't think Ashlee even noticed, though. Her eyes told me that she was as freaked out as I was about Wohlmer's phone calls.

Little by little, we got underway. All the bands, marchers, baton twirlers, local organizations with their banners, and "Roundtree" folks lined up. Three loud whistles, and the Loomis City High School marching band started playing "Strike Up the Band." The parade began to move eastward along Main Street, cheered on by crowds packed five-deep on the sidewalks.

In the past, this parade was surreal enough, but this year, with crazy Harold Wohlmer somewhere out there, even Hitchcock would have plotzed. I hoped Wohlmer had been caught and locked up. Alfie had suggested he might need to be shot on sight, which seemed a little extreme to me because we didn't even know for sure what he'd done.

"Better safe than sorry," Alfie had said.

All this was racing through my mind as I raised my hat and waved to the crowd. I had to keep a smile pasted on my face because I knew Inez was somewhere out there with the film crew.

When we got to 300 East and turned right at the detour from the normal parade routes, the tall Indian reporter from the local paper hopped the barrier. I'd done an interview with her a few years before. I usually don't do local papers because they're generally a waste of time, but I'd felt sorry for what had happened to her people and did that one out of the goodness of my heart. She was walking right towards me. What was her name? Laura or Linda something. Yeah, Linda. Linda Benallie. I never forget a name, especially if it's a woman's, but what the hell was she doing? She stepped right in front of Gooch. If I'd been any worse with horses, I might not have been able to put the brakes on. She could have been trampled. She grabbed the reins from my hands.

"Sorry, honey," I said. "If you want an interview, you'll have to talk to Inez."

Without a word, she put a hand on the pommel of my saddle and swung herself up behind me like a pro.

"Signal Vega to keep going," she whispered in my ear.

She was so serious, and I was so dumbfounded, that I did like she said, raising my arm and pointing Ashlee southward. Ashlee looked at me questioningly, so I pointed again. She took the hint and kept going. I waved my hat for the parade to follow her. It seemed like the thing Vern Roundtree would do at a roundup.

"I was at the Vermillion this evening when you almost got lynched," Benallie said. "You were looking for Harold Wohlmer. Well, we found him."

"Good for you," I said.

She ignored my comment.

"And you're going to help us get him down off Larson's Bluff before he blows the whole town off the map."

I didn't like where this was going, nor did I like where we were going when she took the horse's reins in her hands and started trotting us up the steep bluff. Gooch seemed happy, though, being guided by someone who knew how to ride. At least one of us was happy.

It was damn dark going up that hill, and when some wild animals started wailing, Gooch spooked almost as much as I did, but Benallie kept him calm and on course. About fifty yards from the top of the bluff she stopped and swung herself down, landing like an Olympic gymnast, without an ounce of wasted motion. She handed me the reins.

"You are now Sheriff Vernon Roundtree," she said. "Go up there and talk to Harold Wohlmer. Get him out of there safe and sound so we can all wake up alive tomorrow."

I must have frozen, because she said, "Go ahead, Sheriff. Show's on."

She whacked Gooch on the rump, and I had no choice but to trot up to where Dance and his partner were standing. I couldn't believe what was happening. I'd never had responsibility for anything more serious than raising a concerned right eyebrow in front of a camera, but now the lives of these people, of the whole town, were in my hands.

"Someone here to see you," Dance called out to Wohlmer.

What would Roundtree do? Jesus, help me. What would Roundtree do?

"Sheriff Roundtree!" Wohlmer said. With some difficulty, he found his way to his feet and saluted.

I saluted back.

"Lieutenant Wohlmer," I said, clearing my throat. "On behalf of all the folks of this town, it is my great honor to welcome you to Vermillion." I tipped my hat and slid off Gooch in convincing enough fashion to impress folks who have never ridden a horse.

"Thank you, sir," Wohlmer said. "I know you've had a tough time. Family and all."

Without a script to read from, I hoped I would not step on that land mine.

"Not so bad," I improvised. "Nothing that we can't get through if you and I work together."

Wohlmer didn't respond. Did I say something wrong? Things could go either way. I saw Dance move his hand closer to his gun if Wohlmer's got too close to another match. I suppose he had no choice.

"Will you help me, Harold?" I asked.

"How, Sheriff? How can I help?"

"For starters, there's a mighty pretty young lady waiting for you down the hill. Someone who's missing you bad, who could use some TLC just about now."

"Harriet."

"Yes, Harriet. Will you walk down the hill with me, Harold? To Harriet?"

We waited. I started to say something, but Dance quickly cautioned me with his eyes to hold off. After what seemed ten years of waiting, Harold Wohlmer stumbled out of the shed.

"Let's do this, Sheriff," he said.

"Call me Vern," I said and put my arm around Wohlmer's shoulders. He didn't seem like an arsonist or a killer. He just seemed like an old guy who had had some hard times. My acting job must have been all right because as far as I knew, we were all still alive.

Chapter Nineteen

1:00 a.m.

JEFFERSON DANCE

Poot took the reins of the Palomino and discreetly followed the two men down the hill. Wohlmer was weak and appeared to be suffering from severe dehydration, so Michener helped support him. As soon as they were out of sight, Linda and I ran into the shed. Rao was lying on the ground, his head against a carton of fireworks. He was a little conscious and a lot bewildered. There was a pile of extinguished matches near where Harold Wohlmer had staked himself out. I told Rao everything would be okay. Now that he wasn't worried about being blown up, chances were he'd soon start feeling a lot better.

For the first time, I realized there was a chill in the night desert air. But at least the stars were still shining.

By the time I got back to the sheriff's office, I would have traded all the treasure in the world for a shower and a few hours of shut-eye. I could have fallen asleep on a cactus. I took off my hat, put it on the desk, and stared at it, hoping it would give me some answers.

What would happen to Harold Wohlmer? He was a good man. Confused, suffering from dementia and PTSD, misled, maybe delirious from exposure, he had lost his bearings. He wasn't the only one. The distinction between reality and make-believe had become blurred, intentionally so. Why? In order to sell a television show and prop up a town's economy. Vermillion: Loomis City. Vernon Roundtree: Merle Tuttle. Lyman Honeycut: Sloan Taggert. Go down the list. Harold Wohlmer was a good man. Yet, he had killed Maddison Hadcock, an innocent person. How does one reconcile those things? Aren't we all complicit in one way or another? Staring at my hat wasn't providing any answers.

Suddenly there was a massive explosion. I dived under the desk and drew my gun. Then another explosion and another. Then I heard some distant cheering and realized it was the fireworks. Fortunately, no one had been with me to witness my stupidity. Since I was already on the floor, I didn't even bother to get up. I stretched out and closed my eyes.

The door opened and Poot came in. He sat down next to me.

"You okay?" he asked.

"Yeah."

"You're looking a little frazzled."

"What makes you think that? What's up?"

"They took Harold Wohlmer to the county medical center in an ambulance. He was pretty dried out, so they got an IV going right away. Gimpy followed them in the police car with Mrs. Wohlmer. The DA'll arrive in the morning to book him on some kind of murder charge."

I could only shake my head.

"And Rao?" I asked. Wohlmer would probably be charged for that assault, too.

"Doc Albers treated Rao. Said he'll be okay."

I dragged myself off the floor and sat at the desk. Poot dropped two cell phones next to my hat.

"What're these for?"

"Sloan Taggert's and Maddison Hadcock's. Take a look."

I picked them both up, Hadcock's in my right hand, Taggert's in my left. Poot had opened them to what he wanted me to be looking at. At 9:51 a.m., four minutes after Hadcock's watch was shattered, and presumably when she had been killed, a call went from her phone to Taggert's. The conversation lasted forty-three seconds. There was no recording of the content on Taggert's phone, but in my book that was more than enough of a connection. It corroborated Harold's account that he'd called Taggert. More damning evidence. Or maybe not.

"You ask Taggert about those forty-three seconds?" I asked. "Harold recalled saying two words: 'mission accomplished.' That's pretty slow talking for forty-three seconds."

"I did. And based upon what we made of Wohlmer's account I improvised some details of what he *might* have said to Taggert to fill up the rest of those forty-three seconds. I think that got Taggert scared, because his tongue started waggin' pretty freely after that. He said that he never meant for Wohlmer to harm anyone. He said he had never seen Wohlmer in his life before bumping into him on the street. That Wohlmer was raving about some business in 'Roundtree,' and that's what gave Taggert the idea to convince him to make some mischief that would create bad blood between Loomis City and the 'Roundtree' people so that they would go away and never come back."

"I think that may be part of the truth," I said. "But what I'm thinking is that Wohlmer's conversation with Taggert in front of Outside Influence made him even more confused than usual. Taggert's marching orders excited him, but the import of them also upset him. So first he went back to the Winnebago, maybe erroneously thinking he'd be meeting his wife there. But because he was so distracted, when he left again it was with his walker, and he headed over to the hotel, forgetting he was supposed to meet his wife at the Cowboy Waltz Jamboree."

"You think Taggert really wanted Wohlmer to kill Hadcock?"

"No, on two accounts. I think, like he said, he was toying with Wohlmer's dementia and figured why not push him to cause a little trouble? No one would ever blame a guy in that condition. What I figure is that Taggert tried to convince Wohlmer to bother Ashlee Vega, not Maddison Hadcock, but Wohlmer just couldn't get it out of his head that Alexis Honeycut Roundtree had to be punished for turning her back on her father, husband, and daughter."

"Why do you think that?"

"One, because Mrs. Wohlmer told me that Harold was troubled that Alexis would leave her family. Two, because Sloan Taggert had nothing against Maddison Hadcock. He barely knew who she was. But he did have a big ax to grind with Vega. Taggert believes the relationship between Merle Tuttle and Vega not only dishonored the memory of his sister, Selma, but their dalliance resulted in the ruination of Loomis City, at least in his view."

"So when Harold called him at 9:51, and said, 'mission accomplished' Taggert came to the realization he'd gone too far. That Wohlmer hadn't just made a loud nuisance of himself. That's what took Taggert most of the forty-three seconds to understand."

"And that's why he disavowed knowing Wohlmer."

"I'm sure of it. But the major shock was he believed that it was Ashlee Vega and not Hadcock who Harold Wohlmer had killed, because when we escorted the Taggerts into the jail, Sloan almost fainted when he saw Vega standing there, alive and well. I think that's when he realized that somewhere along the way Harold had gotten his wires crossed. If you recall, Vega's room at the hotel was directly above Hadcock's. The way I see it, Hadcock's death was one big mistake."

"So, who's going to pay?" Poot asked. "Harold or Taggert?"

"Hard to say. They both did it, and they both didn't do it."

I considered what mischief of my own I would like to inflict upon Taggert's person, snoring in his jail cell, for having destroyed the lives of Harold and Harriet Wohlmer and precipitating the murder of Maddison Hadcock.

"I can tell what you're thinking," Poot said. "Don't."

"We'll see."

I scrolled aimlessly up and down through dozens of missed calls on Maddison Hadcock's phone that were made after she had died, which had obviously gone unanswered. Some were just phone numbers, but most were from people whose names were on her contact list—members of the cast and production team who, I imagined, were wondering where the heck she was. Rusty Carlisle's ruse seemed to have worked well, at least for as long as we'd needed it to. Among the calls were the spasms of them from Alfie

Moran, as he had admitted to us. I punched in his number. He answered after the first ring.

"Yes?" he said.

"Just checking," I said. "We've got Hadcock's phone. Just wanted to make sure it was your number. Sorry to call so late."

"*Too* late, I think you mean."

"Whatever. Sorry."

If there had been any doubt, corroborating the number put him in the clear.

There was a knock on the door.

"Come in," I said.

It was Linda.

"Burning the midnight oil ended an hour ago," she said.

"What are you doing up so late?" I asked.

"Why, is there a curfew for Native Americans?"

"Just concerned that Loomis City hasn't been the safest place lately. What brings you here?"

"I told you I got some good dirt on Alfie Moran. Sonny Boy had to cash in extra chips, but I think you'll like this."

"Thanks, but your brother's a little too late," I said.

"What do you mean?"

I gave Linda the lowdown. That Sloan Taggert had goaded Harold Wohlmer to harass Ashlee Vega, but that Wohlmer, confused and demented, ended up killing Maddison Hadcock, whose room was right underneath Vega's, by mistake.

"You mean, now I owe my little brother big time, and it's for nothing?"

It was the first time I'd seen Linda downcast.

"Tell me what you got, anyway," I said.

"Whatever. When Maddison Hadcock was still in her adult film phase, it turns out that Alfie Moran was getting it on with one of her colleagues."

"Tasteless, maybe," Poot said, "but not illegal."

"Except that the colleague was non-consenting, drugged out, and under-age."

185

"How do we know this?" I asked.

"The girl made a video of the two of them and gave it to Maddison for safe-keeping."

"Where's the girl now?"

"Dead. Seven years ago. Overdose."

If Linda hadn't caught my interest until then, that certainly woke me up.

"Let me guess," I said. "Shortly after this escapade took place, Alfie Moran hired Maddison Hadcock for 'Roundtree.' "

"You hit the nail on the head."

"So, it's possible," I thought out loud, "that when he and Hadcock were arguing in her room about her contract, she threatened to expose him if she didn't get what she wanted."

"That would've put a pretty quick end to Moran's career," Poot said, "'specially given the political climate these days."

"Yep," I said, "that would be a darn strong motive for Moran to keep her quiet permanently. Only problem is, we already have Harold Wohlmer's confession and Moran's phone calls to Hadcock trying to find out where she was. He didn't know she was dead."

"How do you know that?" Linda asked. "Just because he told you?"

"They're all listed on the recent calls on her phone."

"Did you also look at her voicemail?" she asked.

"No, I haven't. Until right now, I didn't have a real good reason to think he was lying."

I opened up Hadcock's phone voicemail messages and scrolled down for Moran's. I went to the first one after the time that Harold had called Taggert. Though the call was a half-minute long, there was no message. I went to the next one. Same. I checked voicemails from other callers to see if the phone was working properly and they came through loud and clear. I checked the rest of Moran's voicemails. Nothing.

"Poot," I asked, "when we interviewed Moran, didn't he say he left messages on Hadcock's phone for her to call him back?"

" 'In no uncertain terms,' is what I recollect him saying."

"When Harold came out of the shed," I asked Poot and Linda, "did he have any blood on him?"

"Too dark," Poot said.

"He was wearing an I ♥ VERN T-shirt," Linda said. "I didn't see any blood, but like Poot said, it was pretty dark."

I called Gimpy, who had been under orders to stay at the hospital with Wohlmer. I told him to check on Wohlmer immediately, give him and his clothes a careful look, find out from the staff if they might have washed any blood off him, and call back in a minute or less.

He was out of breath, but he almost made it.

"No blood."

I made another call, apologized for it being so late, and spoke quickly.

"Congratulations," I said before hanging up.

"Come on. Let's go," I said to Poot and Linda.

"Where to?"

"The Vermillion Arms. Room fourteen to visit the Melansons."

"What were the congratulations for?" Poot asked.

"Bob and Dot won the team cribbage competition."

The Melansons' bed was covered with clothes, toiletries, and cartons of "Roundtree" swag.

"Leaving so soon?" I asked.

"No, no!" Dot said. "It's just that we hit the jackpot with the cribbage tournament. We have so much stuff we don't know how we'll pack it. It'll take all night to figure it out."

"Help us celebrate," Bob said. "Last time we drank champagne was on our fortieth anniversary. You aren't Mormon, are you?"

He found five plastic cups in the bathroom and lined them up. Uncorking a bottle, he spilled the bubbling champagne from one cup to another.

"Whoops," he said. "We don't drink champagne often."

"I can see that." I was in a hurry, but I'd learned that Bob did not like to be rushed.

"What can we do for you?" Dot asked.

"*Salud!*" Bob said, and we all raised our glasses.

"Just a few details of what you saw this morning. When the guy with Nikes was running around the corridor," I asked Dot, "what direction was he running?"

"What do you mean?" she asked.

"You were coming from your room, Room fourteen. Is that right?"

"Yes."

"Was he running toward you or away from you?"

"Toward me. Right past me."

"And when you first saw him, was he between you and Room twelve, or on the opposite side of it from you?"

"Between. Yes. Between."

"Thank you kindly," I said. I put my glass down and was ready to go. "And enjoy your trip back to Massachusetts."

Poot and I tipped our hats. Linda curtsied.

CONRAD MICHENER

Believe me, I am not by nature an ambulance chaser. In fact, Ashlee tried to talk me out of it, and the enticements she conjured up to dissuade me stirred me to the depths of my loins.

Nevertheless, I found myself behind the wheel of my Land Cruiser pursuing an ambulance in the middle of the night. That's not entirely accurate. I was behind the police car that was behind the ambulance. The guy with the weird foot was driving the police car—how he pulled off that trick beats me—and I had seen Harold Wohlmer's wife get in with him.

I had no idea how far away the hospital was or where I was. Except for the flashing lights of the police car and ambulance, everything was black. Black on both sides. Black behind me. Black above me. At least, LA at night is light as day. There was no other traffic, and I was scared to death if I lost the two cars in front of me. I felt like I was in a space capsule hurtling into a black hole. We rarely filmed "Roundtree" outdoors at night, and when we did a night scene, of course the lighting had to be set up to convey the feeling of it being dark. But it really wasn't. In fact, those lights were pretty bright. Now, driving through the desert, for the first time in my life I understood how night must have creeped out the cavemen.

We passed a little green road sign that said ENTERING GRANSTAFF, so I suppose we were in the Granstaff outskirts because nothing was there other than the little green sign. I knew when we arrived at the county medical center because a big sign said COUNTY MEDICAL CENTER. I pulled into the parking lot and waited as Harold Wohlmer was taken out of the ambulance on a gurney and wheeled into the hospital emergency entrance. Limper and Mrs. Wohlmer got out of the police car and followed him in.

I realized I didn't have a plan. I didn't know what to do next and just sat there for a while. I was pretty sure they wouldn't let me see Wohlmer, and I knew with Limper hanging around, there would be police questions, and I sure as hell didn't want to deal with that. I got out of the car, walked up to the emergency room entrance, and stood there for a minute. I went back to the car, lit up a jay, and turned on the radio. All I got was static. I listened to static for twenty minutes, thinking. Thinking about Harold Wohlmer. Wondering what he had done and what he hadn't done that had caused all this and wishing him the best. Wondering whether it was even conceivable the old guy had anything to do with Madsie's murder. Hoping he hadn't and beginning to also wonder how it was that Alfie knew about Madsie's murder. Hadn't he asked me at the parade whether Wohlmer could have been involved in Madsie's murder? Yes, he had. Who could have leaked that to Alfie? Actors never could keep their mouths shut.

I left the parking lot, having accomplished nothing, and drove back through the desert to Loomis City. I kept telling myself there was no chance of me getting lost as there was only one road. So why were my knuckles turning white? I don't know exactly what time it was when I got back to the hotel. It was possible Ashlee was still up, and I thought about knocking on her door, but then thought better of it. Back in my own room, I turned out the lights and lay down in bed, and for a while I guess you could say I prayed for Harold Wohlmer.

Chapter Twenty

2:00 a.m.

JEFFERSON DANCE

We jumped into my truck and sped west on Route 12 to Beauville Estates. It wasn't often I exceeded the speed limit, and only a few times I could recall attempting to break the sound barrier. But if I could prevent Moran from skipping town in the dead of night, it was worth the risk of running over a jackrabbit or two.

I parked outside the wall of the development. We continued on foot; the only sound other than our cautious tread was the chatter of nocturnal insects who wait for the coolness of the night to begin their gossip. We passed a BMW sedan parked in the driveway and made our way to the back of the house, where the pool's underwater light illuminated a sickly bruise of untreated yellow-green water. To avoid being seen from inside, we sidled up against the wall as we approached the sliding doors. There were voices from inside. Quiet. Conversational. A small gathering, maybe. Light from the den flickered indecisively. Unexpectedly, a large group started laughing.

I peered inside from a corner of the sliding door. It was no party. It was a television. A late-night talk show. No movement inside. I tapped on the glass. No answer. I tapped again.

I pulled at the door handle. It slid open smoothly and, I hoped, silently enough.

A bare foot extended beyond the end of the couch. Who it was attached to was blocked from our view by the back of the couch. It didn't move when we entered. Poot and I drew our guns. We circled around.

Alfie Moran lay on the couch, a hypodermic needle and empty glass at his side.

"I'll call nine-one-one," Linda said.

"Better you call Doc Albers," Poot said. "He's dead."

On a folding table by the television was a half-empty bottle of whisky, a vaporizer, and a small plastic bag containing pills in assorted colors. Next to it was a legal pad with the top pages hastily scrawled upon. I picked it up and read.

Roundtree, Final Episode: Closing Scene.

Sheriff (SH), accompanied by Sidekick (SK) and Indian Maiden (IM) quietly approach back of Producer's (P) distressingly remote lodging. Late night talk show creates momentary confusion. Sliding doors are unlocked—surprisingly. Enter to find P dead, empty glass and hypodermic needle by his side. (What was the drug? Doesn't matter. Dead is dead.) SH tells IM to call 911, but they are too late by a matter of minutes.

SH discovers legal pad next to assorted drugs and ½-empty bottle of American whisky— just a spoonful of sugar to help the medicine go down. SH reads: Roundtree, Final episode: Closing Scene. *Etc. etc.*

SH scratches his head, wondering what caused P to precipitously off himself, then it dawns on him. "It was the phone call." When SH got his hands on ~~Alexis's~~ Maddison Hadcock's (MH) phone and called P with it, P realized it would only be a matter of time before SH finds P's silent voicemails and determines that the calls P made were a smoke screen. Then, no doubt, SH and IM (who's a reporter) will unearth the video that MH was blackmailing him with. By extension, SH would realize that the gent suffering from dementia delivered MH a haymaker—why he did this will forever remain a mystery to P—rendering her unconscious, and thereafter fled, but that it was P who came back to deliver the coup de grace. [If there's any question in viewers' minds, fingerprints on knife would eventually provide proof.] P, conjecturing that being exposed as a child-molesting, drug-

administering rapist would do little to enhance his career, chooses the easy out: whisky and drugs.

The whole scenario gradually became clear to SH, who is a perceptive bloke, if a bit heavy-footed: First, how P's post-coital argument with MH erupted over contract. (Alas, she was servicing him, not out of love, but only to soften his resolve.) Then MH bringing up the unpleasant ancient history about P forcing himself upon a distressingly young lass who had involuntarily been administered drugs—and threatening to blackmail him with a video of the aforementioned escapade.

P then repairs to the hotel bar for much needed resuscitation and to decide how to appropriately respond, then returns to MH's room for further dialogue. Though he hadn't planned on killing her, P can't allow her to succeed in her blackmail attempts—because they never end, you know—and surprise, surprise, he finds her unconscious on her bed! With this golden opportunity, his primal instincts at self-preservation overtake his better judgment and he stabs her with the breakfast knife that happens to be handily available at her side, providing MH with a new lease on death.

SH, SK, and IM, shaken yet satisfied by the denouement—alas, Harold Wohlmer was indeed innocent—look at each other meaningfully. Jordan (J) rushes in. "Daddy!" she cries to SH. She spies the corpse. "Is he the man who killed Mommy?" SH and J exchange additional meaningful glances. He puts his arm tightly around her shoulders. Family values win the day. Closing Music. Credits.

Final note: A series finale that beats the bloody hell out of "Mash," "Cheers," *or* "Friends."

I finished reading. Linda and Poot looked at me with their mouths open. Ashlee Vega rushed in.

"Oh, my God!" she cried. "Alfie! Is he...?"

"'Fraid so," Poot said.

But Vega wasn't my daughter, and I didn't put my arm around her, either. This was no TV show.

Doc Albers arrived.

"Sorry for waking you up in the middle of the night," I said.

"Well, can't say life hasn't got pretty darn interesting since you showed up,"

Doc said to me.
  "So has death."

CONRAD MICHENER

I couldn't sleep. The little bottles of booze in my mini-fridge were long gone, and the bar downstairs had closed at midnight. I stared at the walls, thought about calling Stewie, then thought better of it. I'd undressed after I'd gotten back to the room, throwing my "Roundtree" outfit in the hallway for Emelda to pick up whenever she did such things. I was glad I wouldn't have to wear it for another six months, when shooting for the season after next was supposed to begin, though I had a strong feeling I'd never be wearing it again.

I took a shower and dressed in street clothes, aptly named because I went out into the street. The shops were shut down and most of the streetlights were off. I turned my back to the traffic light, flashing yellow, at the intersection of Center and Main, and looked up at the sky. The moon was near the horizon and stars were everywhere. I don't think I'd ever noticed that before. The crowd had long gone, having left enough garbage lying around to indicate how many people there had been and how good a time they had. The volunteers would no doubt be out-and-about early to clean up the mess, to again make Loomis City the garden spot of the West, but, in the interim, flocks of crows and magpies and a family of raccoons were having a field day, or I guess it would be more accurate to say a field night. Maybe there wouldn't be much left to clean up after all.

The night had finally cooled things off, and I even started to shiver, though I don't know whether it was from the cold or from the events of the day. What was good was that it was quiet, and I didn't have to be someone else for a while, neither to the fans, the producer, the agent, the public relations person, nor the costar. I wasn't sure who was left when I wasn't being someone else, but whoever it was, it was time to learn how to live with him.

Chapter Twenty-One

3:00 a.m.

JEFFERSON DANCE

We left Doc to complete his tasks. Before leaving, I asked Vega, "How did Moran know you were coming out here in the middle of the night, anyway?"

She shrugged a shoulder. "What do you think?"

Poot, Linda, and I headed back to the sheriff's office. When we got there, we found Merle Tuttle and Sloan Taggert involved in a heated wrestling match. Arm wrestling, that is. On the sheriff's desk. Snipes and Jalen Taggert were officiating. One big, happy family.

"Howdy folks," Merle said to us. Taggert used the distraction to pin Merle's arm.

"What are they doing out of their cells?" I asked Tuttle.

"I *am* the sheriff, ain't I?" he replied.

Merle and Taggert looked awkwardly at each other. They weren't nearly as good actors as the "Roundtree" folks.

"Sheriff," Taggert said to me, "I want to apologize for my rude behavior and for my son's. It was uncalled for, and I promise you it will never happen again."

"We've decided to let bygones be bygones," Tuttle said. "For the good of the town."

"Bury the hatchet," Taggert added.

"And what about the small item of Jalen burning down your stable, Merle?" I asked.

"I ain't pressing charges," Tuttle said.

"You ain't—" And then I remembered the insurance agent, Les Henderson. "So, you're saying it was an accident. Is that it?"

"You got that right. One of my horses must have knocked over the kerosene can."

"And then lit the match?"

"I'm sayin' it was an accident. No need for a criminal investigation."

With the arson charge out of the way, Harold Wohlmer getting the care he needed, and with Alfie Moran the confessed murderer of Maddison Hadcock, the Taggerts couldn't be charged with anything more felonious than planting an idea in the head of a confused old man who, in the throes of dementia, then gave a woman a swollen jaw. I did not favor the odds of such a scenario resulting in a conviction.

"All right," I said.

"We'd hoped you'd see it that way," Merle said.

Taggert extended his hand. I chose not to shake it. Instead, I unpinned the star on my chest and handed it to Tuttle.

"You've had a helluva day," he said to me.

"That's true. But that's not the only reason I'm handing it in. I'm handing it in because if I don't, I'd have to arrest you for any number of reasons, and frankly, I'd rather go hunting."

"What are you talking about, Dance?"

His wrestling match with Taggert finished, the one with me was about to start.

"First of all, Merle, I didn't appreciate the scene you created after you notified your TV buddies that I'd arrested Sloan and Jalen Ray and was bringing them in. I'm no legal eagle, but I imagine that could be construed as obstructing an investigation. Whether it's a misdemeanor or a felony would be up to the prosecutor, of course."

"That true?" Sloan asked. "You did that, Merle?"

I didn't give Tuttle a chance to answer.

"Your new pal here," I said to Sloan, "was trying to make an impression on the 'Roundtree' folks at your expense. But that doesn't compare to some other things."

"Like what?" Tuttle asked. He was starting to get the same dark expression he had when we'd seen him with his rifle almost twenty-four hours earlier.

"The way I see things, you've been letting Leon Snipes peddle drugs in Loomis City for some years now."

"Who's Leon Snipes?"

"Fiddler."

Tuttle looked confused.

"There's a lot more about him than his name that you don't know about," I said.

Tuttle began to protest, but I put up a cautioning hand to signal him to shut his trap.

"It took me a while to piece together why someone who had pledged to uphold law and order would let someone like Snipes roam free in a small town, where it was an open secret he was dealing. I don't know whether you took a share of the profits or not. I don't know if you bought from him like Moran and a lot of the other 'Roundtree' folks had. Maybe you did. Maybe you didn't. But I do know you were intent on being part of the 'in crowd.' You couldn't impress the likes of Ashlee Vega and Alfie Moran with your writing, so you tried to impress them in other ways. So, you put Loomis City up for collateral.

"And you also realized that if folks found out you were aiding and abetting Snipes, you'd lose your job, let alone your standing in the town. You gave Snipes free reign. You gave him a safe haven. Sure, now and then you'd give him a slap on the wrist and put him in jail for a night to make it look like you were doing your duty. But then the way I see it, at some point, things turned ugly. Fiddler, the harmless town vagabond, began blackmailing you. Maybe that's why you were so anxious to get your insurance money. Because if Snipes let the cat out of the bag, your future in Loomis City would be bleak as a foggy night in November. But you couldn't send him to prison, because if there were a trial, he'd squeal. Isn't that right, Leon?"

Snipes had no response. Apparently, he wasn't in the mood to squeal.

Sloan Taggert looked at Merle Tuttle with blood in his eyes.

"Is that true what he says? You sold out the town and your heritage because this piece of cow dung was—"

"Now wait a minute, Sloan. I can explain."

"You do that," I said. "And you can also explain that to the DA when he gets here tomorrow. I'll let you get back to your arm wrestling."

Outside the sheriff's office, Linda and I said our good nights. Poot diplomatically wandered off to smoke a cigarette, something I hadn't seen him do for twenty years.

"I've got to hand it to you," Linda said. "You've solved more crimes in twenty-four hours than Vern Roundtree did in five seasons."

"Maybe."

"I don't know how I'm going to write up what just went on inside."

"Up to you. You could get a Pulitzer if you tried real hard. But there's just one thing that's still eating at my craw."

"Yeah, I know. Who my informant was who told me that Maddison Hadcock had been murdered. I'll tell you if you don't get angry at him."

"I'm done getting angry."

"It was Rusty. Rusty Carlisle."

I thought about his fly-tying in front of Room 12 and Linda's fly casting with Little Zeke.

"I get it. You two fish the streams together."

"From time to time."

That led to an awkward silence. Neither of us could figure out a smooth way to end it.

"Guess I better go," I said.

"You sure you want to sleep in a truck tonight? My bed's a lot more comfortable."

I gave the invitation some serious thought.

"Afraid I'm allergic to ostriches," I said, and tipped my hat.

After Linda left, I looked into the darkness and spotted the glowing ash of Poot's cigarette. I hadn't mentioned to her that my truck was still out at CO_2. Poot drove me there, and, without going into details, we requisitioned a set of new tires from the Taggerts' yard that were even better than the ones they'd shot out. Poot headed off to tend to Sally and get some sleep in his truck before we headed out for our hunting trip at dawn, which was now just over the horizon. I made my way to Getzler Ridge to bed down.

The night being cloudless, the temperature had continued to drop. Dew had begun to settle on the car windows, a sure sign that summer was starting to taper off into autumn. At first, the chill was a welcome relief, but after a while, I have to admit I did start thinking a warm bed had a lot to commend it over my flimsy blanket. I contented myself looking up at the stars, which seemed big as...ostrich eggs. Damn.

Sometime before dawn, I heard footsteps. They were obvious enough for me to understand that someone was making extra sure I'd realize they weren't trying to sneak up on me. Getzler Ridge was pretty out of the way. Who would be here at this sacred site at this time of night? Only one person I could think of. I shimmied to one side of the truck bed. Linda hopped in.

"Figured you might be cold," she said. "Brought an extra blanket."

She lay down next to me. I thought about asking her how, as half-Native American, she felt about white settlers appropriating her mother's ancestral territory and turning it into something now almost unrecognizable. However, this didn't seem quite the right moment for a deep discussion. It wasn't long before I was pretty warm for the rest of the night.

CONRAD MICHENER

I don't know how long someone had been knocking on my door, since it woke me up. I did know that I didn't want to get out of bed to find out who it was, and when it stopped I closed my eyes and hoped whoever it was would go away. But then it started again. I wrapped a towel around my waist and opened the door. It was Ashlee. She looked uncharacteristically lousy. Her eyes were red and her complexion pale and mottled.

"Can I come in?" she asked.

I thought about the hour and almost said no.

"Sure."

She spent the next half-hour telling me about what happened to Alfie, and the hour after that crying in my arms. Then, I suppose, we fell asleep.

Chapter Twenty-Two

6:00 AM

JEFFERSON DANCE

We were up before sunrise. I was making coffee on the camp stove when Poot met up with us. He looked at Linda, then at me.

"Sleep well?" he asked.

I handed him a cup.

He looked at the sky. It was still clear, but you got a sense that the hottest weather was behind us, at least for the time being.

"Good day for hunting," he said.

"Which direction are you headed?" Linda asked.

"West. Out toward Boulder. Bighorn country."

"Who told you that?"

"Some folks we know."

She repeated, "Folks we know," and laughed.

"What's so funny?" I asked.

"You know what your chances are of bagging a bighorn there?" she asked.

"Slim to none?" I asked.

"At best."

"Well," Poot said. "We'll just have to take our chances."

"That would be foolhardy," Linda said, "with a big emphasis on the first syllable. I know a place up in the La Sals. Secret place. Hardly anyone knows how to get there. That's where you'll get your bighorn. There's enough of them there, if you know where to look. I could show you."

Poot and I looked at each other.

"Thanks, Linda," I said. "But we've heard plenty of yarns about secret places from hunters over the years."

"Not to doubt your sincerity," Poot added.

"But no one's ever suggested we'd find any bighorns in the La Sals," I finished.

Linda toed the ground with her boot.

She said, "Yarns, huh? You know that wall-hanging over the bar at the Vermillion?"

"You mean Roaring Meg?" I asked.

"Next to her. The bighorn ram."

"That ram. I'd give an arm to have a shot at a beast like that."

"Guess what? He's mine. I bagged that sucker two years ago. Now, do want me to show you where his friends are, or not?"

Poot and I looked at each other again.

"Can you be ready in fifteen minutes?" I asked.

"Yep. Just need to send my story to *The New York Times* about the weekend. Seems they've taken a particular interest in little old Loomis City."

Linda walked off, with a little more sashay in her step than I'd seen. She might not have been as seductive as Roaring Meg, but she was better. She was real.

CONRAD MICHENER

I lay awake, staring at the ceiling. I tried not to move because Ashlee had finally fallen asleep, but I knew there was no way I could stay in bed.

I managed to extract my arm from under her head and slide off the bed without waking her, and tiptoed to the window. No one was out and about. The sun wasn't up yet, but what light there was cast the motionless town in the pinkish sepia of an old postcard. Somehow, the industrious townsfolk of Loomis City had cleaned the streets while I'd slept. Or maybe the critters had done it. Loomis City would return to its small-town, post-festival self, and the day would be hot as hell again. I raised the creaky old window as quietly as I could and stuck my head out. The air was still cool, with a fragrance I had never noticed before, a fragrance of the desert that flowed into the room with a light breeze. A fragrance worth remembering.

A pair of pickup trucks, one old and one with a horse trailer attached, slowly drove up Center Street. Right below my window, they turned east onto Main, into the rising sun. Probably some *Roundtree* fans heading home. I hope they enjoyed the fireworks.

A Note from the Author

There have been many great fiction writers inspired by the American West. Zane Grey, Tony Hillerman, Larry McMurtry, Wallace Stegner, Edward Abbey. One of my favorites is Craig Johnson, whose novels have been recreated in the popular Netflix series "Longmire." In 2016, while driving cross-country I had the opportunity to stop in Buffalo, Wyoming, where the series is shot. Little did I know when I arrived, anticipating a quiet breakfast at the famed Busy Bee Diner, that it was the town's annual *Longmire Days* festival weekend. The whole town, including the diner, was packed, the majority being senior citizens. My story, *Roundtree Days*, was my flight of fancy for what could happen when the fine line between real life and fiction is obscured.

Acknowledgements

Writing a book is an individual labor of love, but getting it from the author's desk to the book store shelf takes a team of passionately committed professionals. I would like to express my heartfelt gratitude to Josh Getzler, my agent at HG Literary, Meredith Phillips, who patiently proofread my early draft, and Verena Rose and Shawn Reilly Simmons, my editors at Level Best Books, for taking *Roundtree Days* out of the desert and into your living room.

About the Author

Gerald Elias leads a double life as a critically acclaimed author and world-class musician.

His award-winning Daniel Jacobus mystery series takes place in the dark corners of the classical music world. In 2020 he penned *The Beethoven Sequence*, a chilling political thriller. Elias's prize-winning essay, "War & Peace. And Music," excerpted from his insightful musical memoir, *Symphonies & Scorpions*, was the subject of his 2019 TED presentation. In addition to self-published books, Elias's short stories and essays have appeared in prestigious journals ranging from *Ellery Queen Mystery Magazine* to *The Strad*. *Roundtree Days* is his first full-length Western mystery, though its protagonist, Jefferson Dance, made his dramatic debut in the most recent Daniel Jacobus mystery, *Cloudy With a Chance of Murder*.

A former violinist with the Boston Symphony and associate concertmaster of the Utah Symphony, Elias has performed on five continents and has been the conductor of Salt Lake City's popular Vivaldi by Candlelight chamber orchestra series since 2004. He recently made the first complete recording, available on Centaur Records, of the Opus 1 violin sonatas of the Baroque violinist-composer, Pietro Castrucci. Elias divides his time between the shores of Puget Sound in Seattle, and his cottage in the Berkshire hills of Massachusetts, close to the two furthermost points in the continental U.S., where he maintains a vibrant concert career while continuing to expand his literary horizons.

SOCIAL MEDIA HANDLES:
https://www.facebook.com/gerald.elias
https://www.facebook.com/EliasBooks/
https://twitter.com/GeraldEliasSays
https://www.instagram.com/geraldelias504/

AUTHOR WEBSITE:
geraldeliasmanofmystery.wordpress.com

Also by Gerald Elias

The Daniel Jacobus series:
Devil's Trill (also an audiobook)
Danse Macabre (also an audiobook)
Death and the Maiden
Death and Transfiguration
Playing With Fire
Spring Break
Cloudy With a Chance of Murder
Murder at the Royal Albert (2022 release)

The Beethoven Sequence, a political thriller

Self-published:
Symphonies & Scorpions, a musical memoir, *"...an eclectic anthology of 28 short mysteries to chill the warmest heart"*
Maestro the Potbellied Pig, children's book, also an audiobook in English and Spanish versions

CPSIA information can be obtained
at www.ICGtesting.com
Printed in the USA
LVHW030731021222
734411LV00003B/346